Acclaim for *The Unrepentant*

"A gut-wrenching crime thriller. Readers who appreciate depth of character alongside gritty nonstop action will be rewarded."
—*Publishers Weekly*

"Savage, nuanced, and infused with Aymar's signature dry wit, *The Unrepentant* is an enjoyable hard-boiled tale that pulls no punches."
—Jennifer Hillier, author of *Creep* and *Wonderland*

"Gritty and fleet, *The Unrepentant* takes an unflinching look at things that aren't to be forgiven. Aymar's storytelling is timely, thoughtful, and well-informed and will stay with you long after The End."
—Jamie Mason, author of
Three Graves Full and *Monday's Lie*

"*The Unrepentant* is a powerful, darkly evocative story that features an unforgettable protagonist in the wily Charlotte Reyes. These elements combine to make for a thrilling revenge tale peppered with sharp humor and feeling both timely and timeless. E.A. Aymar has arrived."
—Alex Segura, author of
Blackout and *Dangerous Ends*

"Brutal, dark and disturbing, Ed Aymar's *The Unrepentant* packs a punch not easy to forget."

—Zoë Sharp, author of the
Charlie Fox crime thriller series

"Aymar tackles a horrific problem with unflinching courage and wit. *The Unrepentant* rewards readers with crisp prose, relentless thrills, and characters you'd want on your team in what is, at its core, a modern-day brawl between good and evil. I couldn't put it down."

—Wendy Tyson, author of *Rooted in Deceit*

"*The Unrepentant* is a gripping and unnerving tale about the sex trade, American justice, and what it means to be a hero. E.A. Aymar takes on a taboo subject with honesty and courage."

—Allison Leotta, author of *The Last Good Girl*

"A tale of unflinching brutality, told with dark humour and bursting with empathy for both victim and hapless criminal alike, *The Unrepentant* is an action-packed, fast-moving thrill ride sure to leave readers breathless."

—Owen Laukkanen, author of *The Professionals*

THE UNREPENTANT

ALSO BY E.A. AYMAR

The Dead Trilogy
I'll Sleep When You're Dead
You're As Good As Dead

As Co-Editor and Contributor
The Night of the Flood

E.A. AYMAR

THE UNREPENTANT

Down & Out Books
3959 Van Dyke Road, Suite 265
Lutz, FL 33558
DownAndOutBooks.com

The characters and events in this book are fictitious. Any similarity to real persons, living or dead, is coincidental and not intended by the author.

Cover design by JT Lindroos

ISBN: 1-948235-58-7
ISBN-13: 978-1-948235-58-7

AUTHOR'S NOTE

Charlotte's experiences, while not unheard of, are exaggerated for dramatic effect in *The Unrepentant*. Most women don't come to prostitution the same way she does (although some do), but the suffering and subsequent trauma are often similar. And while this is a thriller and a work of fiction, I certainly didn't want to employ suffering as a plot device or diminish abuse. I wanted Charlotte's pain to reach you, like a hand stretching out of the pages.

Know that the trauma Charlotte experiences, as well as her painful sense of identity loss and subsequent emotional repercussions, are all too real in the world of prostitution.

Some of the books I read that had a searing, lasting impact on me, and which I absolutely recommend to anyone interested in learning the truth behind prostitution and all forms of sex trafficking, are Rachel Moran's *Paid For: My Journey Through Prostitution*; Victor Malarek's *The Johns: Sex for Sale and the Men Who Buy It*; Dr. Melissa Farley's *Prostitution, Trafficking, and Traumatic Stress (Journal of Trauma Practice)*; Alisa Jordheim's *Made in the U.S.A.: The Sex Trafficking of America's Children*; Kevin Bales' *The Slave Next Door: Human Trafficking and Slavery in America Today*; Benjamin E. Skinners' *A Crime So Monstrous: Face-to-Face with Modern Day Slavery*; Siddarth Kara's *Sex Trafficking: Inside the Business of Modern Slavery*; Sophie Hayes' *Trafficked: My Story of Surviving, Escaping, and Transcending Abduction into Prostitution*.

I spoke with a number of women about their experiences, or the experiences of prostitutes they've taken into their care, and I owe a debt to Diana Ortiz of Doorways for Women and Families; Taina Bien Aime of the Coalition Against Trafficking in Women; Cherie Jimenez of the Eva Center; Dr. Holly Atkinson; and Stephanie Clark of Amirah, Inc. These women are fighters, their war is ongoing, and their organizations could use your support.

I spoke to other women who do not wish to be named, and I want you each to know that I appreciate your honesty and openness.

And, as always, thank you for reading.

—EA

*"...And there came one of the seven angels
which had the seven vials, and talked
with me, saying unto me, Come hither;
I will show unto thee the judgment
of the great whore that sitteth upon
many waters: With whom the kings
of the earth have committed
fornication, and the inhabitants of the
earth have been made drunk with the
wine of her fornication. So he carried me
away in the spirit into the wilderness..."*
—Revelations 17:1-3

CHAPTER ONE

Mace Peterson expected to see silhouettes of trees, a surprised deer or two, the smudge of a shadowed moon, maybe even a startled snake slithering away at midnight in the woods of Baltimore County.

What he hadn't expected was some man pulling a struggling woman out of a car's trunk.

Another man emerges from the passenger side. Mace shrinks back into the trees on the other side of the road, hoping he doesn't snap a twig.

The second man flips on a flashlight, gathers the woman's legs under one arm. They carry her into the trees as Mace crouches in the shadows. He can hear their grunts, and he hears something else.

Her voice, desperate, cracked with fear: "Stop. Okay? Please? I'll be good. I promise. I'll be good."

And then her voice is muffled. Her words turn unintelligible, but the panic filling them increases as they disappear into the dark.

Mace wants to run back to his apartment building for help, but it's over a mile away and he can't leave this woman with these men. He thinks about trying to stop them but shakes off the idea. Four years in the Army may have taught him how to fight, but that was close to a decade ago. And these men could have weapons. He doesn't.

Well, shit.

1

Mace nervously rubs his arm.

And follows them.

He watches the flashlight's beam bounce through the quiet night, one arm in front to feel for branches, squinting in what little light the moon provides. It's hard to keep quiet, but the two men are walking heavily, and the woman is still making pleading sounds through whatever is muffling her.

Mace worries about his breathing. Either exertion or fear has left his lungs shallow, and he wants to stop and greedily, loudly, suck in air. He reaches under his shirt and presses down over his heart, as if the pressure will calm it, and is surprised to discover his chest is cold with sweat.

The flashlight's beam stops moving.

He hears a thump.

Mace kneels behind a tree, peers into a pear-shaped clearing. One of the men is bent over, hands on his knees. The other man, taller and thinner, is glancing around. The woman's body is curled like a dying fish between them, her hands tied together.

The tall man reaches down, pulls something from her mouth.

Her words rush out like water released from a dam. "I'll be good, I promise. I'll be good."

The tall man kicks her in the stomach. She rolls over. Mace is surprised she doesn't make a sound but hears her gasping after a few seconds and realizes the wind was knocked out of her. She struggles into an arched position, her knees and forehead pressed into the dirt, coughing.

He closes his eyes, tries to control his breathing. Thinks again about running off for help, but he's so close, these men might notice if he moves.

He's trapped.

The shorter man, whose body reminds Mace of a thumb, tosses something and the tall man catches it. Mace leans forward, struggling to see what it is.

The man lifts his arm.

A small axe.

2

Mace's stomach is tightening like a towel being wrung of water. He's still unsure of what to do, what he *can* do.

"Wait," the man shaped like a thumb orders. The tall man lowers his arm. "We forgot the plastic sheets."

"Shit and fuck."

"I'll get them from the car," Thumb says. "Relax. It'll take a second."

"I'll get them," the tall man replies. His rough voice sounds like a chainsaw warming up. He throws the axe into the ground and walks off, passing so close that Mace can smell cigarette smoke on him.

Thumb picks the axe up. He hefts it in his hand, kneels next to the woman.

Mace rushes into the clearing.

He's not exactly sure what he's going to do.

But Thumb seems less dangerous than his counterpart, probably because of his exhausted, bent pose and chubby build. Mace isn't a model of physical fitness either, and he barely remembers the hand-to-hand combat he learned in the Army. Only one thing comes to mind, and it's from years ago, when he played safety for a season on his high school football team.

Thumb turns as Mace's shoulder smashes into the man's face.

Thumb is too surprised to do anything but grunt as his body sails back. Despite everything going on, and somewhere deep inside, Mace is proud of the hit. His old coach would have liked it. All six feet, two hundred pounds of him had gone into the impact. He takes the axe and tosses it into the trees. Then he grabs the woman, pulls her up.

"Come on."

They rush out of the clearing.

Thoughts dart through Mace's mind like scared fish.

Who is this woman?

Who were those men?

Is he going to die?

And also: *Where is he going?*

That's the important one.

Mace stops running and the woman stops with him. He listens to hear if they're being followed, but can't hear anything but his own breathing. He strains to stay silent.

Then he does hear something, a low whisper from the woman.

"Can you cut my hands free?"

Mace shakes his head. "I don't have anything to do it with."

"Why'd you throw away the axe?"

"I didn't want them to get it?"

"Christ. Run."

Mace is a little put off by her attitude, considering he just saved her life. They run again, crashing through the woods. Mace doesn't care about being quiet anymore, he just doesn't want to get caught. He changes path frequently, randomly turning right or left. He has no idea where he's going and is more than a little worried because she's following him faithfully. There's nothing but night around him, two violent men somewhere in it, and he's lost.

Branches grasp at his clothes. Shadows rush and recede. In the dark, the woods seem deep and impenetrable, a vast wilderness. But Mace knows this isn't the case. Baltimore County is a mix of city and nature, as if the two are constantly warring, and everything from the forests to the Chesapeake Bay is being pressed by buildings and roads and other new construction. He knows if they keep running they'll eventually emerge, and they do, onto a dark road.

He doesn't see any cars. "We need to get the cops."

"No cops." It's too dark for her to be anything but a silhouette. All he can see is that she's short and thin, slight even.

"Why not?"

She just shakes her head.

An idea occurs to Mace, and immediately shames him.

He could abandon her.

This woman is in a world of trouble, and he doesn't want to

join her in it. It's easy to imagine returning home and never seeing her again. He's already helped her. There's really no reason for him to do anything further.

But he doesn't leave. He knows the guilt will be too great. Something drew him to her. It was in her voice, the helpless, childlike way she begged.

"My name's Charlotte," she tells him.

"I'm Mace."

"Do you have a phone?"

"It's at my apartment." He pauses. "I got into a fight with my ex-wife and left. Thought about going back for it, but I couldn't. Not after storming out."

"So you don't have a phone?"

"Right."

"Let's stay on the side of the road," Charlotte says, decisively. "That way we can see if someone drives by."

"My apartment's somewhere around here. I just need to get my bearings."

"Get them while we run."

Charlotte hurries down the road.

He follows her, their footsteps softer on flatter ground. His adrenaline seems to be fading; the run is starting to tire him. He's not nearly in as good a shape as he was back when he enlisted, or even when he was married. A lot of sleepless, couch-sitting, Netflix-binging, potato chip-eating nights will do that to a person.

He and Charlotte round a corner. She stops.

Mace doesn't, and nearly knocks her over.

"What?" he starts to ask, and realizes he needs to catch his breath. He puts his hands on his knees, bends over.

When he looks up, he sees a car in front of him.

The car she was held in.

The tall man is standing next to it.

"What are you doing back here?" the tall man asks. "And who's that guy?"

He starts walking toward them.

"Did we just run in a circle?" Charlotte whispers.

"Maybe."

The tall man reaches down, lifts his pants leg. Pulls out a long knife from an ankle sheath.

CHAPTER TWO

Charlotte Reyes wants to run off, but she can't abandon this guy moments after he saved her life. And he's staring at the tall man, seemingly rooted to the ground. She looks around for some type of weapon. Sees a hand-sized rock.

The tall man goes after Mace first. He lunges, the knife even with Mace's eyes. Mace stumbles back into a tree, slips and falls.

The blade ends up quivering in the tree just above Mace's head.

The tall man is staring at the knife. "Shit and..."

Charlotte holds the rock tight between her bound hands.

Uses all her force to smash it into the back of his head.

The impact is sudden and violent, like the sound of someone slamming the soles of two boots together. The tall man goes down to a knee. Charlotte smashes the stone down again, knocking him flat.

She lifts it.

Mace catches her arm.

"Don't kill him."

Charlotte stares at him, confused. "What?"

"He's out. And we need to leave before Thumb comes back."

"Who?"

"We need to go."

Charlotte drops the rock.

A hasty search doesn't reveal the tall man's car keys. Charlotte follows Mace down the road to a trail, relieved the entrance isn't easily visible in the dark. They move as fast as they can without making unnecessary noise. Charlotte stays behind him, fighting the urge to turn and leave, the urge to spare Mace the violence she just escaped.

She knows it will come after her.

Charlotte's not sure how long they spend on the trail, but it seems like a half hour passes before they emerge into a narrow grassy field. Three identical buildings stand across the field from them, each one wide but only a couple of stories high. Mace points to the closest.

"My apartment's there."

A beat passes.

"Maybe we should go in?"

"Oh," Mace says. "Right. I'm trying to figure out what to do. I'm guessing I shouldn't be seen walking into the building with someone tied-up."

Charlotte turns to let Mace undo the knots. The rope cuts into her wrists, into the sores left by handcuffs. She tries to ignore the pain.

"I can't loosen the rope," Mace tells her.

"Can you just pull one of my hands out?"

"Maybe." Charlotte feels his hand over her wrist. He tugs. The rope bites into her skin until she cries out.

"Why'd you stop?" she asks.

"I don't want to hurt you."

"Keep pulling."

She closes her eyes, grits her teeth, feels Mace's hands around her wrist. There's a moment of pain so intense that the insides of her eyelids turn white. She drops to her knees.

But her hands are free.

Mace helps her stand.

"Are you okay?"

"Yeah." Charlotte tries to rub the raw paths cut into her wrists. They're too painful to touch.

They cross the field to the building's back door. Mace unlocks it, holds it open, leads Charlotte up a flight of stairs. The second-floor hall is dark, narrow, quiet and, fortunately, empty. Mace stops outside his apartment. He turns toward Charlotte, opens his mouth to say something, freezes.

He's staring at the bruises on her face, the scabs and dried blood.

She pulls her curly black hair down, looks away.

"Sorry," Mace says. "I just, I was surprised…"

"Can we go inside?"

He unlocks the door, pushes it open. Charlotte enters first. Mace follows and closes and locks the door behind them. She watches him do it.

The apartment is small and dimly-lit, very much a bachelor pad. The walls are all white and Charlotte only sees one picture hung, a framed black and white movie poster for some depressing-looking movie. A tiny square kitchen with the absolute basics—dirty stove, thin refrigerator, old toaster, outdated microwave on a crumb-covered counter—is to her right. The front door opened into the living room, and the only furniture is a black leather recliner facing a wall-mounted television. Closed doors bookend either side of the room. There's a scent of mustiness in the air, as if the room is rarely opened to the outside.

"Eve?" Mace calls out.

No answer.

"Who's Eve?"

"My ex-wife."

"Your ex lives with you?"

"She came over to talk."

Something about that doesn't make sense to Charlotte. She doesn't show it, but suspicion tightens her body. "Why'd you leave your own apartment?"

"I just needed to get out of there." Mace has his own questions. "Who were those men?"

She stays guarded. "They were holding me. Doing things I didn't want them to."

Mace shifts his weight. "And we can't call the cops?"

"No."

"Why not?"

Charlotte ignores him. "Can I use your bathroom?"

Mace wants to ask again about the cops but decides against it. He nods.

Charlotte walks quickly, enters the bathroom, closes and locks the door behind her. She sees a sink, toilet, cramped standing shower and, inside the shower, old grooming supplies. A hand towel hangs on a hook near the door, a small frosted window is set in the wall tiles. She tries to open the window. It won't budge.

Charlotte sits on the closed toilet seat and rubs her eyes.

She wants to keep running.

She can't end up back in that basement, blind in the dark, her body jerking whenever a man's hand touched her skin. Begging for them to stop or let her go, that helplessness when they'd ignore her. Weight pressing down, suffocating Charlotte until she was finally free to gasp and cry.

She stands, turns on the faucet, gingerly touches her face with warm water. She tries to notice how much blood and dirt are swirling down the drain. She's careful not to look at herself in the mirror.

Charlotte turns off the water, softly pats her aching face with the hand towel. She spots a small pair of curved scissors in Mace's grooming supplies, digs them out, touches the tips.

Charlotte slips the scissors into her pocket.

She opens the bathroom door. Mace is still standing in the living room.

"Are you being honest with me?" he asks. "Why can't we go to the cops?"

"One of the men who had me was a cop. He said they'd help him get me back if I told."

"Oh." Mace swallows. "I'm sorry."

She can't completely let her guard down, but something about Mace seems trustworthy. Maybe it's because all the men Charlotte's come across recently have been cruel and Mace, somehow, seems softer.

"Are you Native American?" she asks.

"Because I knew my way around the woods so well?"

That makes her smile. "I was just wondering where you're from."

"Maryland. But my dad was black and my mom was white, if you're really asking about my tan."

Charlotte looks at him more carefully. "Wouldn't have guessed that."

"No one does. What about you?"

"Mexican."

"I thought so because of the accent but...Charlotte's a Mexican name?"

"It's not, I am. Is Mace short for something?"

"No."

"That's your real name?"

He looks sheepish. "My real name's Marcus but, when I was in high school, I was sitting in the back of a class playing with pepper spray and sprayed myself in the face. After that, everyone called me Mace."

Charlotte stares at him, then briskly shakes her head. "What were you doing in the woods?"

"I wanted to be alone after the fight with Eve. She's a lawyer. I never win our arguments."

"How long has Eve been your ex?"

"We were together a decade. Been apart a year."

"A decade?" Charlotte squints at Mace. "How old are you?"

"Thirty-seven. You?"

"Eighteen."

"You are?" He sounds surprised. "You don't look that young."

"I'm starting to see why she left you."

Mace smiles.

Charlotte can't remember the last time she saw a man smile.

But then he walks toward her and she backs away. Her hand digs for the scissors in her pocket.

Mace lifts his hands. "I'm just going to sit in this chair. Okay?"

"Yeah." The tension is back in her body, like a cat readying itself to jump. Mace walks around the wide recliner and settles into it.

Charlotte's hand stays in her pocket.

"If you want to talk about what happened," Mace offers, "you can. That's all I wanted to tell you."

"I thought maybe you were going to hug me, say 'it's not your fault' over and over."

Mace laughs, and his laugh is nice and low and rhythmic. It surprises Charlotte, but not in a bad way.

After what's happened, the idea of a comforting man seemed impossible. But there's a kindness in his caution toward her, in his smile and eyes and laugh.

Mace rubs his chin, the beginning of a beard more careless than intentional. "Well, it's *not* your fault, but I wasn't going to tell you that. Just wanted to sit."

They're quiet for a few moments.

"You only have the one recliner?"

"Yeah. And a microwave. Want some mac and cheese?"

"Not really."

"That's okay. I'd have to toast it. Microwave's busted."

Charlotte almost smiles at that, even if she suspects it's true.

"You got family nearby?" Mace asks.

Charlotte studies him. "Not sure I want to go into that."

"Okay." Mace scratches his unkempt hair and a few gray strands blink out of the black. "I just meant, is there anyone nearby who can protect you?"

"I should get going."

"Where?" Mace asks, startled. "You just said you didn't have anywhere to turn."

"I can't put you in danger. And you're in danger as long as I'm with you."

"There's no way anyone followed us here," Mace assures her.

Their conversation is interrupted by a knock on the door.

CHAPTER THREE

"Crap." Charlotte glances around the room. Scared, she seems even smaller.

"It's them," she whispers.

"It's probably just a neighbor." Mace looks down at her hands. "Why do you have my toenail clippers?"

Another knock.

"Is there a place to hide?" Charlotte's voice is still low.

"You don't need to—"

She darts back into the bathroom, softly closes the door. He hears it lock.

A third knock.

Mace opens the door.

He doesn't recognize the man on the other side. Tall, good-looking, brown hair, blue eyes, wearing jeans and an open leather jacket with a plain black shirt underneath.

The man smiles, shows Mace a shiny silver badge. "Officer David Baker. Baltimore County P.D."

"One of the men who had me was a cop."

Mace keeps his expression blank. "Okay."

"We're searching for a missing fugitive. Hispanic female. Late teens, dark hair, brown eyes, slim build. Five-foot-even. You seen anyone matching that description tonight?"

Mace shakes his head.

"Are you sure?"

"I haven't been out all night."

Officer Baker looks down at Mace's feet. Mace follows his gaze, sees his own muddy sneakers.

Baker glances back up, studies him. Mace stares right back, keeping his expression blank.

Mace hasn't suffered from cops the way some of his black friends had, but that's largely because of his uncle. Any time he'd been stopped by a police officer, and Mace sensed the situation could turn threatening, he casually mentioned his uncle's work with Baltimore County P.D., even after his uncle had suffered a heart attack and passed on.

Mace is about to mention his uncle, but Officer Baker leans close. "This woman is extremely dangerous. If she's inside and threatening you…"

"No one's in here but me."

The cop gives Mace the long look black people are used to receiving. Then he steps back and smiles, baring big, white teeth. "If you see something, report it. Call the station and ask for me."

Mace watches him go to the next apartment. Then he closes his door, locks it. He's not breathing right, almost as if he's forgotten how. He takes a few moments, then heads to the bathroom.

He knocks on the door.

Charlotte opens it, the scissors tight in her hand.

"Okay?" she asks.

Mace still has questions, but he has enough answers. The bruises on Charlotte's face are enough. The red raw rings over her wrists are enough.

"Okay."

CHAPTER FOUR

Will Hasting's insides feel like a bag of cats being stomped to death. He hopes he doesn't look that nervous, hopes his expression is calm while Frank, his older brother, talks on the phone and paces.

"How many more in the area?" Frank asks. "And you're hitting every apartment? Every single one?"

He glances at Will, who looks down at his lap.

"Okay." Frank hangs up the phone, stares at it like he's going to hurl it into the wall. Instead he tosses it onto the bed.

"How the fuck did they lose Charlotte?" he asks Will.

Will shrugs. "I mean, I wasn't there."

"They told Dave someone attacked them in the woods and ran off with her."

That piques Will's interest, despite how uncomfortable he feels. "Really?"

"No fucking idea." Frank walks to the other side of the room, puts both hands flat against the wall, leans his forehead against it. Will stays on the floor, too nervous to say something and incur Frank's wrath.

He's not sure why his older brother intimidates him. They share the same height and build: both about five-ten and a hundred sixty pounds, sandy-blond hair, thin limbs, narrow faces, lines for lips.

Then again, he's never seen Frank this agitated.

"Maybe we shouldn't have…" Will's voice trails away.

15

Frank turns, stares him down. "Shouldn't have what?"

"Nothing."

"Shouldn't have *what*?"

"Shouldn't have gotten involved with this stuff."

The stare turns hard.

"We were doing fine," Will adds.

The gaze softens. "Well, don't worry about it because, chances are, we're not doing it again. No way Barnes is trusting us with this shit anymore."

"What happened to his two guys? Are they coming back here?"

"Dave has no idea. Doesn't even know where they are."

"I didn't like them." Will says. He didn't like the brusque way they showed up and took charge, or the sense of menace they carried, of blood and violence.

"Anyway," Frank says, dismissively, "Dave's hitting all the houses and apartments nearby, seeing what he can turn up."

"What if he can't find her?" Will hopes Frank can't hear the nervousness in his voice.

He hopes Frank can't tell part of him wants Charlotte to escape.

Frank rans a hand through his hair before he speaks. "We keep looking. Find her, finish her off."

"But if we don't?"

Frank gazes at Will and shakes his head. "Dave told me we need to wipe this place clean."

Will looks around the little basement room. A small bed with chains and handcuffs looped over two hooks. The hooks are bolted into the stone wall on either side of the bed.

"There's not much to clean," Will observes. "You want me to wash the sheets?"

"We need to burn them. Dave said that if she gets to the cops and he can't stop her, she might bring them back here. This place has to look normal."

"Not like the kind of house where you hide kidnapped women?"

"Right. The chains have to go, too. We'll leave the hooks up. Can't get them out anyway." He gives Will another hard look. "What?"

"It was easier when we were just selling weed to white kids in the 'burbs."

Frank's expression softens again. "I get that. But like Dave said, holding that girl for a month should pay what we make in three. Unless you want to try selling inside Baltimore. Fuck with those gangs."

Will shakes his head.

"We can't go back." Frank reaches into his pocket, pulls out a pair of medical gloves, starts tugging one on. "All we can do is go forward. And cover our tracks." He pulls on the other glove. It slaps down on his skin. "Which means finding that bitch and covering her with dirt."

CHAPTER FIVE

"How do you not have a gun?" Charlotte asks, as she paces back and forth. "What kind of American are you?"

"We need the cops," Mace tells her. "Not a weapon."

"He *is* the cops."

"Not all of them. There has to be someone else. The FBI. The CIA. Magnum."

"Who?"

"Never mind." For a moment, Mace thinks about the men he served with, the few who became friends. But it's been too long to turn to them. The separation was too severe.

Except for what drove him out, his military service seems like it happened to someone else.

"I think we're okay for now," Mace goes on. "That cop was stopping at every apartment in the building. He had no idea you were here. Just thought I was some awkward lonely guy."

Charlotte stops pacing, looks at Mace.

"I'm only a *little* awkward," he amends.

Charlotte ignores him. "My guess is they're keeping an eye on the buildings around here. They know someone helped me. So don't mention it, like, on Facebook."

"I don't have Facebook," Mace tells her.

"You make me sad." Charlotte meant it as a joke, but it sounds harsher than she intended. She's relieved when he grins.

"Anyway," she says, "I know you're worried. You're not sure who I am or who those men were. I'll leave. Trust me, I can take care of myself."

Mace walks into the kitchen, pulls out a water bottle from the fridge, offers it to Charlotte. She catches it when he tosses it to her. He takes out another, twists off the top and drinks.

She wipes her mouth with the back of her hand, pressing gingerly on the bruises.

"How'd you even get involved with those men?"

Charlotte takes another drink. "That's not something I want to talk about now. And, honestly, I'm kind of tired. Like everything just hit me."

Mace believes her. He remembers soldiers in Iraq after they returned from missions. How tired they were from the adrenaline loss, eyes half-open and unfocused, dead on their feet. And exhaustion is spreading through him too, like a fog filling and dulling his body.

"You can stay here," he tells her. "I have a spare bedroom. There's a lock on the door."

Charlotte hesitates. "You sure?"

"Yeah."

"It's just for the night."

Mace nods.

"And, also, were you serious about that mac and cheese?"

CHAPTER SIX

Despite how tired he is, Mace struggles to sleep.

He closes his eyes and feels branches pulling at his clothes. Hears the thud of that knife plunging into the tree. The heavy stone smashing a man's skull.

He gets up, pulls sweatpants over his boxers, limps into the living room, legs sore from running and tension. He sits in his only chair and reclines it.

The argument with Eve earlier tonight seems like years ago. Mace remembers a trip they once took to San Diego, a spontaneous vacation. How odd it was to stand on one coast and then, hours later, another. As if it wasn't possible the same person had stood in two such distant places in one single day. That's what the argument feels like. But not just removed by time.

Mace almost feels like it happened to a different person.

He leans over, tries to rub the ache out of his calves. Bending hurts his back.

Jesus, he thinks. *Charlotte doesn't even know who Magnum P.I. is.*

I'm getting old.

Mace stretches his legs, wonders what to do about Charlotte. He can't just let her leave, go off alone into a world where vicious men are hunting her.

And he promised her he wouldn't call the cops.

Mace pulls his phone out of his sweatpants, taps it against his palm.

He understands why she wants to avoid them.

But that doesn't mean every cop in Maryland's on the take.

If he called, Charlotte would be furious, but she'd be safe.

And so would he.

Mace dials 9-1-1 but doesn't press SEND.

He hangs up.

Something gnaws at his insides.

Guilt.

He doesn't want to lie to Charlotte. Seems like she's had enough shitty people in her life.

Tomorrow, Mace decides. Tomorrow he'll talk with her, try and convince her that the cops or feds can help.

Mace settles deeper in the chair, rests his head back into the soft cushion. He sends an email to his office from his phone, telling them he had a family emergency and he'll need a day or two off. The website development company he works for lets him telecommute, but Mace figures it'll be hard to concentrate on coding with Charlotte hiding out in his home.

The argument with Eve returns to him. He never should have married an attorney. Mace has lost every argument they've ever had, from which cable package to buy to whether pancakes counted as dinner to tonight's, whether or not Mace should see someone for his depression.

He'd try to explain that he wasn't depressed.

"You don't think so?" Eve had asked, skeptically.

"I'm good."

Her eyes narrowed. "You're in an apartment the size of a Hyundai with barely any furniture and..." She sniffed. "It always smells like pancakes in here. You're lonely, Mace. I don't want you to be lonely. You deserve more."

There was an implication there that Mace didn't want to pursue. Eve wanted him to be with someone, just not necessarily her. She wanted him to move on. And that was hard for Mace to believe...unless Eve had met someone else.

"Have you..." he asked, and let the question drop.

"Have I what?"

"Met someone."

Eve didn't look away, didn't change her expression. Stared at him with those analyzing lawyer eyes. "This is about you, not me. And I want you to be happy." Her expression changed, softened by empathy. "Wouldn't you want that for me?"

"I'd prefer that you're alone, too."

A small trace of a smile. "Really? Even if you'd met someone else?"

"Yeah. Absolutely."

Mace drifts back to the present, looks at the only picture in his apartment, a framed movie poster of Woody Allen's *Manhattan*. The poster is black and white and depicts one of the iconic scenes in the movie—Woody Allen and Diane Keaton's silhouettes on a park bench, staring at a morning mist-shrouded Queensboro Bridge. Mace has never seen the movie, but something about the image drew him to buy the poster. He liked the intimacy of the couple, the way they're alone in a public place. It's hard to tell, but it seems like Diane Keaton is facing Allen as he looks forward, his figure forlorn. Everything in the picture is shadowed but decipherable: the wooden park bench, a thin tree, authoritative street signs, the small dog next to Keaton.

Even the bridge is faded to the point that it almost blends into the white background, yet it dominates the picture.

Mace stares at the poster until his eyes close.

CHAPTER SEVEN

Mace could be a saint or a psychopath and, after everything she's been through, Charlotte's nowhere near comfortable enough to fall asleep in a stranger's apartment.

Plus, she's lactose intolerant and the mac and cheese hurt her stomach.

She sits up in bed. There's not much in the room aside from the bed and a dresser full of Mace's clothes. She's wearing her jeans and one of his T-shirts, a grey one that hangs to her knees and smells like wood, as if it's spent years in a dresser drawer.

She can't stop watching the doorknob, waiting for Mace to try the lock.

She slides off the bed.

Charlotte pulls the door open and peers outside. The kitchen light is on, the living room dimly illuminated. She's surprised that Mace is sleeping in the recliner and not in his bedroom.

There's no way she can stay here.

Even if Mace was honest about everything he said, Charlotte doesn't feel safe in this apartment, less than a mile from where she was almost murdered. And that cop already came. What if something aroused his suspicion? What if he comes back with the rest of them and they force their way in?

Her wrists burn from the ropes. Her mind is jumpy with memories of those men coming into the room she was held in, lying on top of her, pulling her out of the car's trunk, dragging her through the woods. Men controlling her for weeks, maybe months, she has no idea. Those hands pushing and pulling and forcing her to bend until she nearly broke, like dried clay.

Charlotte walks across the apartment noiselessly, past snoring Mace, slips into his bedroom. She reaches for the light switch but decides not to turn it on. She leaves the door open, using the light from the kitchen.

She finds his wallet on the dresser, the same place her uncle kept his.

There's not much, about eighty dollars.

Charlotte takes it all.

She figures she can use the money to get a cab, but she didn't see much traffic outside the apartment building and has no idea how close the nearest major street is. Good thing the key fob to Mace's car is right next to his wallet. Charlotte grabs the key and is about to stuff it into her pocket, but pauses.

What if Mace calls the police and reports her? The last thing she needs is to get arrested, brought back to that cop.

And Charlotte doesn't want to steal his car. Despite her distrust, Mace has been nothing but nice to her.

She's growing nervous, worried he'll wake. Whatever she's going to do, she needs to do it quickly.

She takes the car key.

Mace is still sleeping in the chair. She sees the thinning dark hair on top of his head, hears his soft snore. She tries to think of anything else she needs—food, water, more money—but everything she can think of runs the risk of waking him.

Charlotte walks to the front door, turns the knob, steps outside.

The hall is empty.

She closes the door and hurries to the stairs. Heads down. Pushes open the door leading outside. Peers through it.

Steps out into the cool night.

Charlotte runs over to a dark inlet in the building. From here she can see the parking lot and the sign for the apartment complex: Garden Crossing.

What garden?

She pushes a button on the key fob. A truck's red taillights blink at her.

Charlotte hurries to the truck, pulls open the door, climbs inside. She has no idea where she's going.

Just away.

CHAPTER EIGHT

Frank's phone rings.

Will and Frank watch it, too nervous to answer. Their partner, Seth Yates, strides out of the bathroom, his curiosity gone the moment he sees the caller ID.

He puts the phone on speaker.

"Why isn't Charlotte dead?" Barnes asks, his voice raspy, harsh.

No one says anything.

Will doesn't know much about Barnes, and he's not sure if the rumors are true. That Barnes spent time in the military, either Iraq or Afghanistan. But some people say he never went overseas. They say he stayed in the Southwest, traveled back and forth to Mexico to train the Mexican military to fight the cartels. No one is sure of the truth. Everyone is too intimidated to ask.

Will isn't even sure if Barnes is his first or last name. If it's real at all.

"She was with a couple of your guys," Frank puts in, nervously. "Someone attacked them in the woods."

"Was it one of you?"

"What?" Will asks. "No!"

"You think we're that dumb?" Will can hear the fear in Frank's voice.

"Maybe," Barnes says. "I'm not sure how dumb you are. But my guys were in the middle of the woods somewhere in fucking Maryland, in the middle of the night, and they were jumped by someone who just happened to be in that same spot at the same time. That sound suspicious to you?"

"Well," Frank admits, "when you say it like that..."

"Where's Dave, the cop?" Barnes interrupts. "He there?"

"He's out looking for her," Seth says. "But he didn't have anything to do with it."

Seth's voice doesn't hold the same fear that Frank and Will share. He's always reminded Will of a worn wall; scarred but standing.

Barnes doesn't sound convinced. Will understands why. It's too unlikely a coincidence. He'd been with Frank that night, but Dave and Seth were both out. One of their group of four could have tried to save her.

But that doesn't make sense.

Not after what they'd done to her.

"No one double-crossed you," Frank is saying. "We're looking for her. Dave's checking all the buildings near the woods where they lost her. We'll find her."

"Three days," Barnes tells them. "Three days from now, if she's still out there, your gang of four is cut down to three."

His line disconnects.

CHAPTER NINE

Mace can't believe he didn't hear Charlotte leave.

But its morning, her door is open, and the guest bedroom is empty.

He's alone in the apartment.

He also can't believe he slept as long as he did. He woke around nine a.m., and it's been years since he slept past six. Eve used to hate that he was an early-riser.

It was part of his makeup. Even as a child, Mace liked structure, the more rigid the better. He put his toys away as a toddler, ate cleanly, woke and went to bed at the same time for years. Any disruption to his daily schedule caused tears. He relaxed as he grew older, but some of those early habits manifested in different ways: he was always on time, happily predictable.

And then his grandfather committed suicide when he was just out of college, and order was gone.

His grandfather had grappled with depression and lost. Mace remembered visiting him, the bleary way his grandfather greeted him, trying to speak through a haze of drugs. And when they heard the news, that he'd sliced his wrists open, everything about Mace's mother collapsed.

It was like déjà vu from his childhood visits with his grandfather. Mace and Eve would find his mother sleeping on the couch, barely able to wake up for their visit. Mace tried to help, begged her to continue counseling, offered to move her into their house or even move in with her, but she refused. She had moments of sobriety where it almost seemed as if she'd recovered, when she smiled through tears, joked with Eve about Mace's childhood or mischievously hinted at hopes for grandchildren.

She seemed happy the last time Mace saw her, a year and a half ago. She moved aside pillows and blankets, so he could sit next to her, and talked with him about her depression. She said it was genetic, said her struggles had grown worse. Claimed it caused her divorce, her listlessness, her absence from friends and family. She cried when she told Mace she was happy it hadn't affected him.

Mace didn't have the heart to tell her that he was on antidepressants.

Had been ever since he left the Army.

Where the hell did Charlotte go? Mace rubs his face. He's tired, and the soreness in his legs has spread through his chest and arms and back. But he needs to find her: for her safety, and for another reason he can't quite understand. The more he'd spoken with Charlotte, the more familiar she seemed. Almost as if he's known her for years.

He heads to the bathroom and strips down to take a quick shower before he goes searching. Mace turns on the water, looks at himself in the mirror, at the chest fighting a losing battle to hold definition, the softening biceps that used to be boulders.

At least, that's how he remembers them.

Mace steps in the shower and lets hot water run down his back. The heat leaves his skin tingling. He closes his eyes.

And hears his front door open.

His head pops up, hand on the faucet, about to turn the water off. He leaves it on, figures it better whoever's out there is unaware he's heard them. Mace slides open the shower curtain, grabs a towel, wraps it around his waist.

"Mace?"

The tension disappears.

He opens the bathroom door and steps outside.

Eve's sitting on his recliner, long legs leisurely crossed.

She looks more relaxed than she did when he stormed out the night before. She's wearing black pants, brown boots and a brown blazer. The way she's sitting accentuates her legs and lean body, and the colors in her outfit contrast nicely with her black skin. She's bound her braids at the bottom and turned her hair into one long lovely rope. He can smell her lotion from where he stands. Like its drawing him closer to her.

It's hard for him to look at her face, her full lips and soft eyes, and not feel overwhelmed by love.

But Eve's trying to play it cool. He plays it cooler. "I thought we were done talking."

Water's running down his face, and Mace runs his hands through his wet hair.

The movement accidentally causes the towel to fall to the floor.

"You're not happy to see me?" Eve asks.

In his bedroom, Mace pulls on a pair of boxers, jeans, and a T-shirt. He hears Eve changing television channels in the living room, staying on each channel longer than he would, one of those meaningless married habits that used to inexplicably irritate him.

Mace walks into the living room, leans against the wall. Eve is watching some show about people renovating a house.

"I thought we were done talking."

She turns toward him. "I'm worried about you."

Mace shrugs, tries to make the motion nonchalant. "You said that last night. I'm fine."

He wonders about Charlotte. Wonders where she went, if she's okay. He'd planned on searching for her, taking his truck around the neighborhood, seeing if he can spot her. The odds are slim, but he has to do something.

And if that doesn't work, he'll call the cops. Tell them everything that happened.

"You don't seem fine," Eve is saying. "And how long do you plan on living here?"

"What's wrong with this place? It gets cable."

Her forehead furrows. "Cable? Who still has cable?"

"I'm not coming back."

"I'm not asking." Eve doesn't let the sentence linger; this is the point that caused their explosive fight the night before. "I don't want to look after you. I'm not your babysitter."

"Right." He's not sure where she's going with this.

"All I want is for you to talk to somebody."

"Another counselor?"

"I think you should try someone else. There's nothing wrong with trying, right?"

Mace takes a moment before he speaks.

"I appreciate you coming back here," he tells Eve. "I do. But you don't have to." He walks to the window, pulls open the blinds, looks out to the wooded path that leads to the Jones Fall River.

"You're not going to kill yourself," Eve says. "You're not her."

"You have no idea what it's like when you're down. Really down." It feels easier to talk this way, looking out the window instead of at Eve. "Doesn't feel like you're ever going to come up."

"You're taking your medicine, right?"

Mace nods.

"Then it's not going to drag you down forever. When depression hits, it's not real. And the sadness won't last. When you're on your pills, that's the real you."

"What if it's not? What if the real me is the person without pills?"

"Remember what that doctor said? How the body naturally heals bruises? We're not meant to suffer. Our bodies recover. The medicine helps with that."

Mace doesn't say anything.

"I'm worried about you, no matter what you tell me. Especially because you don't seem like you want to get better."

And at that, like a suddenly struck match, anger flares. He faces her. "You don't understand."

"Then tell me." Eve's expression is blank, refusing to let emotion in. "What don't I understand?"

"When I talk about that stuff, it feels like it'll drag me down. I don't want to talk about it."

"You don't want to talk about it, and you won't turn to someone else?"

Mace nods. "That sounds about right."

Eve stands. "I'm not doing this. I'm not having this conversation again."

"Go ahead then. Like you left our marriage."

That stops her, just as Mace knew it would.

"You didn't make it easy to be around," Eve tells him, struggling to keep her anger controlled. "I tried."

The word "tried" stirs something in Mace, sends him back to the time when he'd found his mother's body on the couch, pills spilled on the floor like confetti, smiling childhood pictures of him on the table. After her funeral, he couldn't be close to anyone. He pushed her away emotionally and, eventually, they stayed in different corners of their house. Mace was downing Paxil and Xanax, numbed and alone, turning cold whenever Eve approached.

She tried to help, her family tried to help. He rebuffed their efforts. And Eve was alone, and she was never the type to be alone. She turned to Mace helplessly, begged him. He held her with limp arms. When Eve gave up, Mace didn't begrudge her. Helping someone who's sick is a romantic notion; in reality, it's a superhuman effort. He couldn't ask it of her.

He left.

The new situation didn't feel better, but it did feel natural.

They stayed in infrequent touch for months but, a few weeks ago, Eve had returned. Showed up at his door and tried to get him to talk.

"You don't owe me anything," he says now. "Just a goodbye."

Something in Eve's expression cracks, almost breaks. She starts to say something but goes to the door instead.

Mace wants to call out to her.

But he doesn't.

A few minutes later Mace is chewing his thumb knuckle and wondering if he should go after her.

Yeah…

On one hand, Eve's got a good future ahead of her without him dragging her down. She's smart, beautiful, tough, funny, ethical…Mace should let her go, let her step away from him and his dips into depression.

Let her leave you. Let her start over. Find what she needs.

She deserves more.

On the other hand…

When she finds more, it'll be with someone else.

Mace hurries after her.

He spots Eve at the end of the parking lot, striding toward her black Toyota sedan. He's about call to her when someone touches him.

Mace turns, sees a grinning man, and recognizes him immediately.

It's the man from the woods, the one he knocked to the ground. The one who had been holding an axe.

Thumb.

Mace has no idea what to say.

"Oh, hey."

Doesn't sound right.

Thumb doesn't say hello back. Just keeps grinning. He lifts the bottom of his coat to show Mace a gun. Points to a van at the other end of the lot.

CHAPTER TEN

A few hours earlier Charlotte sits on a bench, arms wrapped around her knees, and stares dourly at Baltimore's Greyhound bus terminal, unaware of what's about to befall Mace.

It hasn't been easy to find. She'd driven until she found an all-night gas station, and the attendant working there gave her directions she somehow forgot minutes later. She stopped at a second gas station, bought a Snickers bar, and drove until she found the bus terminal off a dark side road.

The terminal is closed until morning. And Charlotte has passed so many cops that she doesn't feel comfortable waiting inside of the truck she's stolen from Mace. She parked, left the key on the front tire, and sat on a bench across the street.

Charlotte isn't sure where she was going; she just planned to take a bus as far as eighty dollars (minus a Snickers bar) would take her. Pennsylvania? North Carolina? She has no idea how far Barnes's reach extended. He'd gotten her to Baltimore from all the way across the country, had planned on sending her to Russia.

He must have people all over the U.S., maybe the world.

She hugs her knees tight to her chest, as if she can eventually shrink away into nothing.

A homeless man limps past the bench, muttering to himself. She eyes him but he doesn't glance at her. Just keeps limping.

Charlotte watches him walk away. She always wondered what turned someone homeless; imagined those men and women as babies that were loved and cared for enough to grow into children, and then adults. When had they been cast aside?

Or had they jumped, like she had, blindly and desperately?

And landed in chains?

She remembers those moments when she'd see sunlight in the basement, when one of those men opened the door at the top of the stairs. She's always loved sunlight, basks in its warmth whenever she can. But back then, sunlight couldn't reach her. And even if it had, it wouldn't have broken through her grief.

Grief and resignation had consumed her.

Until something else had grown.

Something dark. Impenetrable.

Charlotte rubs her eyes, presses her palms into them.

"Shit," she says to herself.

It's easy to get lost in her thoughts, so easy that she realizes an hour must have passed. Cars and trucks are starting to rumble over roads. Birds chatter. Dawn is coming.

She wonders if Mace will help, maybe get her across the country. She can go back to California, try and start over, lose herself in that state's long stretch of land. Barnes will never know she's no longer in Baltimore, or even in one of the surrounding states.

And maybe, with Mace, she landed somewhere safe. If she runs off again, she has no idea where she'll end up.

She couldn't confidently stay in his apartment, but what women could after what she'd gone through? But now, some distance removed, she isn't nearly as worried about him.

Charlotte just hopes he isn't too mad about the truck.

She leaves the bench, takes the key from the tire, climbs back into the cab. She pulls out of the station and drives and then exhaustion hits her. Hard, like a punch to the back of her head, leaving her groggy. She finds an open parking garage, spots a secluded corner, pulls into it, her head nodding as she turns off the ignition.

Charlotte sleeps for a couple of hours, wakes confused. Remembers where she is, then leaves the garage and gets directions back to Garden Crossing Apartments.

When she returns she parks and collects her thoughts. Tries to think of what she'll tell Mace.

And sees him. Walking across the lot.

A short stumpy man is behind him, keeping close. They reach a van and the man opens the side door. Mace says something, and the man pulls a gun from his jacket pocket.

Mace nods.

Charlotte takes a closer look at the man, recognizes him from last night. The one Mace knocked over.

That same feeling she had in the basement, that sense of something cold and dangerous growing inside of her, returns.

She thinks about the way that man had held the axe over her, how he'd pulled her by her hair out of the trunk. Thinks about the terrible things he'd whispered to her.

She feels like she's burning.

Charlotte opens the truck door and steps out into the cold morning.

CHAPTER ELEVEN

Mace reflects on the various regrets of his life as Thumb leads him to the van.

He regrets not shouting for help. He wanted to keep Eve out of danger, but ever since she climbed into her car and sped away, Mace has second-guessed that choice.

He regrets not having a child. Neither he or Eve ever wanted children, but the absence of a child, particularly around their friends' large families, often felt stark. He wondered how much that absence affected Eve. She never said anything about it, never indicated any unhappiness, but Mace wasn't sure he believed her. And she would have made a wonderful mother. It would be nice to have an older child now, perhaps fully grown. Who could save him.

Speaking of children, he regrets saving Charlotte.

No, he doesn't.

Maybe a little.

Mace wonders if he should try and make a break for the woods, suddenly take off running. But he wouldn't make it more than a few steps before Thumb shot him.

Then again, he has one more option.

He can beg. Shamelessly.

"I don't know what you want or who you are, but I can't help you."

Thumb reaches past Mace, grabs the van door, slides it open.

Mace sees nothing but a floor and walls covered with dark plastic.

"Don't act dumb. You remember me. Get in the van."

Mace shakes his head, tries to look confused. "I don't."

Thumb pulls his gun out.

"I don't," Mace whispers, his hands rising in surrender.

The man's other fist flies out of his pocket and smashes Mace's left cheek. It's a hard punch. Mace stumbles backward, trips, falls butt first inside the van. His cheek feels shattered. Pain spiderwebs through his skull.

His legs are shoved inside. The door creaks shut.

The door slides back open.

Charlotte is standing behind Thumb.

Mace blinks, sees her hand in Thumb's pocket.

Mace can tell from the bulge that she's holding his weapon.

"Close the door," Charlotte tells Mace.

He looks at her.

Charlotte grabs the door with her free hand and slams it closed. Thumb's eyes widen as he realizes what's happening, just as his head is caught between the door and the edge. Charlotte closes the door on the man's head again.

"Give me a hand," she tells Mace.

Mace can't stop staring at Thumb, now slumped unconscious halfway inside.

"Mace! I can't lift him by myself."

Mace numbly grabs him under the shoulders and pulls Thumb inside. Charlotte climbs in and closes the door.

"We have to move. They'll check in with him. Come looking when he doesn't answer." She reaches into the man's pocket, pulls out his keys, and tosses them to Mace. They bounce off his chest. "Go up front, start driving."

Mace picks up the keys. "Where?"

"Start with 'away.' We'll figure out the rest later."

Mace climbs into the front and starts the engine. There is no back window, so he uses the side windows to reverse. He pulls out of the parking lot and heads down the road. Wipes his forehead on his sleeve. He's surprised at how much he's sweating. He slides a hand under his shirt and feels his damp chest.

Mace hears Thumb groaning, moving.

"What's your name?" Charlotte asks.

"Mace," Mace replies.

Thumb laughs.

"Him, stupid," Charlotte snaps. "Tell me your name." Thumb doesn't respond. Charlotte tries again. "Why are you looking for me? Why can't you just let me go?"

Another laugh from Thumb. "Come on, you saw too much. Can't let you just walk. And I'm not telling you shit, cunt."

The shot is loud, sudden, a thunderclap.

Mace yelps, swings the van over to the side of the road, pulls out the brake.

He turns. Sees Charlotte holding the gun, looking at him quizzically.

Thumb is lying on his back.

Mace looks at Thumb's caved-in face and sees blood.

Nothing but pooling blood.

"Why'd you kill him?" His voice sounds different, insecure and young. It's good that Mace is sitting because he doesn't think he could stand. His arms and legs are rubber, his heart a terrified rabbit. The van smells of metal and smoke.

"No way this guy could walk after finding out where you live," Charlotte is saying. "And he wasn't going to tell me anything." She pauses. "And I hate the word *cunt*."

"We could have taken him to the police." Mace feels distant from his body, as if his soul and voice are about to float away.

"Remember that nice officer you met last night?" Charlotte reminds him.

Mace touches his forehead. He's surprised at how soft it is. It feels like this is the first time he's ever touched his own skin.

"You killed him."

"You got a one-track mind." Charlotte's hunting through

the dead man's pockets. She pulls out his wallet, takes the money, and dumps everything else on the floor.

"Change of plans," she announces. "Let's get your truck. They're going to be looking for us, and we need to lose this van."

CHAPTER TWELVE

They drive back to the Garden Crossing apartment complex. Mace tumbles out and Charlotte joins him, happy to get away from the corpse. She hadn't noticed until now how chilly the day is. The grayness of the sky. Everything seems slowed down, vivid, like she's carefully watching a movie.

She can still feel the imprint from the shot, the jolt against her hand.

She wills it away.

"Where can we go?"

Mace is pale, his hand over his stomach. "To do what?"

"To get rid of the van and the dead guy."

"I don't, I don't know."

"How about where you found me? Those woods?"

Mace throws up. Charlotte looks around. The parking lot is half-full of cars, but no people.

"It's been a while since I've seen someone dead," he tells her.

"But you have?"

"I was in the Army."

Charlotte stares at him. "I'm not getting that impression from you, but we'll talk about it later. Let's go. I'll drive the van. You follow me."

Mace walks to his truck, climbs inside, and sits.

Charlotte re-enters the van. The pungent smell of the corpse has filled it. Her hands clench the wheel and something rustles inside of her. She grips the wheel hard until the rustling goes away.

It takes ten minutes of driving, but Charlotte finds a small turnoff along the wooded road and steers the van up it. Mace follows her. She turns down a second small side road, rounds a wide curve, pulls the van over to the side. It's an empty road, rarely driven, shrouded by thick tall trees with brown leaves dangling like pennies.

Mace parks behind Charlotte and steps out when she does.

"God," she tells him, walking toward his truck. "Smells like hell in there."

Mace doesn't respond.

"Can you tell me anything about this place? Do people come here a lot?"

"I don't think so. I don't know."

"There has to be some type of tracking device on the van," Charlotte tells him. "They'll find us."

"Who?"

She ignores the question. "Then again, I don't care if they find the van. But if the cops do, we're in a lot of trouble. You got any rags on you?"

"What?"

Charlotte pulls off her shirt, starts gnawing at the bottom.

Mace looks away from her bare skin and bra.

She rips her shirt, then pulls the tear until the bottom half is separated. She puts the top half back on. It doesn't even reach her belly button. She unscrews the gas cap, rolls the strip of T-shirt into a rope, pushes it in. She pulls her shirt out, along with a dripping trail of gasoline.

"Good thing he was a smoker." Charlotte takes a lighter out of her pocket.

"You're going to set him on fire?"

She opens the van door. "You should start your truck."

"Shouldn't we..."

She disappears inside.

Charlotte exits the van a few moments later, coughing.

"Let's go."

They drive back the way they came. When they reach the main road, Mace glances at her. "How'd you learn to do that?"

"Use the gas to start a fire? Some TV show." She looks out the window, drums her fingers on her knee. "Where are we going?"

"Back to my apartment."

Charlotte grabs the dashboard. "What? Why?"

"The only bad person who knows I live there is on fire right now."

"You don't know that."

"I need to get a few things."

"That's stupid. If we go back there, you're going in alone."

"I'll be quick."

Charlotte's not happy, but she doesn't say anything else. They drive in silence for a few minutes.

"He's not the first person you've killed, is he?"

She doesn't answer.

Mace doesn't press.

No, Charlotte thinks, *he's not.*

But this time, the killing left her cold. The other time, the only other time, she was a wreck.

Now that feeling inside of her, that fire, feels like its devoured her guilt or fear. She touches the trigger's fading indent in her index finger.

If anything, she's relieved.

Relieved that one less man is chasing her, that she's a little closer to being free. Further away from being forced back into that basement.

And that's when Charlotte understands what she needs to do.

She's going to kill all the men who held her.

No matter where she goes, no matter where she runs, she'll never be safe until they're dead. Either she has to die, or they do.

She won't rest until that happens.

Charlotte knows they won't, either.

CHAPTER THIRTEEN

Mace sprints up the stairs of his apartment building two at a time, reaches his floor, runs down the empty hall. He hurries into his apartment and sinks to the ground.

He breathes deeply until he calms down, at least enough to take stock of the situation. Charlotte's right; whoever's looking for her could realize she was in this apartment building. There are places he can go—friends' houses, both close and far away. And Mace can find someplace safe for Charlotte, to pay her back for saving his life.

He has to hurry, but it feels impossible to stand. His legs are soft, his entire body unwilling to move.

He wonders if that's because he wants to stay away from Charlotte. She was casual when she killed that man. It shouldn't be that easy.

But he knows the men chasing her are worse.

Mace pulls himself up. He opens the hall closet, takes out a gym bag, throws random handfuls of clothes inside. He unlocks the safe in his closet and grabs his emergency credit card.

And then an idea hits him so hard it stops him in his tracks.

Now's the time to call the cops.

His phone is in his hand, but Mace doesn't dial. Instead he thinks of what to tell them, how to explain everything that's happened in the last twenty-four hours.

"Mace?"

He shouts.

"Hell's wrong with you?" Eve asks.

She's standing in the doorway.

"What are you doing back here? How'd you get in?"

"Your key was in the door." She holds it out to him. "And I forgot my jacket."

"Oh."

Eve looks at the bag slung over his shoulder. "Going to the gym?"

"No."

She walks into his apartment, maddeningly slow.

"Now's not a good time," Mace tells her.

"Are you going away?"

"Maybe. Yes. Maybe."

Eve purses her lips. "You don't sound like yourself."

"A lot's changed. I've changed. I'm going through changes."

Eve touches his arm. "What's going on?"

"I really just need to go."

"Then tell me quickly."

Mace doesn't think it's possible, but he manages to relay the events of the past day in under two minutes. Eve's expression changes from humor to horror while he talks.

"...And I don't know what to do," he finishes. "I mean, I do. I need to go to the cops. Tell them everything and turn her in."

Eve walks over to the chair and leans on it, as if for support.

Mace had set the bag down, but now he picks it back up and loops it over his shoulder. "Are you okay?"

"I need to think this through." Eve stares down at her hands. "Have you been taking your medicine?"

"Even if I don't, it's not like I start hallucinating Hispanics. Charlotte's downstairs in my truck. You can go see her for yourself."

"I think I believe you."

"What I do tell the cops? Everything I just told you?"

"The guy in the woods. The one she beat with a rock. What happened to him?"

"We didn't stick around."

"Is he dead?"

"I don't think so."

"And you saw his partner today, and she did kill him?"

"Well, she saved my life, then she killed him."

Eve crosses her arms. "Why?"

"She said he knew too much about her. Also, he called her a cunt. If you meet her, don't call her that. She hates it."

"What did you do after she killed him?"

"She said we needed to burn the van, so we did."

Her eyes turn puzzled. "Why?"

"Because I don't want those men to find me," Charlotte says.

She's standing by the front door of his apartment. Mace hadn't even heard her enter.

He sees, unhappily, that Charlotte's holding the gun that belonged to Thumb. It's loose in her hand, hanging by her side, pointed at the floor.

"Hi, Charlotte," Eve says coolly. "I'm Eve, Mace's ex-wife. He's told me a lot about you."

"He doesn't know much."

"Well, he's told me what he does."

"That's great," Charlotte replies, and she gives Eve a thumbs-up with her free hand. "Pleased to make your acquaintance and all, but I need to go. Mace, if you want to stay, that's fine. But can I borrow your truck?"

"Where are you going?" Eve asks.

"I'll find somewhere."

"We need the cops," Mace says.

Charlotte's hand tightens. "I told you, no cops."

"I'm not sure that's the best idea, either," Eve puts in. "Considering they'll charge Mace as an accessory to murder."

"What?"

"It was self-defense," Charlotte says.

Eve taps her index finger against her palm, a habit she has when explaining something. "Right now, I don't have proof of anything that happened to you, Charlotte. Even if you're telling the truth, chances are those men destroyed any evidence at their house. A house that, from what Mace said, you wouldn't be able to locate. All we can prove is that you two murdered someone…"

Eve pauses. Her voice is uncertain, small, when she speaks again.

"I can't believe I'm saying this. But you two murdered someone and destroyed his body."

Mace shifts uncomfortably.

"You might be able to explain what happened," Eve finishes, quietly, "but we need to go over this a few more times. Before we call any authorities."

"That does sound like fun," Charlotte says, "but I don't have time to discuss this. Those men are on their way here."

Mace makes a quick decision.

"I'm coming with you. I don't want you to be alone."

Charlotte turns toward the door. "Then let's go."

"Wait." Eve raises her hand. "I may have a place."

Charlotte stops. "Where?"

"My house. Just until I figure out the next step."

Mace shakes his head. "I don't want to put you in danger."

"I meant the rental. It's been empty for half a year."

Mace takes a quick moment to think about it. "We just need a place to hide out and regroup. No one would find us there. And it gives us a chance to figure out the next step."

Charlotte opens the front door. "Let's go." Her voice is curt.

Mace grabs his antidepressants from the bathroom, shoves them in his bag. The three of them walk down the hallway. Mace tries to focus his thoughts, but he can't stop thinking about the killing.

Or Charlotte's ruthlessness.

Or that he's put Eve in danger now, too.

CHAPTER FOURTEEN

Officer Dave Baker turns off his phone and chews his thumbnail. Will and Frank, sitting on the couch opposite him, exchange glances.

"Who was that?" Frank asks.

Dave hurls his phone into the wall behind them.

Will dives to the other end of the couch, hands shielding his face. Frank sits in the same spot, unfazed, a bottle of Guinness in one hand, a dead joint in the other.

Dave walks over to his phone, picks it up. Turns it back on.

"Strong phone," he remarks.

"Not good news?" Frank takes a swig from his beer.

Will eases back to his spot on the couch, eyeing Dave warily.

"No," Dave elaborates. "Not good news. They tracked down Tyson's van."

"That sounds good," Frank observes.

"His burnt body was in it."

"Who did it?"

"Charlotte, you dumbass."

Frank cocks his head. "You're telling me a sixteen-year-old killed him?"

"Eighteen. And I don't think it was her. Not her alone. Maybe that guy she found helped her. Maybe she's fucking someone new." Dave glares at Frank, voice rising as he speaks. "But unless you have some helpful fucking suggestions, don't get too flippant. How do you think Barnes is going to take this? One of the men he sent is dead."

"Okay, okay." Frank lifts his hands. "I got it. Chill."

Dave glares at him, then looks at the floor.

"It just doesn't seem like her," Frank presses. "That chick used to lie there and take it."

"She fought back at the end," Dave counters.

"Not this much. Or this well."

"Maybe she's changed," Will offers.

Frank and Dave turn toward him.

"Like, maybe she wants revenge."

Dave rubs his chin. "Maybe she does."

"She didn't just fight back," Will goes on. "Something else about her was different. You guys didn't hang with her. I did. And those last days, it was like some switch in her got turned off. She's not normal. Not anymore."

Silence.

"We can't let her stay in public too long," Dave decides, "and we can't let her escape. We need to keep an eye on the bus stations, train stations, hand out photos, pay men to tell us if they see her. And wait for her to poke her head up at the wrong time."

"We're going to watch train and buses?" Frank asks. "And hope we catch her before Barnes comes after us? That's it?"

Dave smiles. "No. That's not it."

Will glances at Frank, worried about Frank's ominous tone, hoping his brother shares his concern. But Frank is watching Dave, a smile playing on his lips.

And Will has never felt more alone.

It's been three years since Will has seen anyone in his family other than Frank.

He thinks that's strange.

Strange because he has three other brothers and two sisters, and he assumed that, at some point, he'd run into one of them. They only live a state away.

And he's always expected his parents to come looking for him.

But they never have.

Their father was a serious man with a body like a barrel and short blond hair, tight eyes, thin lips. Never smiled, never laughed, never showed pleasure. Their mother was soft and small, a timid brunette who gave her children love only when her husband was out. When he was home, she reverted to quiet passivity, unquestioning, everything about her downcast.

They lived a few miles outside of Richmond, Virginia, in a giant unkempt house. The children were all a year apart, with Frank the oldest at nineteen, followed by Will at seventeen, all the way down to their youngest sister, Alice, at seven. Their days were a mix of homeschool taught by their mother and prayer led by their father.

Frank never got along with their father. Part of that was because as soon as he and Will moved into their own room, Frank promptly began sneaking out, heading a mile or two into Richmond. He'd leave just after ten and get back before dawn. Will was terrified by his brother's audacity, even if he admired it. Frank would come home and tell Will about the streets, the men, the women; to Will, it was as if Frank was visiting some exotic land.

One of the worst beatings Will ever witnessed was when their father caught Frank sneaking back in one night. Their father hit Frank so hard that he stumbled against the wall, fell flat on his face with a thick sound. He turned Frank over, hitting him until Will cried out and rushed over and pulled his father's shoulder.

That night, the family prayed. Except for Frank, who was lying in bed, and their mother, who was tending to his wounds.

Frank's right eye, grossly red and swollen, bulged for a week. But the change wasn't just physical. A few days later, he told Will he was leaving.

"Where?"

"Baltimore."

"Baltimore?" It sounded a million miles away.

"This guy I met has a friend there. He said he could get me a job and a place to live. Beats here, right?"

"I guess."

Two nights later they each packed a suitcase full of clothes, slipped out the window, waited a half mile down the road for a car to show up. Will had meant to leave something for their mother, a note telling her that he and Frank would be okay, but he forgot in the excitement.

By morning, Frank and Will were in a house in Towson, receiving instructions for their new job from a man with sharp blue eyes and a way of looking at them that felt like a shark swimming past.

"Most of the weed you sell is going to be at the college," Dave Baker told them. "You go to any of the rec centers or student buildings on campus, kids will come up to you. Find someone with Greek letters on a sweatshirt, tell them what you do, and they'll buy from you in a heartbeat. These kids are all suburban yuppies, and being able to tell someone they have a dealer will make their dicks explode. But don't give them your numbers. These little shits get caught, the first thing they do is rat you out. In fact, you should just carry burners with you."

Will had no idea what Dave Baker was saying, but Frank was listening intently.

"The other good thing about campuses is they're not controlled by gangs. Colleges are too strict. They see a suspicious black guy on campus, they freak the fuck out. You two West Virginians won't have that problem."

"We're from Richmond," Frank said.

Dave ignored him. "You're not going to hang at the campus all day. We're not working corners here. You sell at the university for an hour or so, then you head to the town center. And whatever you do, stay the fuck away from Baltimore. You try and sell there, you'll get shot to pieces. Trust me. You'll make all the money you need off the college kids."

Dave drove them around the town that night, showed them Towson University and the area around the town center. Frank sat up front and asked question after question. Will stayed quiet in the back. He was so nervous that he wondered if Frank and Dave could feel the tension radiating off him.

Will looked out at the night, thinking about his mother. Thinking about the way she must feel.

It's okay, Will told himself. *I can always go back.*

Dave let Frank drive a beat-up Toyota Camry with deeply-tinted windows. "Got it off a dead banger," Dave told them, with pride. "Nobody wanted it at the auction." But Frank wasn't used to driving, and it took thirty minutes of jerky starts and stops to get to the college the next morning.

Will had been to Towson University the night before, but he was stunned at the change during the day. He had never seen this many people in one location; it was almost its own small town. He couldn't help looking at the students, all about his age. They drove past brick buildings and manicured lawns, past a team of soccer players jogging across a field and pulled into a parking garage.

Will carried a backpack full of small sealed bags of weed and followed Frank to a student union, just a short walk away. They made their way to an empty couch through groups of students talking, eating, or shooting pool. Will set the backpack between him and his brother.

"We should have had this," Frank said, his voice low.

"What?"

"All this," Frank told Will. "We should have had this. Gone to school. Instead of growing up in that fucking compound."

"It wasn't a compound," Will said.

Frank ignored him. "All that praying. And everything was quiet all the time. Everyone shutting up whenever dad was around."

"Mom wasn't bad."

"She was a coward. Scared whenever dad was in the room. Even if she knew the stuff he was doing was wrong. One time I begged her to help us."

"You did?"

Frank nodded tersely. "She just stood there, hands under her chin, shook her head. Started crying, the same way she always did. She knew it was wrong."

"She was scared."

"She was a bitch."

That last word hung so thickly Will could almost see it floating between him and his brother.

Frank grabbed Will's backpack and slung it over his shoulder. "We got the chance to start over. Let's make the most of it." He pushed himself to his feet, approached a young guy wearing a sweatshirt with strange letters on it and a baseball cap.

Will didn't talk to anyone that first day, but Frank was a natural. He sold almost everything in the backpack by the end of two hours. "Come on," Frank told him. "Let's get more from the car then head to the mall."

Will followed his brother out of the student union. And as he followed his brother out, it was hard to let one thing go.

Will missed his mother.

He even felt like crying and had to swallow down tears.

Eventually, like Will's shyness toward Dave, his worry about leaving home, and his nervousness at walking around the university, that feeling would fade.

CHAPTER FIFTEEN

Eve's rental in Pikesville is nicer than Charlotte expected. The house smells of fresh paint and is empty of furniture. The rooms are wide, the walls bare, the carpets plush.

"You're selling it?" Mace asks, surprised.

Charlotte notices how uncomfortable the question makes Eve. "Can't keep it forever."

"I guess."

They'd walked up to a living room with a separated kitchen and an opening to a den. Another staircase led to the bedrooms.

"We used to live here," Eve explains to Charlotte.

"Wait," Charlotte says. "Is this place under Mace's name? Because if they find out he was involved..."

"It's under my maiden name," Eve assures her. "They'd have to jump through a lot of hoops, and we won't be here that long."

Charlotte walks over to a window and peers outside. The houses here are detached from each other. The closest is almost twenty yards away, and separated from them by a row of tall, winter-bare trees.

The house reminds Charlotte of a girlfriend of hers whose family was looking for a larger house, and Charlotte had occasionally accompanied them on their search for a new home. She'd loved going to the open houses, imagining the empty rooms filled with furniture and family, walking past cheerful, chattering ghosts.

"You can stay in any room you like," Eve tells her. "And the alarm system is still working. The passcode is Mace's birthday."

Mace looks surprised as he heads into another room.

Eve turns toward Charlotte. "Where are you from?"

Charlotte has decided that she likes Eve. She seems self-reliant and has the charm of being both pretty and approachable. And it's nice to be around another woman again. It helps to distance her even further from what happened this afternoon.

"California," Charlotte tells her. "San Diego."

"I've never been there," Eve replies. "But I've heard it's beautiful. Mace and I went to San Francisco once, but we never went anywhere else in California. I've lived in Maryland my entire life."

"You've never left?"

"I've traveled, just never lived anywhere else. Maryland's home to me." Eve scratches her shoulder. "It's okay, except for the crime. Mace and I moved out of Baltimore back when we got married, and..."

The sentence slips away.

"Mace saved your life?" Eve asks, changing the subject. "Or is that some sort of metaphor?"

Charlotte smiles. The sensation feels good. "He did."

As if on cue, Mace walks into the living room. "I'll take this room. Charlotte, you sleep upstairs."

"Shouldn't I be close to the door?" Charlotte asks.

"Why?"

"What if someone comes in?"

"Then they'll have to get past me."

Charlotte and Eve look at each other.

"Don't look like that," Mace tells them. "I can handle the door. And it'd feel weird to sleep in our old bedroom."

Again, Charlotte notices Eve's expression, how the edges of her eyes and mouth tighten.

Mace is glancing around the empty room. "We don't have any pillows or blankets, right?"

"I'll bring some tomorrow." Eve pauses. "Are you sure I should go?"

"Why wouldn't you?" Charlotte asks.

"Because someone tried to kill you today." Eve turns toward her. "And because you've been through some shit, and you're just a young girl. You might seem fine, but you can't be. You can't be."

Charlotte rubs her elbow. "I'm okay."

Eve looks at Mace. "And even though you and I are separated, I care about you. After you told me what happened..." Eve leans against the wall. "After you told me what happened, I felt like God had shaken me or something."

Mace doesn't say anything.

"I can't open this door tomorrow and find you two dead." Eve's voice softens.

Mace nods. "Okay."

"I can sleep in the other bedroom. It'll be..."

"No."

Charlotte's arms are crossed over her chest.

"Sorry?" Mace asks.

"You're right about a lot of stuff," Charlotte tells Eve. "Our lives were in danger. They still are. Maybe the men who had me will find us. They're looking, for sure. They don't know how much I learned about them, and they can't risk me telling anyone. But I don't think they'll find us tonight. I'm not sure how they even could. But let's say they do, let's say they come here and kill us. And you open the door tomorrow and find our bodies."

"Remember," Mace interrupts. "I'll be sleeping near the door, so they'd have to get past..."

"If they kill us," Charlotte continues, "then we'll need you to find them. Get them arrested, throw them in jail. If you're here, and they kill all of us, then they go free. I can't let that happen. We need you to make sure they pay for what they did."

Eve gazes at Charlotte.

Then she nods.

"You're persuasive for an eighteen-year-old."

"I grew up fast."

Eve gives Charlotte a hug and walks downstairs with Mace. Charlotte listens to their low voices by the door but can't make out what they're saying.

She heads upstairs.

She stops at the top of the stairs and sits down. The hug from Eve was a surprise, and not in a good way. It felt like a cold shadow fell over her. Charlotte shivers.

She hasn't felt another body since the basement.

Charlotte runs her hands through her hair, tightens her fingers, pulls until she feels the roots stretch. She stands and walks through a thin dark hallway with three doorways. Two doors lead into empty bedrooms, the other to a small bathroom. She walks into the largest bedroom and sits in the corner furthest from the door.

The memory of the man she shot that afternoon starts to push through. Charlotte fights the memory, the same way she has in the past.

She stares at the wall until she's lost in its whiteness, blank.

Until that ghost vanishes, along with all the others.

CHAPTER SIXTEEN

Mace walks Eve out to her car, a silver BMW sedan.

"Sit with me a minute," Eve tells him. "Let's talk."

She opens her door and climbs in. The door shuts and the outside noise is silenced. She watches Mace as he slouches into the passenger seat, hands shoved in the pockets of his hoodie, knees nearly touching the glove compartment. He's always had this relaxed style, and there's something about the casual disregard that Eve loves.

He rubs his forehead, then his eyes.

Eve wants to touch him but doesn't. "How you doing?"

"I don't know."

"Charlotte felt like she was going to jump away when I hugged her. Should I stay?"

Mace plays with the strings tightening his hoodie before he shakes his head. "Charlotte was right. We shouldn't all be together. I'm just not sure if we should call the cops."

Eve taps her index finger against her palm. "Nothing's changed from earlier. They'd still charge you as an accessory to murder. It doesn't look like Charlotte has any proof of what happened to her. And the two of you killed somebody and deliberately tried to cover it up. I can promise you, the court won't let you walk away."

"But she can identify the cop who was holding her. The one who came by my apartment. Baker or something."

"Maybe," Eve acknowledges. "But then it's her word against

his. That doesn't work well in cases of sexual assault, and definitely not if the accused has any type of distinguished record. If he was a repeat offender instead of a cop, that would be different."

"But she said they raped her! Can't the cops do a test or something?"

"It depends on how long ago she was assaulted," Eve explains. "And whether or not she has his semen in her. She was held by several men. That cop may not have been the only one."

"Then what else can we do? Legally?"

"I have a friend who might be able to help. But you're safe here. Just keep an eye on Charlotte. I'll be back in the morning."

Mace stares out the window. "It sounds like you're telling me to break the law by not going to the police."

"I'm not." Eve sighs. "Or maybe I am. I don't want you to end up in prison. And if she's telling the truth, then I'm not sure the law can give her the help she needs." She pauses. "If she's telling the truth."

Mace is silent. Eve watches a brown leaf hanging on a branch, the breeze pushing it back and forth. Little moments like this have always captivated Eve, a sight or smell that brings her back to childhood. She looks at the leaf and remembers the fall days spent in Baltimore, the Saturday afternoons when she'd go to the Enoch Pratt Free Library on Eastern Avenue where her mother worked, and the quiet hours she'd spend reading at a table. Eve would lose herself in books, immersed in the pages until her mother's hand on her back brought her blinking into the world. They'd walk home, heading past the row houses that run through Baltimore like brightly-colored jewels in an aged necklace.

Eve can remember where the paint peeled on certain houses, and she can remember which of their neighbors would sit on their porch steps, smoking and drinking and laughing. She can remember the smell of cigarettes on her father when he would come in, and the playful way he would try and hide from her mother, so she wouldn't chide him. The smells of hamburger or corn on the grill in their tiny backyard. The day her older brother left for basic training, and how stiff and coarse his uniform felt when she hugged him goodbye.

Those moments stick out, despite the rest of her life seeming to rush by, like a movie fast-forwarded that is suddenly stopped, the screen frozen, before it moves on.

Eve looks at Mace, still slouched, staring despondently out the windshield. She remembers how J.T., a lawyer in a different firm, first kissed her. It's been months, but she can still feel his chapped rough lips, and the heavy feeling of his hand on her back. Eve had left Mace by then, and it had been years since she'd kissed someone else. She worried she was doing it right, if she should even be doing it, if someone would be able to see them leaning into a doorway down the street from the bar where they'd just left happy hour, if that even mattered. She knew, technically, she wasn't doing anything wrong, but something about it was unsettling.

Maybe it was the secrecy. Eve had explained to J.T. that her marriage with Mace was over and told him about Mace's struggles with depression. "I'm only telling you this," Eve said, a week later when she and J.T. were in bed, "because I don't want you to think I'm still attached. I'm not. But he gets depressed and finding out about us might put him over the edge."

"I got you," J.T. told her. Her head was on his chest, and she liked feeling his chin nudge the back of her head when he spoke. "It's fine to keep this a secret."

"Good." She didn't want to go into detail about Mace's mood swings, his solitude, the way what *could* happen worried him more than what *had* happened. Eve and Mace were opposites this way. She preferred intimacy with people, sharing as a way of emotional commune. Mace stayed distant, kept everything and everyone an arm's length away. And after his mother's suicide, that distance increased. Eve tried to bring him back, but the more she tried, the further away he went.

She knew, early on, that J.T. wasn't anything more than a

fling. He was five years younger than she was, and more social. Eve liked spending her Saturday nights in, watching a movie or reading or doing work, but J.T. always wanted to go out. They didn't go anywhere together, but he wanted her to meet up with him, and was irritated when she didn't. "I'm just past that scene," she'd explain. "Everyone there is younger than me. I can't tell you how old I feel."

"You're crazy. You fit right in."

But she didn't. Eve always felt out-of-place in those environments and wondered if that had something to do with Mace. Not in his influence over her, but in how they got along. Mace always seemed like he was between worlds, not entirely belonging to one, mentally, emotionally, racially. After years of being together, something of that stuck in her.

After a few months, she broke things off with J.T. and decided to see how Mace was doing. They'd kept in touch infrequently, but she could never let go.

It always seemed unreal not to have him in her life.

"I'll be back in the morning," she tells him now.

"When you get here," Mace replies, "call me. I'll walk you from your car to the door."

"Why?"

"Because of the sex traffickers."

"You're going to protect me?"

"Well, I was in the Army."

"But that didn't work out."

"If they try to kidnap you and force you to become a sex slave, they can kidnap me instead. And then they'll end up broke and out of business. That's my plan. It's a long con."

Eve laughs. "I'm sorry. I sounded bitchy just now. I appreciate it. I guess I am a little scared. Charlotte killed that man right in front of you?"

Eve sees a shadow pass over his face.

He nods.

"Call me if you need anything." She puts her hand on his arm.

It's just a quick touch, but Eve can't remember the last time she touched him.

After a few moments, he places his hand over hers.

Then she leaves.

CHAPTER SEVENTEEN

Charlotte's sitting on the staircase leading to the bedrooms when Mace walks back in. He looks up at her, his expression clouded.

"What?" she asks.

He takes a moment to respond.

"I'm bothered that you're not bothered."

Charlotte cocks her head. "What do you mean?"

"You killed that guy without any remorse. And you were held and..." Mace pauses. "...tortured, and you're not acting like someone should."

That curious expression stays. "How should I be acting?"

Mace feels like he's walking on uncertain ground. "Scared? Closed off?"

"I kept the bedroom door locked last night. And I made sure the room I'm staying in tonight has a lock. And I have that guy's gun. So, yeah, you could say I have trust issues."

"But I just...how can you not hate *everyone*, most of all men, after what happened to you?"

"You don't know what happened to me." Charlotte averts her eyes. "And it's not like that. I may not trust you, but I don't *hate* you. You're not those men." She scratches her ankle. "But you're right. I don't feel bad about killing him. I'm worried I will, that it's going to catch up to me. But I just don't. I told you that you don't know what happened to me. Something inside me is gone. Like any sympathy I'd have for those men was..." Charlotte pauses.

"Complicated?" Mace suggests.

"Destroyed."

Silence.

"I'm sorry," Mace offers.

"I'm sorry I left last night. I should have told you. I freaked out."

"You want to talk about it?"

"This has been the longest day. I'm not sure I'm up for talking right now."

"Want to get something to eat instead?"

They order a pizza and Mace pays the driver with a twenty. Charlotte notices his eyelids drooping as they finish. Her own are weighing down. She heads upstairs.

It's a rough, restless night. Charlotte dreams of the man she shot, his naked body stalking her in the back of the van. His face keeps sliding off, revealing blood and skull. She runs to corner after corner of the van, but he won't stop pursuing her.

Charlotte wakes abruptly, her heart beating so hard it hurts. She sits up, a hand on her chest, trying to calm her breathing. She's relieved that the room is empty of furniture, that there are no hiding places, few shadows in the dark.

She tries to sleep again but that corpse returns. This time she's back in the basement, chained to the wall, and he's coming down the stairs. She can't see him, but she knows it's him; she hears his heavy footsteps just outside the door. The chains bite her wrists.

Charlotte wakes sitting up. She stands, walks to the window, peers out into the night. The neighborhood is still and quiet, windless. And suddenly Charlotte wants to be in it, as if this frozen moment is a chance for her to run off, the world paused so she can dart through it unseen, until it eventually resumes.

She remembers that Mace is sleeping next to the front door.

He said he'd protect her.

But he's actually trapped her.

Charlotte lowers herself to the floor. Reminds herself that

Mace isn't bad. Thinks about Eve. Eve will help her.

She can trust in her.

And Eve will be back in the morning.

Charlotte sits with her back against the wall, the window above her, and stares at the door to the bedroom. And waits.

CHAPTER EIGHTEEN

He stands outside Baltimore Washington International Airport in a line of people waiting for taxis.

Barnes is bigger than everyone else around him, not just in height, but girth. There's something threatening about his presence, immediately intimidating. A woman cuts through the line and bumps into him, turns to apologize. Their eyes meet.

Barnes smiles at her, but it's not a friendly smile. There's cruelty to it, in the way his eyes travel up and down her body, in the way they pointedly stop at her breasts.

Under normal circumstances, she would have said something rude. She's dealt with leering men before, takes pride in not backing down.

But this man is different. She senses the danger.

She crosses her arms over her chest, turns away.

Barnes adjusts the duffel bag slung over his shoulder, then reaches down and adjusts his cock as a cab pulls to the curb.

He's come for Charlotte.

But there's someone else he needs to find first.

CHAPTER NINETEEN

Charlotte wakes to footsteps on the stairs. She can't believe she fell asleep, has no idea how long she was out. She looks around the empty room for a weapon and sees nothing useful.

"Can I come in?" Eve asks through the door.

Charlotte relaxes, but only a little. She walks over to the bedroom door and unlocks it.

"I brought breakfast." Eve holds out a crinkled paper bag. Charlotte smells pancakes. "McDonalds."

Charlotte blinks and looks back at the light seeping around the edges of the window blind. "It's morning?"

"You two must be tired. Mace was asleep when I came in. Still is."

"That makes me feel safe," Charlotte says wryly.

But moments later, she's too distracted by the pancakes to care. Charlotte isn't embarrassed by the ferocity with which she attacks her food. She barely notices until she sees Eve looking at her, mouth open.

"Sorry." Charlotte swallows hard.

"Didn't Mace feed you last night?"

"He ordered a pizza, but it was from Domino's."

Eve frowns. "I'm not sure how he survives on his own."

Charlotte's noticed something off about Eve ever since she walked into the room, but can't put her finger on what it is.

She uses a napkin to wipe syrup from her chin. "Something on your mind?"

"I told a friend about you," Eve blurts out. "She's a lawyer and works with a group that helps victims of sex trafficking and domestic violence."

"You told someone?"

"You can trust her. I promise."

Charlotte doesn't say anything.

"It's just, after you told me that stuff yesterday, I thought you could use some help. And she can do a lot more for you than Mace or I can."

"Okay."

"And—" Eve takes a moment to exhale, "—she's downstairs."

"What?"

"I thought you should talk with her right away."

Charlotte's quiet.

The silence lasts. Eve crosses her arms loosely over her chest and waits.

"I get what you were trying to do," Charlotte tells her. "And I appreciate it. But I didn't ask for your help. Everything you and Mace has done means a lot. But I'm not ready to talk to anyone else. Especially a complete stranger."

Eve touches her braids, pulls one nervously. "If you have to run, she can help."

Charlotte is quiet again, but not for as long this time. "It's like this. I was trapped in a dark box for a month. And everything in there was pitch black. Then the top was pulled off and I'm blinking into the light. The only thing is, I can't see very well."

"Let me help you."

Charlotte shakes her head. "I need to get out on my own."

"Why?"

"It's just hard for me to trust anybody."

Eve nods, slowly. "Do you want me to tell her to leave?"

"I think so. I'm just not ready yet."

Charlotte hopes Eve's not upset. And she's surprised at her own resistance.

She reminds herself of her mother.

Charlotte's mother, Olivia Reyes, had moved to America with her boyfriend when she was just nineteen years old. Her family had warned her, told her not to trust him, said that America hated Mexicans. Olivia just smiled, told them she was moving there legally and they had nothing to worry about. Her boyfriend—she never told Charlotte his name—had dual citizenship. He'd gone to college in the United States and returned to Mexico to teach for a year. He met Olivia her first year at the university. And disappeared when they moved to the states and she told him she was pregnant.

Charlotte's earliest memories of her mother are of a stout woman with a round face and thick black hair and a constant smile, so happy that it was always on the verge of turning to laughter. But then that smile fades the more Charlotte remembers, and lines furrow into her mother's smooth brown skin, grey lines shine in her black hair, and her expression turns pained.

She seemed to enjoy holding a grudge, relished it the way someone else might treasure finding a hundred-dollar bill. They lived in Long Beach, in a small apartment in a crowded building down the street from the restaurant where Olivia cooked, and one-time Olivia asked their neighbor, a heavyset black man who always wore dark sunglasses, even at night, to keep the noise down.

"Suck my dick."

Charlotte, twelve at the time, looked up at her mother. Her cheeks had turned red, her jaw tight. She felt her mother's hand squeeze her own.

"I sorry?" Olivia asked.

He leaned an elbow against his doorframe. Sucked a cigarette, lifted his chin, blew smoke to the ceiling. "Suck. My. Dick."

Olivia pulled Charlotte out of his doorway and hurried back to her apartment. Charlotte heard him laugh as her mother closed the door.

Olivia paced all over the apartment that evening, muttering to herself while Charlotte watched her from the kitchen table, where she was doing her homework.

"Mom," she said, "there's nothing you can do. *Olvidalo.*"

Olivia stopped, glared at her daughter. "What you say, Carlota?"

"We should tell the landlord."

"He can't help us. We help us."

Her mother was waiting for her when Charlotte came home from school the next day.

"What are you doing?" Her mom, who had found work in a local library, didn't get home till close to dinner.

"You don't let men talk to you in that way," Olivia said sternly. "*Diga?*"

They went back to his apartment, but this time Olivia didn't knock. Instead, she reached into her pocket, looked up and down the hallway, and took out a paper clip. She unfolded it and used the clip to pick the lock to his front door.

"Mom?"

Olivia hushed Charlotte, ushered her inside.

"What are you doing?"

Olivia's smile was tight. "He went work. I wait."

"You took the day off for this?"

Olivia didn't answer. Just led her daughter to his bedroom.

The bed was unmade, the sheets in a crumpled ball at the end. Clothes were strewn all over the floor, and the television was still on. Charlotte watched her mother look around, grunt, and then hurry back to the living room.

She returned with an ashtray. She set it on the bed, took a pack of cigarettes from the nightstand, pulled out a cigarette and placed it on the tray.

Charlotte still wasn't sure what was happening until her mother took out a small bottle of lighter fluid from her purse.

"What are you doing?" she exclaimed, as Olivia lightly dabbed it on the bed.

"*Mi amor,*" Olivia said, and she capped the lighter fluid, "no one talk like that to you."

She lit a match and set his bed on fire.

Charlotte and her mother left the apartment. They hurried downstairs and crossed the street.

Charlotte was worried.

"The building might burn down!" Charlotte whispered, her voice high. "Someone could die."

Olivia waited until she could see dark smoke in the window. Then she pretended to turn hysterical, shrieking and pointing until someone called the fire department. They arrived in minutes, and Olivia and Charlotte waited in a small crowd of onlookers, watching the firemen work.

Olivia calmly rubbed her daughter's back.

A burning cigarette was blamed. Their neighbor was evicted.

But there were other, less vengeance-filled memories that Charlotte enjoyed. She loved the nights they went to the roof. The building's residents would head up there for cookouts or parties, and Charlotte and Olivia would sit on lawn chairs and listen to the happy conversations, and stare at the ocean a few blocks away. Charlotte would tell her mother about her day at school and her friends and what she was reading. Sometimes they gossiped, sometimes they sat still and watched the giant sun sink until it was just the two of them and the cars on the street below drove past, the sound like surf.

But even then, a distant worry started to gnaw in Charlotte. A worry that this happiness was temporary, that something big and foreboding loomed. That the safety and loveliness of moments like this would end.

She told her mother this, one of those nights.

Olivia listened to her daughter and took a while to respond.

Olivia almost always spoke in English, in an effort to better her understanding of the language. But this time, she spoke Spanish.

"When I was young," she said, "I used to go fishing with my

father. He was a very good fisherman and would bring home enough for our family to eat and to give to the neighbors." Olivia laughed. "I was terrible. I never caught any.

"My father always did a thing that surprised me. If there was a fish that struggled well, he would fight it, and bring it into the boat, but he wouldn't kill it. Instead, he would unhook it and throw it back into the sea.

"I always wondered why he did that, since that was often the biggest fish of the day. Maybe he thought that fish was a good fighter, and this was a gesture of respect. Or maybe the fight had damaged the fish in some way."

"Did you ask him?"

Olivia nodded. "He said it was the same fish every time. That he and this fish had a promise to always meet and fight. That they were friends.

"Now, I knew it wasn't the same fish, and he knew that. But it meant something to your grandfather to have that promise, that idea that there is always a reason to return. Even if it's not the same thing, it's close. Sometimes, that's enough."

CHAPTER TWENTY

Mace downs a spoonful of Lucky Charms and stares at the woman who had come with Eve. Dory Jones is pale and overweight with a short crewcut. Mace figures her for her forties. She seems tired—the way the edges of her eyelids sag, the yawn she stifles as she types into her phone.

Something occurs to him.

"Want some?" Mace asks. Aside from brief introductions when Eve brought her in, and a quick recitation of the events that had led him and Charlotte to this house, this is the only thing Mace and Dory have said to each other.

"Some what?"

"Lucky Charms. Green marshmallows, stuff like that."

"No."

Eve comes down the stairs.

"Charlotte doesn't want to talk," Eve tells them. "Doesn't feel ready."

Dory nods. "I thought that might be the case."

"Why'd you come?"

The two women look at Mace.

"This didn't seem like a good idea," he adds. "Not without running it by Charlotte first."

"Some victims want help right away," Dory tells him. "Others refuse to trust anyone. Women in Charlotte's circumstance usually fall into the former category."

"What circumstance is that?" Mace asks.

"Younger, inexperienced, violently assaulted, away from familiar surroundings. Older women tend to be more reticent." Dory removes a notepad from her briefcase, flips it open. "That said, regardless of how she feels now, our goal should be for her to turn to me and the resources I'll provide."

"That shouldn't be hard. You seem pretty warm."

"Mace!"

"Do you have another approach?" Dory asks him.

"I'd start with finding out what Charlotte wants."

Eve glares at him. "She's eighteen. And confused."

"For right now," Dory puts in, "let's get some basic information. I might be able to use it to locate her family or friends. Is that fair?"

Mace considers it, nods.

"Can you tell me her full name?"

"Her first name is Charlotte," Mace says. "And her last name is…" He thinks for a few moments. "Shit."

"I'll find it out. How old is she?"

"Eighteen. Like Eve told you."

Dory ignores his tone. "Where she's originally from?"

"San Diego," Eve says.

"What's her ethnicity?"

"Spanish," Mace puts in.

"Hispanic?"

"Right. Hispanic."

Dory drums her pen on the pad. "There's a good chance that Charlotte may not be her real name."

Mace hadn't thought about that. And he wonders if Charlotte's eavesdropping, just out of sight on the stairs. He leans forward and looks, doesn't see her, eats another spoonful of cereal.

Mace isn't sure why, but he woke up with a sense of calm. He'd been worried that he'd wake panicked, but his dreamless night helped. His resolve has strengthened. His goal—his only goal—is to make sure Charlotte's safe.

There's no complexity or complications.

And for Mace, the simpler the better.

"Does she know where those men were holding her?"

"I don't think so," Mace answers.

"Tell me more about the cop that stopped by your apartment."

"Officer David Baker. Tall, good-looking. Brown hair, blue eyes. Seemed friendly." He pauses, then adds thoughtfully, "Didn't remind me of a sex trafficker."

"What do you think a sex trafficker looks like?" Eve asks.

"Shorter?"

Dory ignores him. "I understand her hesitancy about contacting the police. She could be right. He may not be the only officer involved."

Eve touches her chest. "Really?"

Dory taps her pen on the notepad. "Trafficking is a multi-billion-dollar industry. That pays for a lot of crooked cops."

"What can we do?"

"We won't go through the police. That's not something Charlotte wants, and not something we've always done. Not that we necessarily do anything illegal."

Mace notices the word "necessarily."

"We have a network spread throughout the U.S. We can move her to another state, set her up with people who can help her out."

"But those men will still be able to find her," Eve points out.

"Not when we give her a new name. That takes time, but we'll put her somewhere remote. And it'll be easier since she has no connections, no children or family that she needs to take with her."

"Do you think we can trust her?" Eve asks.

"Do you have reason not to?"

Eve looks at Mace. "It kind of feels like she's hiding something."

"She is," Dory tells them. "Something happened to her that

can't be reached. It's hidden."

Eve nervously tugs a braid. "What do we do?"

"Wait for her to reach out to you."

"Like I said!" Mace points out, triumphantly.

"*And* make sure she understands you'll do everything you can for her," Dory adds. "You're both right."

Silence.

"But I was little more right, yeah?" Mace asks.

CHAPTER TWENTY-ONE

From their car, Will and Frank stare at Baltimore's Shelter for Victims of Domestic Violence.

It's different than Will expected. He thought it would be a large building, like a hospital. But the shelter is a regular three-story house in a residential neighborhood. The shelter surprises him, and so does the city. His assumption, from news reports and television shows, had been that Baltimore was nothing but a gang-infested slum. He's surprised to see a quiet block with kids playing, dogs being walked, houses that look like they'd belong in any suburb.

They've been parked down the street from the shelter for hours, Frank slouched in his seat, occasionally rolling down the window to blow weed smoke out. Will busies himself on his phone, playing games or searching for more safe houses.

There aren't many in the area. This surprises Will, although it makes their job easier.

Then again, he wonders how many simply don't list themselves publicly.

"I dunno," Frank replies, when Will raises the question. "Seems like they'd want to be public. Otherwise how would anyone find them?"

"I guess. But other people would find them too."

"How many more did you come up with? Two, three?"

"About that."

"Well, there's nothing happening here. No one's stepped in

or out all day. We ought to check inside."

"How?"

Frank takes a puff, waits a few seconds, cracks the window open and blows the smoke outside.

"We can't sneak in. Don't want to risk getting caught or let them know someone's being hunted. We ring the doorbell and ask."

"Yeah?"

"Yeah."

Will takes a moment to think about it. "Maybe I tell them Charlotte's my sister. She got beat up by her husband, and I'm worried about her."

Frank rubs his chin, nods. "That could work. What if she sees you?"

"Then I run."

Will steps out of the car, the chill in the air a welcome contrast to the warm sweet aroma of weed that had wrapped around the car. He glances around, walks to the safe house.

Much like the night Charlotte escaped, Will's not sure if he wants her to be found. He can't forget her whimpers or cries, the sounds of her suffering, how he ignored her those first days when she begged for help. He wishes he could confide his feelings to his brother, but Frank—like Dave and Seth—is determined. Desperate to recover Charlotte.

Find that bitch and cover her with dirt.

Will walks up the porch steps, swallows hard, rings the doorbell.

An intercom blares. "Can I help you?"

Will presses the button, leans down to speak into the microphone. "Yeah, I'm looking for my sister Charlotte. She's a... guest here."

"Guest?"

"Yeah."

"We don't give out the names of our *guests*."

He glances back at his brother sitting in the car, sees Frank on the phone.

"Well, the thing is, I'm worried about her. Her husband beat her hard. Can you just tell me if she's okay?"

A pause. "What's her name?"

"Charlotte Reyes."

The response comes fast, too fast for him to believe it. "No one here by that name."

Will accepts it, tries to hide his relief as he hurries back. Frank leans over, pushes open the passenger door for his brother.

"Not there," Will says, as he climbs inside.

Frank doesn't respond. He's been looking into his own phone.

"What's wrong?"

"Dave's heard rumors," Frank says, slowly. "Barnes is coming to town. Might even be here already."

Will feels like something died in his throat. He turns away from Frank, stares out the windshield. A woman is slowly jogging toward them, jogging and simultaneously trying to secure her headphones. A dog walker, with three leashes attached to his belt, is ordering three small unruly dogs to sit at the corner. A car slowly slides backwards out of a driveway.

"We need to find her," Frank says.

Will keeps looking out the windshield.

"Yeah," he eventually agrees.

CHAPTER TWENTY-TWO

Charlotte hears the front door close and stops trying to fix her hair in the bathroom. She doesn't have a brush. The best she can do is run her fingers through the long dark curls, try and position it so they cover some of the bruises on her face.

The bruises still surprise her: the raised redness on her right cheek, the tender lump over her left eye, the scratchy patches on her forehead and chin. It masks her, makes her feel like she's been given a new face, a face that belongs to someone else.

She heads downstairs and finds Eve in the living room, going through a handful of plastic shopping bags.

"Did she leave?"

Eve's squinting at the back of a shampoo bottle. "Just now. Mace is putting groceries away in the kitchen."

"She brought all this?"

Eve sets the bottle down. "All for you. Clothes, blankets, personal care, lots of other stuff. She brought some magazines, too. I didn't know what you liked, so I told her to get a bunch of different ones."

Charlotte studies Eve. Then she walks over and sits down next to her. She leans into Eve, takes her arm, pulls it over her shoulders.

"Oh," Eve says, surprised.

Charlotte feels the light weight of the other woman's arm, the caution in it, the wariness in case Charlotte changes her mind. She appreciates that contrast from the men; their blunt force, their disregard, the way they seized her body like flags piercing land.

Neither she or Eve move when Mace walks in.

"Want to make dinner? Dory brought groceries."

"It's not even noon," Eve replies.

"Watch a movie? Eve brought her iPad."

Charlotte considers it. "Eh."

"How about we play Twenty Questions?"

"Nah," Eve tells him.

"Do you want to just sit here and shoot down my ideas?"

Eve smiles, and Charlotte warms at the sight, at the familiarity and affection in Eve's expression. "That works," Eve says.

"Okay. We could make parachutes with the blankets and jump off the stairs."

"Nope."

"How about freeze tag?"

"Hard pass."

The three of them end up falling asleep instead, sprawled out on the living room floor, the tension from the past few days uncurling like smoke wafting upwards.

Hours later, Mace is the first to wake. He glances at Eve's watch, surprised to see that it's six at night. Charlotte and Eve are still asleep.

A small helpless sound is coming from Charlotte. He leans over to her. She's asleep, but whimpering. Tears run down her face.

"Charlotte?" Mace whispers. He touches her arm.

She jerks away, sits up and wipes her eyes, then lies back down. All without waking up.

Mace stays silent, waiting to see if she's okay. Charlotte stays asleep, still whimpering, but softer.

He stands, knees cracking, rubs his calves. The soreness from the run through the woods and the stress of everything that's happened has finally caught up with him; the muscles in his legs feel brittle, about to snap at any moment. He hobbles to the kitchen, pulls a frozen pizza out of the freezer, turns on the oven.

"What's up with you and pizza?" Charlotte asks.

She's standing at the kitchen door.

"You were crying in your sleep."

Charlotte nods. "I had nightmares. The kind I don't want to remember. Let's change the subject. You and pizza. What's the deal?"

"It's easy? And it has vegetables. Like a flat salad."

Charlotte grins, lifts herself onto a counter and sits. "You and Eve lived here?"

Mace nods. "After we moved out of the city."

"Why'd you leave Baltimore?"

"We thought maybe we'd want a family someday."

"Why didn't you have one?"

Mace hesitates, unsure if he wants to tell Charlotte about his depression, his fear of passing it onto his child. His worry of exposing someone else to that pain.

Fortunately, Eve walks into the room.

"Pizza?" She frowns at Mace. "What's up with you and pizza?"

"It's easy."

"He called it a flat salad," Charlotte tells Eve.

"He always says that."

"I do?" Mace asks.

"Hey, I'm going to take a walk," Charlotte tells them. "Just around the neighborhood."

"Not going to happen," Eve says. Mace nods.

"But I'm bored!" Charlotte exclaims, and, to Mace and Eve, she's turned from a hardened survivor to a whiny teen. "And I hate being indoors. Can I go out? I saw a hoodie in one of the bags. I'll put the hood over my head and keep my face down. Just around the block?"

Eve makes a quick decision. "Only if I go with you."

"What?" Mace's arms are wide, in shock. "You're serious?"

"It'll just be a quick walk." Eve looks to Charlotte.

Charlotte nods.

* * *

It's colder outside than Eve expected. She looks enviously at Charlotte's hooded sweatshirt.

Charlotte points across the street. "There's a bench over there. Want to sit?"

"I thought you wanted to walk?"

"I just wanted to be outside."

Eve follows Charlotte to the bench, takes a seat next to her. The wood is knotty and cold. Eve crosses her arms and her legs and blows into her cupped hands.

Charlotte smiles a little. "Sorry. We can go in."

"I'm okay."

Charlotte slouches down, hands deep in her pockets, and looks up into the night. Eve glances around the neighborhood. A few cars nestle next to the curb, but they're empty and the houses are mostly dark, only a window or two lit. Eve used to find the seclusion of this neighborhood off-putting. Now, she welcomes it.

Charlotte slouches and stretches her legs. "What do you want me to tell you?"

Eve's taken aback by her forwardness. "Nothing you don't want."

Again, Charlotte's half-smile. "That's not true."

"Okay," Eve admits. "I want to know everything. But, really, only what you want to share."

Charlotte keeps staring up. Her face looks rounder to Eve from this angle, younger, any blemishes or bruises hidden by the dark. "I feel like something's missing from me."

Eve waits. She doesn't want to accidentally say something that will stop Charlotte from talking.

"There was a time when those men had me, and I felt like my body didn't belong to me anymore. Like it never would again. It still doesn't feel like it's mine."

"What do you mean?"

"It's like…like I'm someone else. Like I'm outside myself watching me. Stuff happens, and I can't believe it's happening. Like when that guy died." Charlotte lifts her foot to the bench and rests her chin on her knee. "And I have these bad nightmares. I keep dreaming I'm still trapped. You know what I mean?"

"I can imagine," Eve tells her. "But that's it. Only imagine."

"That's okay."

"No, it's not." She changes positions on the bench so she's facing Charlotte. "Mace and I can help you with some things, but not everything. You didn't want to see her earlier today, but my friend Dory is the only person who might understand what you're going through."

"You really want me to talk to her, huh?"

"I really do."

Charlotte shrugs. "Okay."

Eve leans back. "Just like that?"

Charlotte slowly nods. "You and Mace have been really nice to me, but I know I can't stay here forever. I know I need to figure out the next thing to do. I just don't want to end up sitting on a couch telling someone all my problems."

Eve thinks about it. "Yeah, that's not Dory. She's not the most…approachable."

"I shot a man in the face yesterday."

The night stops like a sharp intake of breath. The cars in the distance, the sound of wind, the cold wooden bench underneath her…all of it leaves Eve.

"And I didn't feel bad about it," Charlotte continues. "Is that strange?"

"How do you feel?"

"The nightmares are bad, but when I'm awake and I think about him and what happened, I kind of don't feel anything."

"Well…I mean, you…"

"He's not the first person I've killed, Eve. And he might not be the last. Not if I see those guys again."

"Who was the first person?" Eve's voice is smaller than she expected.

"Someone I do feel bad about." Charlotte stands. "Let's go back in."

CHAPTER TWENTY-THREE

At seven the next morning, Dory King closes the door to her Grand Cherokee, pulls a Five-Hour Energy out of the glove compartment and downs it. She starts the car and heads to Eve's rental.

She reaches a stop light and leans back in her seat, closes her eyes, and hopes the drink will kick in soon. She doesn't feel as tired this morning as she usually does, but the caffeine is more habit than anything else, at this point. Dory is almost positive her terrible diet is killing her, and she has definite plans to consider changing it. Once she's not so tired.

A car horn startles her awake. Her eyes flick to the rearview mirror. An angry woman is gesturing. Dory waves and drives.

What she needs, she thinks, is more sleep. Or drugs. She remembers her law school days at Penn State, when everyone was swallowing Adderall. Everyone except her. Strange she didn't, Dory often thinks, since her body is ninety percent caffeine at this point. Sometimes she thinks about trying it now but can't imagine anything sadder than a thirty-five-year-old woman hooked on Adderall.

Another stoplight.

Dory leans forward, grips the wheel, determined not to doze off.

It's all last night's fault. She'd scoured the web, first looking for information about Charlotte—nothing, no surprise—and then going through the personals posted on sites like BackPage and

Craigslist, exchanging emails with women offering themselves up, trying to determine their involvement in the sex trade.

It was a loser's gamble. The emails that weren't monitored by pimps were written by women scared of crossing theirs. In the five years she's been doing this work, Dory has never rescued anyone that way. She's come close a few times, when women would start to admit they needed help.

But that's when the emails would abruptly end.

After Dory had finished her search, around two in the morning, she reviewed the files for a client going through a divorce. That took another hour.

The light turns green.

Her Jeep rolls forward.

She's never thought of herself as the type of person who'd be married to their job, but she's not married to anyone else. At this rate, she never will be. She hasn't dated for a year, not since Yolanda dumped her.

There had been a time when Yolanda was everything.

Soft brown hair, light kind eyes, occasionally bringing home a cat from her vet practice that they'd end up boarding. They'd been together four years and were planning on marriage, a baby or two, trips to Europe, mornings snuggling in a sunroom.

But then that girl showed up in Dory's office, an eighteen-year-old Filipina named Mara who'd just moved to the states for an older American man. Mara had met him online, exchanged emails, fallen in love, and moved away from her family. She'd arrived a month ago. The abuse started within a week, the prostitution a week later. Mara had seen the sign for Dory's practice and thought she could help her.

Dory didn't have any idea what she could possibly do, she'd never even come across anything like this.

She kept Mara with her in the office that day, cancelled all her other appointments, spent the afternoon on the phone with colleagues and law enforcement, trying to find anyone who could help. Someone suggested a home that cared for survivors of domestic violence. Dory took Mara there.

She never heard from Mara again, but Dory struck up a friendship with the woman who ran the house, an older white-haired lady named Carol. Dory went back to the house a week later, after Mara had been given safe passage back home, determined to learn more about women in similar situations.

"It's more common than you can imagine," Carol had told her, "and it happens in every country in the world. People don't understand how these predators work. They think it's like that *Taken* movie. That's not the case at all. The truth of the matter is that poor or vulnerable women are targeted, lured by false promises, then forced into prostitution. And there's no one to help them. The authorities are corrupt, the women are considered outcasts by society, and their families refuse them when they escape or return. No one is on their side."

"I had no idea about any of this," Dory told her. "I sort of hate myself for that. I'd always thought prostitution was a victimless crime. I thought it should be legalized."

Carol's expression hardens. "So it'd be easier for men to treat women like commodities? So men can buy people who, in most cases, don't have the desire to sell their bodies? They just have no choice?"

"But I've seen people defend sex work."

"Usually those people have the privilege to defend it. And that's a small percentage of prostitutes worldwide."

Dory went home and did her homework. She read studies, lost herself in books, attended seminars and lectures. To say the work engrossed her would be an understatement. She'd always been this way; when something interested her, Dory threw herself into it. The last time she had been this determined, this focused and passionate, was during law school.

And that was well before she'd been involved with Yolanda.

"It is prostitution," Dory read aloud from Rachel Moran's *Paid For*, one night during dinner:

"...itself which is corrupt and the women who are abused in

it and by it are expected not only to bear the burden of its corruption on their bodies, but on their characters as well. This is a slur and an injustice, because the act of prostituting oneself has nothing to do with a woman's nature; it has to do with a woman's circumstance."

"Can we talk about something else?"

Dory blinked. "Why?"

"I mean, it's powerful," Yolanda said, uneasily. "Don't get me wrong. And I don't want to sound like I don't care. I do. But it's all we talk about now."

"You never said anything."

"I'm sorry." One of their cats, Marbles, jumped into Yolanda's lap. She bent down, buried her face in its fur, kissed it, and looked back up.

"Is this dangerous? What you're doing?"

"I'm not sure," Dory said. "But you're right, I do want to do more."

Yolanda nods.

"I'll try and be around more often. I promise."

It wasn't a promise Dory kept, not after Carol put her in touch with an underground network dedicated to hiding women who'd been abducted and escaped. "You can't tell anyone about it," Carol told her. "We don't always work with authorities. Everything we do is secret, and we're much smaller than you think. A dozen people in the states, trying to find ways to give women new lives. We only work with a few at a time, and just with extreme cases. We have other channels for women trying to escape abusive husbands or boyfriends. This is for women caught up by gangs or organized crime. And we could use your help."

Dory didn't hesitate.

She plunged herself even deeper into her research, stayed later at the office, saw less of Yolanda. One weekend she drove a scared beaten woman to Boston. She returned the next day to find Yolanda sitting on the couch, a small suitcase by the door.

"I didn't want to leave without talking to you," Yolanda said.

Dory pulls to a stop outside of Eve's house, lets the car idle while she prepares herself. She reviews what she needs to tell Charlotte, tries to anticipate what questions she's going to get asked. She's still tired, but the fog of exhaustion is clearing, the way it always does when she's about to go to work.

CHAPTER TWENTY-FOUR

There's a knock on Charlotte's door.

It had been another nearly sleepless night, but Charlotte doesn't feel as tired as she should. A nervous energy runs through her.

It's not like she's a psychologist, she tells herself, as she paces around the bedroom, arms crossed over her chest. She steps over the magazines that Eve brought her, the confused mix you'd find in a doctor's waiting room: *Elle, Sports Illustrated, Cosmopolitan, The New Yorker.*

"Come in," she calls out.

The door opens.

"Charlotte?" Dory's wearing glasses and a loose sweater over jeans. "I'm Dory." She closes the door behind herself, opens her handbag, pulls out a writing pad. "The men who kidnapped you. Do they know about your family?"

Charlotte blinks. "Straight to business, huh?"

Dory relaxes. "Sorry. I need to work on my bedside manner." She tries to smile and half-succeeds.

Charlotte takes a seat on the floor, Dory sits across from her. "It's okay. But what do you mean, my family?"

"Did those men threaten them?" Dory's tone has grown kinder. "Can they locate them?"

"It was just me and my uncle. My dad was never around, and my mom died a few years back. But, no, they don't know where I lived."

"It was just you two? No siblings, aunts or other uncles who came by? Grandparents?"

"I hadn't seen anyone else in my family for years. And none of the men who were holding me knew where I was from."

"Did you ever tell them your last name?"

"I don't think so. It's Reyes."

Dory writes in her notebook, then stops and chews the end of the pen.

"It may be possible for them to find your uncle."

"I don't care."

Dory raises an eye.

"I ran away from him. He wasn't nice." Charlotte wonders where Mace and Eve are. The house is quiet, as if its listening.

"Would he be able to find you?"

Charlotte shakes her head.

"The men who held you. Any names?"

"Barnes. One was named Barnes. He's in Arizona."

"What was his nationality?"

"American, I think."

"Not Russian or eastern European?"

"I don't think so."

"Hispanic?"

"Just white. Why?"

Dory starts over. "Let me explain. We're going to try to find somewhere safe for you to go, but I need more details about these men to make sure it's completely safe. Ethnically-based sex traffickers are concentrated in certain regions in the United States, and the groups don't work together that often. For example, I'm not going to put you in Las Vegas if you tell me Albanians had you. I need to make sure you're protected. And that means most of what I ask is going to be personal."

Charlotte crosses her arms over her chest. "Like what?"

"For example, did those men use condoms? We'll have to get you tested regardless, but that's important. Were you photographed or videotaped? When did the most recent incident occur? Do you want to make this a legal matter? And if you do, then that's a whole series of other questions, but Eve and Mace didn't seem to think you did. Is that right?"

Charlotte nods again.

"You just want to get away." Dory leans back. "I understand. But I need to have a clear idea of what happened to you. You can tell me anything. This information stays between us. It doesn't leave these walls."

"You don't work with anyone?"

"I don't work with anyone local. I have associates around the country, but we only tell each other necessities."

"That makes sense."

"Along those same lines, I realize you don't want to discuss your past. That's understandable. PTSD can result in an emotional numbing that often gives way to avoidance. But..."

"I want to talk. But I want Mace and Eve here."

If Dory is surprised or offended, her expression doesn't show it. "Can I stay in the room?"

Charlotte nods.

Dory stands, opens the bedroom door and calls down.

Charlotte picks at her thumbnail as she hears rustling downstairs, the sounds of Mace and Eve coming up the stairs.

"I want to tell you what happened," she says when they reach the bedroom. "My past feels like its pressing down on me. I need to breathe."

"You don't have to," Mace says.

"I know. But I think it'll help." Charlotte stands, paces a bit, leans against a wall. "I never knew my dad, and my mom died when I was fifteen. I was sent to live with her brother."

CHAPTER TWENTY-FIVE

"The bedroom in the attic is yours," Raúl, Charlotte's uncle, told her. "Got a bathroom down the hall, and there's a TV on the dresser. Doesn't get cable, but I figure you should be studying, right? Your mom let you watch a lot of TV?"

Charlotte shook her head. She was still holding her suitcase and wanted to set it down but doing that would feel like acceptance. And she wasn't ready to call this place home.

"Shame about Olivia," Raúl said. "Not that she and I talked much."

Charlotte nodded, felt a rock in her throat at her mother's name.

"At least you weren't the one to find her, right? That would have been worse."

Another nod.

Raúl studied her face. He wasn't much taller than she was, but he was stocky, with rolls of muscles on the verge of relaxing into fat. "They say there's no pain with an aneurysm. Just like a snap of the fingers. She didn't suffer."

"Okay."

"Like I said, you should thank God you didn't find her. Because that would have—"

"Will you please stop talking?"

Raúl seemed startled. "Well, shit, Carlota. Just trying to help."

"You're not helping."

Raúl's expression darkened, and he brushed his curly dark

hair out of his face. "You got Olivia's ungratefulness. I could see that right away. She didn't have any patience. Never listened when someone tried to do something for her. You're just like her."

Charlotte held her tongue. She liked the comparison.

"And you don't have any other family up here," Raúl went on. "It's just me. You understand that, right?"

"Yeah."

"It's yes, not yeah. I'm not taking shit from some fifteen-year-old girl."

She'd moved from her mom's house in Long Beach to her uncle's in San Diego, and the two cities might as well have been on other sides of the country. Olivia's death had distanced Charlotte from her friends. None of them understood her withdrawal or could relate. She'd felt alone in Long Beach.

San Diego wasn't much better. Raúl drank heavily on the weekends, and Charlotte would stay in her room when his voice rose, and he started knocking things over. She'd hear glass clink and the television would stay on the same channel for too long and her uncle would grow too loud. She'd read until his voice died down, until she could emerge from her bedroom and find him passed out on the couch or floor. Then Charlotte would sleep.

It took a month, but Charlotte noticed a change in him, and a change in herself. They both seemed to realize the permanence in their situation, that Charlotte had nowhere else to go. It happened when Raúl asked if she wanted to tag along to his mixed martial arts class. His day job was a security guard for an office building downtown, but he taught mixed martial arts several nights a week.

She didn't have much interest in the sport, even though she'd watched a couple of fights on television with Raúl. But she thought the class might be a good place to make new friends, and she was curious to see Raúl in charge of something. The gym was in a small narrow strip mall, and it smelled musty, of men and sweat. There were a dozen people in the class, most in their twenties and thirties, and only two were women. Charlotte felt uncomfortable in the judo gi Raúl had loaned her. The pants were tight around her waist and loose at the ankles, and the heavy white jacket was stiff. She stood in the corner, trying not to be conspicuous, stretching her arms to loosen the jacket.

"Line up!"

Charlotte was startled at how deep Raúl's voice was when he emerged from the back office, wearing a worn gi loosely tied over his waist. Something about him was different. His appearance hadn't changed—curly long black hair, a hanging belly, not an inch over five-foot-five. But now he had presence. She followed the other students as they scrambled into two rows. Raúl stood in front of them, his expression stern.

"Today is going to be devoted to ground. Chokes and submissions. Let's stretch out."

The class's obedience surprised Charlotte. She was used to arguing with Raúl, but now she saw him through their eyes, and Charlotte realized there was a side of him she hadn't grasped. He walked up and down the rows of students, adjusting their stretches, once or twice exchanging pleasantries.

After stretching, Raúl had every student in the class partner up. Charlotte wanted to approach one of the women, but they had paired up with each other immediately. Another student, who looked to be in his early twenties, asked if he could work with her. She nodded.

"I'll show you how to do it," he said. "Then you can try it on me."

"Okay."

"Sit down with your back to me," he told her, and pointed to a pair of students in front of them. "Like he's doing."

Charlotte did, and she felt him behind her, his chest pressing against her back. Then his arm wrapped around her chin and slipped beneath it, over her neck.

"Tap when you can't breathe," he said.

His forearm pressed into her windpipe and Charlotte's breathing turned coarse, but she could still breathe. Barely.

"You okay?"

"Yeah." The word came out a grunt.

"Try this, Eric," Raúl said. Charlotte hadn't realized he was near them. Raúl guided Eric's arm up, lifted her chin.

"Now press back," Raúl told him. "Up and back, lightly."

The effect was immediate. Charlotte's air was gone. Her arms flailed, her legs kicked. The room turned dark.

She looked up into a circle of faces peering down. Raúl was closest to her.

"You have to tap your opponent on the arm," he told her. "Otherwise they think you're struggling to get away, not giving up. Understand?"

"Did I pass out?"

His face broke into a grin, although everyone else stayed tense. "You did," he confirmed. "But you'll be okay. Go take a break."

Charlotte stood, rubbing her neck.

"I'm sorry," Eric told her, frightened. "Are you sure you're all right?"

Charlotte nodded. "Just surprised."

She sat to the side of the class and watched the others grapple. She couldn't believe how easily she'd been knocked unconscious. But she wasn't frightened. Instead, the experience thrilled her. She watched the other students with renewed interest.

After about ten minutes, she rejoined the class.

Mixed martial arts happily overwhelmed Charlotte. The sport was exhausting and challenging, but something about the struggle resonated in her. Charlotte loved perfecting grappling techniques, the minutiae behind a slight adjustment that turned a firm hold excruciating, the feeling of an opponent frantically tapping her arm. She didn't like the kickboxing portion as much; Charlotte had the speed to avoid fists and land her own punches, but not the strength to hit hard. She knew it was because she punched the way she applied a choke or arm bar, steadily, like a powerful storm gathering speed.

After a few months, she was considered one of the best in the room, and even helped Raúl coach the other students. She still didn't have close friends, and memories of her mother hit her like a knife in her neck, but mixed martial arts made her happy.

And it brought her closer to Raúl, which was something she needed. They were never as close as Charlotte and her mother had been, and he still drank on the weekends, but a relationship grew. Raúl had fought MMA as an amateur a dozen times in Mexico, and Charlotte was captivated by his stories. She had no desire to compete, but an admiration for those who did.

But even with this new passion, she was still lonely.

Her high school was starkly divided into cliques, and often those cliques were racial. She'd lived all her life in the United States and, because of Olivia's hopes to master English and assimilate, Latin culture had always been kept an arm's length away. And Charlotte's darker skin color automatically excluded her from the white kids. This hadn't been a problem in Long Beach because Charlotte and her friends had been too young to care. Now she was in a different school and it might as well have been a different world. She was a good student and kept to herself, but she fervently wished that her mother was still alive. That she was sitting next to her on that apartment building roof, looking out over the water and the city.

Charlotte had been living with Raúl for about a year before he climbed into her bed.

She was startled awake by the motion of the bed shifting. She sat up and saw her uncle lying next to her, fists over his eyes. He wore boxers and a T-shirt. She felt uncomfortable in her soft flannel shorts.

"You get lonely, Carlota?"

"What?"

Raúl moved his fists and looked at her with wide, soulful eyes. "Loneliness. Does it ever get to you? Come on, I'm just trying to talk."

"Sometimes I miss my mom."

"I miss my daughter."

"You haven't seen her at all since the divorce?"

He shakes his head. "We used to lie here at night before they left."

"Sometimes I'd fall asleep on my mom's bed," Charlotte offered. "We'd be talking, and I'd wake up the next day in her bed." She smiled. "I'd be confused when I woke up. She and I both."

"Can I lie here with you?"

Raúl came back the next night, and soon they were going to bed together. Sometimes Charlotte would wake and find him holding her. Sometimes his hand was under her shirt, touching her stomach, her breasts. Once he guided her hand into his shorts.

Charlotte knew it wasn't right. The next night, she wouldn't let him touch her.

"What's wrong?"

"We shouldn't do this."

"It just feels nice to be with you. Makes me feel better. Look, I haven't had as much to drink because of you."

Charlotte didn't say anything.

"Can't we just lie here?"

But a few nights later, he moved her hand again.

She stopped him, but he begged her until she relented.

Completely.

Most nights Raúl was gentle, guiding her, telling her what to do. Some nights he was too drunk to tell her anything, and those nights he was rough and clumsy and hurt her.

But it's not that bad, Charlotte would think. She and Raúl went to movies, dinners, shopping, mixed martial arts. He took her shooting, off-roading, fishing.

She sometimes wondered if they were dating.

Sometimes other kids made fun of her, told her she and Raúl were too close, and that stung.

After almost two years of this Charlotte told him she was leaving.

"Yeah?"

"When I graduate. I'm moving out."

"Why's that?"

She never liked it when Raúl only answered in one to two-word sentences, when he kept his emotions hidden

But she'd anticipated it, practiced what she was going to say.

"I need to live my own life."

He put his foot on the edge of the kitchen table, leaned back in the chair he was sitting in. Drank from his beer.

"Going to break my heart."

She heard the sadness in his words. And it did hurt.

That night the bedroom door slammed open and he stumbled in. Charlotte sat up and his hand was on her chin, forcing her down. He grabbed the waistband of her pajamas and his other hand tried to disappear inside her.

He left her shaking on the floor.

She stayed that way for hours.

Then she stood.

Raúl was in the kitchen the next morning when she walked up to him, shirtless, braless, and pressed a knife into his hand.

"Do it," she told him.

He took the knife from her, held it dumbly, and took a step back. Charlotte had seen her uncle as imposing but now, with uncertainty clouding his face, he was different, slight.

"Carlota, what are you doing?"

Charlotte took his hand, pressed the blade of the knife between her bare breasts.

"Push it in."

He didn't move.

Her hand over his, she drove the tip of the blade into her

skin. A drop of blood ran down her stomach.

"Come on."

She dug the knife deeper but didn't make a sound. And didn't look away from her uncle's face.

His eyes widened.

Charlotte left him standing there. She walked into her bedroom, dressed, and grabbed the bag she'd packed that morning.

She didn't see her uncle when she left.

CHAPTER TWENTY-SIX

Will and Frank had visited a dozen women's shelters the day before with no luck. Even when they were allowed in, some sort of security—a locked door, a guard, a curious reception-ist—prevented them from going in farther.

They sat in Frank's car, eating fast food, trying to figure out their next step.

Frank speaks through a mouthful of hamburger. "We can't keep checking those places. I'm pretty sure we're on some sort of watch list by now."

Will dips a fry in ketchup and downs it. "We should try something else. And tell Dave we can cross the shelters off the list."

"Right. Well, technically, she could be at any of the ones we went to. We have no proof."

"Let's not tell Dave that."

"He's not our parent or teacher...or anything. We don't have to lie to him."

"I don't like making him mad."

"Yeah, me neither." Frank washes down his hamburger with a mouthful of Coke. He snaps his fingers. "We're idiots!"

"Why?"

"She has to eat, doesn't she? Why don't we just watch res-taur...never mind. Thought about it as I was saying it."

"You mean," Will says, "you don't think we should try and keep an eye on every restaurant in the area?"

"Shut up."

"Maybe she'll make a reservation at The Rib Joint. Let's ask Seth."

Frank bristles. "I don't see you with anything to offer."

"Well, look, we know where she was last. The woods where the body and van were."

"So?"

Will finishes off his fries. "Maybe she's still around there. I don't think she hopped on a plane or anything. And don't criminals return to the scene of the crime?"

"Yeah, but *Tyson* was the criminal."

"Oh, right."

"Seth and Dave are hitting train and bus stations again. Let's see if they come up with anything." Frank reclines his seat, pulls out a joint from the glove compartment. "I don't feel like working today anyway."

Will nods, inclined to agree with his brother.

CHAPTER TWENTY-SEVEN

Neither Mace, Eve, or Dory have moved since Charlotte started speaking.

Charlotte doesn't notice.

She's lost in her past.

Charlotte thought about heading back to Long Beach, but she didn't want Raúl to find her. She picked Tucson. She liked the idea of another state.

Hitchhiking took her a day and a half. Much of that was because of her determination not to accept rides from cars only occupied by men. And a lot of the women she saw, in the cars that zipped past, were with families, and Charlotte rightly assumed a family would be less likely to pick up a hitchhiker.

She walked on the side of the road, her backpack bumping her, eyeing cars as they approached, trying to determine if she should stick out her thumb. Finally, a car driven by two college girls pulled over. They let her in and asked a few questions, and then talked with each other so much that Charlotte wondered if they remembered she was in the backseat. They dropped her off a rest stop, and she thought about trying to find a hotel, but the day had been exhausting. She decided to sleep there.

It was more of a tiny shopping center than a truck stop, complete with a Subway, some type of frozen yogurt stand, stores selling magazines and cheap souvenirs, and mounted TVs showing cable news or sports. Charlotte ate McDonalds, bought a *People* magazine, found an empty bench, and read. She didn't follow celebrities that closely, but she knew them, and liked seeing their easy happiness and matter-of-fact wealth. The magazine was more engaging than she expected and, when she finished it, Charlotte was surprised at how late it was.

Other people were sleeping on benches; she did the same. She stretched out on the wooden slats and waited for sleep. It didn't come. She lay on the bench, counted sheep, quietly recited a lullaby, re-read the magazine.

Nothing worked.

The bench hurt her back. And there were too many people around. Charlotte couldn't stop looking at them, marking where they slept, wondering if they would move near her once her eyes closed.

The night was painfully slipping away.

She had to pee, so she took her backpack and headed to the restroom. She wasn't that worried about keeping her bench. It couldn't be much more comfortable than the floor.

The restroom was empty. A long row of sinks were on one side, stalls on the other. She walked into a large handicapped stall, locked it, and hung her backpack on the hook behind the door. She tore off some toilet paper and wiped down the seat, then covered it with more toilet paper.

She peed, flushed, stood, and fastened her pants. Then she sat back down.

Charlotte couldn't explain why, but she felt more comfortable in this small restroom stall than she did outside. She stretched her legs, closed her eyes.

Something nudged her foot.

Charlotte's eyes opened. She'd been asleep, no idea for how long.

She looked down and saw a man's head in the space between the bottom of the door and the floor, staring up at her.

She inhaled sharply and drew her legs back.

"Hi," he said.

Charlotte didn't know what to do.

"Hi," he said again. "Let me in."

"What? No."

"Come on." He withdrew his head. The door shook. "Hurry up."

"No!" Charlotte said, forcefully. She stood.

The door shook harder. "Come on."

Charlotte's anger surprised her. She twisted the lock and shoved the door out.

It smacked the man in the face. He staggered backward, bumped into the sink. He was short and thin with short brown hair and glasses.

"What the fuck's wrong with you?" he asked.

Charlotte grabbed her bag and swung it at his head. The man raised an arm, went back even further, ended up leaning against a sink. She bent down, grabbed his legs and pulled. The back of his head smacked the counter as he fell.

"Shit," he said, sitting on the ground. Charlotte kicked him in the ribs. He cried out. She did it again.

"Okay," the man said, and he stood and limped to the door. He unlocked it and let himself out.

Charlotte ran to the door, watched him hurry away.

She went back to the sink, splashed water on her face, rinsed her mouth. Ran some water through her hair. She was breathing fast.

She felt like that little man had been some sort of test, as if his harassment was part of running away, becoming herself.

Until then, she'd never thought of herself as a fighter.

That morning, Charlotte ate breakfast next to a young couple heading to Tucson. They offered to give her a ride.

The trip took two hours but, once Tucson came into view, things seemed better. Charlotte felt lighter. Tucson rested inside an uneven ring of mountains; a potter's broken bowl half-buried in dirt. A few tall buildings were clustered in the middle of the city, as white as sunbaked bones. They drove past dry brown land as they got closer, punctuated by the kind of cacti Charlotte had only seen in cartoons. She couldn't believe how tiny Tucson was compared to the surrounding mountains. Nature dominated the city.

They drove in on wide roads with low buildings on either side. The streets weren't crowded with cars or people until they reached Fourth Avenue, where Charlotte and the couple parted ways. Fourth Avenue was full of shops and shoppers, and Charlotte loved the feeling of getting lost in people, disappearing into the cheerful crowds. She wandered into stores of trendy clothes or southwestern souvenirs; an overabundance of turquoise stones and long soft dresses.

Charlotte had no idea where she was going to spend the night, but she had about six hundred dollars between what she'd saved and stolen from her uncle. She kept walking down Fourth, turned on a few side streets and stumbled upon an outdated two-story motel.

A week cost her a hundred and fifty dollars. She figured it was worth it. Her room had peeled blue paint and a stained comforter covering the bed. She didn't care.

She was hundreds of miles away, but Charlotte still worried about her uncle finding her. That first night, worry shook her awake whenever she caught a few moments of sleep. She kept the lights and television on. At dawn, the sun rose over Tucson's mountains, like a cover slipped off a painting. Charlotte opened her door, stepped barefoot into the warm, beautiful morning. Watched the little city wake.

CHAPTER TWENTY-EIGHT

"I never knew you were in Tucson," Mace says.

Dory, Eve, and Charlotte all look at him.

"*That's* what you took from everything she's told us?" Eve asks.

"Well, I mean, I heard Tucson's nice."

Eve turns toward Charlotte. "How're you doing?"

"I'm okay."

Dory stretches her neck. "We've been talking for a while. Let's take twenty minutes. I'm going to get some water."

Charlotte lifts her arms and slowly exhales. Dory stands, rubs her knees, and heads out of the bedroom. Eve follows her. She hears Mace ask Charlotte, "It's a dry heat, right?"

Dory waits for Eve and they head down the stairs together. They reach the lower level and walk to the kitchen. Eve waits until she's sure they're out of earshot before she speaks.

"I think we need to call the police."

Dory stares at her with patient, relentless eyes.

"Why?"

"Half of what she's telling us may not even be true. I'm not sure I trust her story, but I trust what Mace said. About the man she killed."

Dory walks to the kitchen entrance, glances out, and walks back to Eve.

"Seems like they had to do that."

"You know that won't matter much in court," Eve presses.

"They killed a man and burned his corpse in a deliberate attempt to hide evidence from an enemy they can't produce. Or even identify. And that means we may have two threats. The men hunting Charlotte. And Charlotte."

"How's Charlotte a threat?" Patient. Relentless.

"She's a killer. And an unrepentant one."

"I'm not a psychologist," Dory says, "but I've worked with enough survivors to understand that trauma strikes people in different ways. Most respond in somewhat predictable fashions, but there is an occasional outlier. Right now Charlotte's hurt, and she's scared. And I don't believe we need to worry about her in that way."

"I bet the man she killed had the same thought. And so did her uncle."

"Her uncle?" Dory frowns. "She didn't kill Raúl."

"Are you sure?"

"I don't know. But I *feel* like she's telling us the truth. And I know she's someplace, mentally and emotionally, that we can't understand. Or even bridge. But I always give victims the benefit of the doubt, and there's something about her I trust. In my gut."

"Yeah," Eve says, uneasily. "I *feel* like she's being honest, I get that. But my mind keeps questioning everything. Even if my gut hasn't steered me wrong yet when it comes to people."

"To be fair, you married Mace, and now you're separated."

"My gut had indigestion that day?" Eve smiles. "Sorry, that's a Mace joke. I catch his sense of humor whenever we hang out. It's awful."

Dory offers a small smile back.

"We'll listen to what else she tells us," Eve concedes. "And I'll think about if I should go to the police or not."

CHAPTER TWENTY-NINE

Charlotte lived in the motel, which was shady but cheap, and found a job as a hostess at a nearby Applebee's. She didn't have a lot of money, but she didn't need a lot. She had enough for the motel and her manager let her eat for free.

Charlotte loved Tucson's relaxed prettiness. She spent her days exploring the city, reading in her room, sitting by the teardrop-shaped motel pool, watching television on the bed. She grew familiar with the cleaning staff and the other long-term residents: the old woman a floor below her, the creepy guy a few doors down, the mother and infant she'd occasionally see at the vending machine. It was an unspoken rule that no one asked questions about each other's past or what had brought them there. They talked about the weather and television shows and, in the case of the mother, her baby. Charlotte occasionally inquired about babysitting—not for money, just because she thought the baby was cute—but the other woman politely declined. Charlotte understood.

She didn't trust anyone either.

One day Charlotte was reading an Anne Tyler novel by the pool when a girl, about her age, sat in the chair next to her.

"I'm Sofia."

"Charlotte." She'd given to calling herself Charlotte rather than Carlota. The Spanish version reminded her too much of Raúl.

Sofia was wearing a long T-shirt over a two-piece swimming

suit, and she pulled the T-shirt off and set it next to her. She had dark eyes, long hair, and a natural tan. Maybe Hispanic or a mix.

"How long have you been here?"

"At the pool?"

"The motel."

"Oh." Charlotte laughed. "I live here. What about you?"

"Yeah," Sofia replied, absent-mindedly running a hand through her hair. It was thicker than Charlotte's, and more styled. "My daddy's here for work for a few weeks. Wish we'd stayed somewhere nicer. Like, in the car."

"It's not that bad. I kind of like it."

"What about your folks?"

"I'm here by myself," Charlotte told her, and it was hard not to say that without a touch of pride.

"Really?" Sofia seemed dutifully impressed. "Or, like, with a boyfriend?"

"Just me."

"I was seeing this one guy a while back, but we broke up."

Charlotte felt like Sofia mentioned a boyfriend to try to compete with her independence. But she didn't mind. "Why?"

Sofia swept her hair to her other shoulder with a quick motion. Charlotte smelled the flowery scent of her shampoo or lotion. "He turned out to be a freak show. Wouldn't leave me alone. I needed my space."

Charlotte nodded.

"You date much?"

She didn't want to talk about her personal life, but she felt like she had to give something. "Not really."

Saying that left her insecure. Sofia was too pretty not to have had a dozen boyfriends. Leaving Raúl and starting her own life had seemed like a mature decision. Now Charlotte felt hopelessly young.

Sofia reached into her purse, pulled out her phone, glanced at it and frowned. She put it away. "Sorry for grilling you. I'm just surprised. You don't meet many people who live here. You like it?"

"It took me a while, but now it's kind of home."

"Well, that's sad," Sofia said, but with a smile. "I'm burning up. Keep an eye on my stuff?"

"Sure."

Charlotte watched Sofia grab the railing and carefully slip one leg in the water, then the other.

Sofia turned to her back, smiled at Charlotte, and drifted away.

Charlotte saw Sofia at the pool every day. They talked about guys, Tucson, TV, clothes, hair, makeup. They also talked about their families, but not much. Charlotte never saw Sofia's father. Sofia said he was always working, all day and into the nights. She didn't seem to mind.

"Are you planning to stay at this motel forever?" Sofia asked once. They were in the pool, holding themselves up with their elbows on the edge.

"Maybe," Charlotte said. "Are you and your dad leaving soon?"

Sofia gave her an exasperated look. "Hopefully. As soon as he makes enough for us to move somewhere else."

Charlotte was hurt by Sofia's eagerness to leave.

"I mean," Sofia said, "you and I will keep in touch. Or get our own place."

Charlotte warmed. "That'd be nice."

"Are you going to make enough to afford rent, being a waitress?"

"I'm not a waitress," Charlotte corrected her. "I'm a hostess."

"So, no?"

"No."

"Maybe we should, like, take out student loans and go to college and better ourselves. Although that seems like a lot of work."

"Right?" Charlotte kicked her legs slightly, let them drift.

She closed her eyes, enjoying the combination of Arizona heat and the water. It reminded her of nice times in California, when she visited the beach, lying between sun and sand, letting her back bake.

Having Sofia with her made things better. She hadn't thought she was lonely, but talking with her was easy and natural and Charlotte hungered for the connection. She missed Sofia when she would leave and, as they spent more time together, realized her friend felt the same way about her.

She opened her eyes and watched Sofia lift herself out of the water, grab a Corona from her handbag, and slip back into the pool. Sofia dragged the top of the bottle against the edge of the pool and popped off the cap. She took a drink, then turned toward Charlotte.

"Seriously," Sofia said, "have you ever thought about it? Going to school or something?"

"I don't plan on staying here forever," Charlotte clarified. "But for now, it's fine. I did think about maybe taking a couple of community college classes. What about you?"

Sofia frowned. "My daddy makes enough so I don't have to work, but I should be more, like, self-reliant or something."

Charlotte nodded.

"I don't mind borrowing from him, but sometimes I think it'd be nice to have my own money. My own life."

"Yeah."

"Maybe we should find a couple of rich guys."

After everything with her uncle, the idea of dating filled Charlotte with dread. "Haven't seen many rich guys at Applebee's."

"Yeah, or Tucson for that matter." Sofia smiled, then turned serious. "Hey, how come you don't speak Spanish?"

"What?"

"You said your mom was Mexican. She didn't teach it to you?"

"No. I mean, she was always working on her English. I

guess that's why she never tried to teach me. And the rest of her family was somewhere in Mexico."

Sofia drank.

"You never tried to find them?"

Charlotte shook her head. "What happened to your mom?"

"She left us."

Sofia turned away and Charlotte decided not to ask anything else.

She watched Sofia finish off the bottle and toss it into the water.

CHAPTER THIRTY

"Seriously," Sofia told Charlotte, as she sat on her bed, fastening on a pair of earrings, "I can't go to Applebee's for dinner again. Don't you get tired of it?"

"I don't think I'll ever get tired of a free meal."

"There are so many other places," Sofia whined. "We could go for Mexican. That's super cheap."

"How cheap is super cheap?" Charlotte tried to remember how much money she had. Less than two hundred, about one hundred and eighty. And that had to last five days.

"I dunno. Like fifteen bucks or something."

A key scraped the door lock. The door opened. Charlotte turned and saw a man she'd never seen before. She glanced at Sofia.

"Hi, Daddy," Sofia said. She fastened her second earring. "This is my friend Charlotte. I told you about her."

"Nice to meet you." Sofia's father was tall with bushy dark hair and small eyes. Everything about him seemed big—easily over six feet with a long gut and thick arms and legs. He wore an open flannel over a T-shirt and jeans with a large, fist-sized belt buckle.

"Good to meet you, too." She'd been about to add "sir." Something about Sofia's father seemed to command authority.

"We're going out to eat," Sofia told him. "You want us to bring you back anything?"

"I'm good." He closed the door behind him but stayed standing in the doorway, staring at Charlotte.

"She's broke," Sofia complained. "We're going to have to go somewhere gross."

"It's not that…" Charlotte started.

"How much do you need? Fifty dollars cover you?"

"That should be good." Sofia bounced off the bed, trotted over to her father, gave him a quick kiss on the lips.

"Charlotte, you live here, right? By yourself?"

Charlotte didn't like that Sofia had said anything about her to her father.

"Yeah."

He nodded but didn't move from the doorway.

Sofia stood a few feet in front of him, arms crossed over her chest, foot tapping. She sighed and marched back to Charlotte.

"Give me a kiss," Sofia told her.

"What?"

"It's my daddy. He'll give me the money if I kiss you."

Charlotte tried to laugh it off, but the motel room seemed darker. "Are you serious?"

Sofia laughed with her, rolled her eyes. "He's, like, such a sicko. But come on, just do it so we can get out of here. I'm hungry."

"But I'm not, I'm not like that."

"Me neither!" Sofia seemed offended. "But come on, you've never kissed another girl? Like, just to show off?"

Charlotte felt embarrassed when she shook her head. She glanced at Sofia's father.

He hadn't moved from the doorway.

"Come here," Sofia said. "It'll be quick." She turned to Charlotte and, before Charlotte had time to respond, kissed her.

Charlotte took a step back.

"You call that a kiss?" Sofia's father asked.

Sofia looked at Charlotte, sadness in her eyes. And something in Charlotte broke.

She remembered Raúl.

Maybe this was just how men were.

The second kiss lasted longer. Charlotte didn't stop until Sofia did. The entire time, she hoped it would be enough to make Sofia's father happy.

He was holding out a fifty-dollar bill when they stopped. "Have fun tonight."

CHAPTER THIRTY-ONE

"Are you okay?" Mace asks.

"Yeah, why?"

He and Eve trade uneasy glances. "Because you're crying."

"I am?" Charlotte touches her eyes, surprised.

"Maybe we should take a longer break," Eve suggests.

"I do feel kind of shaky inside," Charlotte admits. "Could we stop for the night? Start again in the morning?"

Dory seems reluctant, but agrees instead of pressing her point. She says her goodbyes and leaves.

"I'm sorry about your uncle," Mace tells her, when he hears Dory walking down the stairs. "That sounds awful."

"It wasn't that bad."

Again, that uneasy glance between Mace and Eve.

"What do you mean?" Eve asks.

"I went along with it. It's not like he held me down and made me. Except for a few times."

"You were a child!" Mace sounds alarmed. "He took advantage of you."

"But I went along with it. Most of the time he didn't force me."

Mace stands. "You weren't old enough to choose. He manipulated you."

Charlotte looks down at her hands. "I guess. It's just that I knew Raúl so well, it's hard to hate him."

"You don't have to hate him," Mace says. "But it wasn't right."

118

* * *

Eve left for the night, and Mace and Charlotte kill time before falling asleep by watching *The Avengers* on Eve's iPad.

"I'm glad you're talking to us about all this," Mace tells her. "It can't be easy."

"It's not," Charlotte agrees. "But I want to tell you. It's important, for some reason."

Charlotte hasn't looked up from the screen. She's watching Scarlett Johansson being questioned by gangsters as she's tied to a chair, and the image leads Mace to wonder if this movie was the best idea. But Charlotte doesn't seem bothered by it.

"Is talking about it bringing up bad stuff?"

Charlotte pauses the movie just as Johansson starts to fight back. "I think I'll always have nightmares." She's silent for a moment. "But I'm tired of talking about myself. Are you and Eve getting back together?"

"What? No. I don't know. Maybe. No."

"I like her. She's nice. And pretty. And smart. How'd you get her?"

"Waited till she was slumming."

Charlotte grins. "Why'd you split up?"

"I have a family history of depression. Makes me tough to live with."

Mace is surprised by his own admission; he hadn't planned on telling Charlotte.

"Like, just bummed out or hardcore?"

"Little bit of both. It gets worse when things are bad. My mom dying took me under. And that led to me and Eve splitting up."

"How'd your mom die?"

"Suicide. Like her father."

"I'm sorry."

Now it's Mace's turn to grin. "After everything you've been through, you're sorry *I* had a hard time?"

Charlotte nods gravely. "I have my problems, you have yours. And it makes me sad to think about you depressed."

"I take medication to help." Mace reflects. "But this is the first time I've even thought about it since I met you."

"Well, I like to keep you busy."

"Thanks for that."

Charlotte laughs and turns off the lights. He presses play and the movie resumes.

He's seen the movie before but, even if he hadn't, Mace is too distracted to pay attention. Out of the corner of his eye, he watches Charlotte watch the movie, her eyes tracking the action, her face lightening when humor pushes through.

In the dark, he wonders again why he told her about his depression, wonders if he'll regret it. He's only talked about it with Eve and a couple of short-term psychologists.

Why had he said it?

Charlotte laughs and looks at Mace the way people do when they laugh—eagerly, expecting confirmation. He smiles, and a realization hits him: he wanted to share something with her.

He hasn't felt that for years.

CHAPTER THIRTY-TWO

Eve answers after one ring.

"Did you call the cops?"

"Dory?"

"Eve, did you call the cops?"

Eve sighs, stares out her apartment window at Columbia in night. Living in Columbia, Maryland, was a bit further out from the city than Eve originally wanted–she still found herself surprised that she wasn't in Baltimore proper–but she does love how quiet everything here was. How distant it is from the crime and poverty occasionally found in Maryland. Columbia was one of the country's first planned communities, and the town is fiercely protective of its safety and reputation.

Still, there's an artificial suburban quality to living here that bothers Eve. Especially after spending most of her life in Baltimore, where everything in the city always seemed like it was happening down the block from wherever you were.

And Eve wonders if she's grown accustomed to that distance. If she needs it.

And she wonders if Charlotte is threatening that artificiality.

Is that what truly worries her?

"I understand your concern," Dory is telling her, "given that if our assumptions of criminality for Mace and Charlotte hold up, you would likely be charged with aiding a—"

"This isn't about me," Eve interrupts, and she turns away from the window, her arms crossed tightly, shoulder pressing the phone into her ear. "It's about Charlotte. And whether or not we can give her what she needs."

"The state won't provide her with the type of environment she needs or deserves."

"I don't disagree with you. But I don't think it makes sense to let a killer go free."

"Please," Dory says. "I've worked as an advocate for years now. Don't do anything until we find out more about her. At least until she's told us the rest of her story. Please."

"What you're asking is unethical."

"That's why I called. Did you tell the cops?"

Eve relaxes her arms. "No."

Dory exhales. "Thank you."

"But I'll be pissed," Eve tells her, "if we all end up dead."

Dory chuckles, and Eve realizes it may be the first time she's ever heard Dory laugh, or at least come close. "I'll apologize in heaven."

CHAPTER THIRTY-THREE

The knocks on the motel door interrupt *Family Feud*.

Zeke turns down the television with the remote, gingerly lifts the ice pack off his head.

"Yeah?"

"Open up, Zeke."

The three words turn Zeke cold. He takes his gun off the nightstand and slips it under the pillow. He sits up on the bed. "It's open."

Barnes walks into the room. He glances at the blue wallpaper, the box television set, the paint-chipped door leading to a bathroom. Scrunches his nose at the faint smell of smoke, then closes the door behind himself.

"I didn't know you were coming to town," Zeke tells him. He offers his hand.

The big man leans against the door, hands in his coat pockets, with a smile on his face. He makes no move to shake hands. After a few moments, Zeke withdraws his.

"How'd you find me?"

"You ain't Richard Kimble, Zeke."

"Who?"

"Guy from *The Fugitive*."

Zeke frowns. "I never saw it."

Barnes doesn't respond.

"You want something to eat or drink? I got beer and pretzels."

"I don't want anything, Zeke. Tell me what happened to

Charlotte. And Tyson."

Zeke plays dumb. "Is that why you're here?"

"You didn't answer my questions, Zeke."

"Can I be honest about something? Just real quick? I don't like how you keep saying my name."

"Zeke, what happened in the woods, Zeke?"

"She had help. Some guy came out of nowhere. Hit me with a rock a bunch of times."

Barnes walks over to the bed with its faded floral comforter and thin sheets. Zeke casually leans back, his hand closer to the pillow.

The big man reaches out, runs his hand over Zeke's head and feels the bumps. "That where these came from?"

"Yeah she…"

Barnes uses his thumb and forefinger to squeeze the largest lump. Zeke squeals and his legs kick out.

"You let her go."

"Not on purpose!" Zeke's hands are over the big man's, his legs still kicking the comforter. "Not on purpose!"

"I don't care for failure, Zeke."

He lets go of the lump and Zeke flops back on the bed. He turns, scrabbles at the pillow and pulls out his gun.

"You fucking touch me like that again and I'll put a bullet in you!"

Barnes isn't fazed. "I've had a bullet in me."

Zeke doesn't lower his arm. "Then you get how this goes."

"What happened to Tyson?"

"No idea, okay? He was looking for her and all I know is they found his body in the van. All burned up. Not sure who did it. Maybe it was Charlotte, maybe it was some banger."

"Yeah."

Barnes slaps the gun out of his hand so fast Zeke doesn't have time to fire. He turns and sees it bouncing off the motel's wallpaper.

When he turns around, Barnes' hands are around his throat.

"Don't much care for failure, Zeke."

The big man squeezes.

CHAPTER THIRTY-FOUR

Eve and Dory arrive at the same time the next morning. They find Mace sitting on the floor of the living room, a bowl of cereal in his lap.

"Weird to see a grown man eating cereal," Eve observes. "Feels like we caught you doing something wrong."

"Where's Charlotte?" Dory asks.

Mace hard swallows the cereal in his mouth. "Still sleeping. I tried to wake her before I went to the store, see if she wanted anything. She said she was fine, just tired. But I bought an extra bowl and spoon for her." He holds the spoon out. "Want some?"

"I'm going to check on her," Dory heads to the second floor.

"It's Fruit Loops," Mace tells Eve.

"Well, in that case..." Eve settles next to Mace, takes his spoon, scoops up and swallows a bite.

They eat in silence, passing the spoon back and forth.

"How was last night?" Mace asks.

Eve wipes her mouth with the back of her hand, decides not to mention the phone call with Dory. "Fine."

"Good." Mace nods. "By the way, we should get another spoon. What we're doing, eating with one spoon...this isn't right. Reminds me of when we were starting out."

"We had more than one spoon, didn't we?"

"I've just been thinking about Bolton Hill a lot recently."

"I liked living there."

"We needed someplace bigger, but yeah." Mace stretches his

legs. "Charlotte asked if we were getting back together."

Eve gives the spoon back to Mace. "What'd you tell her?"

"Told her I had no idea."

"I'm good with that."

They eat some more.

Mace moves one of Eve's braids out of her face.

"You guys ready?" Dory calls down.

CHAPTER THIRTY-FIVE

Charlotte's showered and her hair is still wet. She's wearing black sweatpants and a white long-sleeve shirt with *LOVE* across the front in pink.

Dory is sitting on the floor, her notepad spread open over her legs. "Like I told you, be honest. All we want to do is help, and we need the truth to give you the best help we can."

She pauses.

"And listen," Dory continues. "I know you don't know me as well as you know Mace and Charlotte. I understand you might have some concerns about trusting me."

Charlotte nods.

Dory reaches into her pocket, pulls out a dollar, sets it on floor in front of Charlotte. "Here."

Charlotte picks up the dollar, looks at it doubtfully. "What's this for?"

"Give it back to me."

Charlotte does.

"Fifty cents to me, fifty cents to Eve. We work for you now. And we can't go to the cops unless you tell us you're about to commit a crime. You can trust me."

"Okay," Charlotte says.

Eve can't hide her surprise, but she doesn't say anything.

She doesn't know what she can say.

And Dory doesn't turn to see her reaction, but Eve can feel the other woman's satisfaction.

Dammit, Dory.

* * *

Charlotte didn't know the second man in Sofia's motel room.

The girls had been on their way out to dinner, but Sofia had forgotten her purse, so Charlotte followed her back inside. Sofia's dad was standing against the far wall. The second man was sitting on the bed.

Sofia didn't seem surprised or concerned. She tossed off a bright, "Hi, Daddy!"

Charlotte stayed by the door. She'd grown used to Sofia's father, even if she wasn't comfortable around him. It had been weeks since he'd first had them kiss. He'd asked them to do it a few times since then, once having them lie on the bed, but he never went beyond that. Charlotte still wasn't sure how to respond. She went along with his requests, mainly because that's what Sofia wanted.

"This is my friend Bill," Sofia's father told them.

"Nice to meet you," Sofia said, as she passed Bill on her way to the bathroom. She touched his leg, let her hand drag from his knee to his thigh.

Bill didn't say anything. He was a small white man, thin with a green baseball cap. The room was too dark for Charlotte to get a good look at his face.

"You girls going out tonight?" Sofia's father asked.

"Yeah," Charlotte said quietly. She hadn't realized her hands were clasped, her fingers nervously rubbing together.

Sofia emerged from the bathroom, wearing jeans and a bra.

"I thought you were just getting your purse," Charlotte said.

Sofia ignored her. "Daddy, have you seen my shirt? The black one with the zipper on the side?"

"No."

Sofia ducked back into the bathroom.

"You going to change too?" her father asked Charlotte.

"I'll wear this." Charlotte's voice was soft, uncertain.

"You need money?"

"No."

"I could use some." Sofia emerged from the bathroom and walked toward Charlotte, now wearing only a bra and panties, carrying a Corona.

Bill stared hard at Sofia.

"You two make yourselves comfortable," Sofia's father said. "Sit on the bed. Next to Bill."

Sofia slipped an arm over Charlotte's shoulders, kissed her on the cheek. Gave her the bottle.

Charlotte drank. Alcohol seemed like a good idea.

"How much money are you thinking?" Sofia asked.

"Couple of hundred, at least."

Charlotte felt Sofia's hands lifting her shirt. She moved away from her friend.

"I should go."

Bill spoke up. "So soon?"

"Yeah, I guess." It was hard for her to concentrate.

"How long you in town?" Bill asked Sofia's dad.

"Not long."

"Wish I'd met you before."

Charlotte's lack of concentration was compounded by light-headedness. "Can I use the bathroom?"

"Sure," someone said. Charlotte wasn't sure who.

She struggled to keep her balance until she reached the bathroom. She closed the door behind her, realized it had no lock.

Charlotte sat on the toilet, head in hands, and tried to think. Something was wrong with her eyes.

She didn't remember slumping over or falling to the floor.

Or the bathroom door opening.

Charlotte felt the bars pressed against her back.

She couldn't see a thing. She tried to stand. Her head smacked something solid. She stayed on her knees, reached up. Touched metal.

Her head ached, felt like someone was dragging the blunt edge of a shovel through her skull. She rubbed her eyes. It was dark, but she made out something in front of her. Bars. A cage.

Panic rushed, and she cried out.

A door opened. Charlotte twisted around, saw a man walking toward her. He crouched, and she could only see his legs and boots.

She recognized the boots.

Sofia's father.

"Hello?" Her voice was raspy. She hadn't realized how thirsty she was.

He didn't respond.

"What are you doing? Where's Sofia?"

He rose. Charlotte felt the cage rattle, and the door opened. A hand reached inside.

"Come out."

Charlotte took the hand, awkwardly crawled. She stood, back aching, wanted to run to the front door. But his hand firmly held hers.

"Next to me," he told her. He sat on the bed.

Charlotte didn't see a choice.

"You never even got my name, did you? Sofia never told you."

Charlotte shook her head.

"Barnes."

She could smell him, the stench men get when they spend time sweating outdoors.

Barnes stared at her. His stare was menacing, his eyes lined with anger.

"You're not even nineteen, are you?"

"I'm eighteen."

"But you could pass for sixteen, maybe fifteen. Men ever tell you that?"

Charlotte kept trying not to look at the closed door. She wanted to jump off the bed and rush out, but she was too scared.

Charlotte hadn't been this scared since her mother died.

Barnes reached down and loosened his shoelaces. Kicked off his boots. Charlotte watched one hit the opposite wall and fall to the floor. "Sofia and I are only in town for another week. She tell you that?"

Charlotte shook her head.

"Then we're heading somewhere new. I thought maybe you could join us, maybe I could break you in. But it doesn't look like I can, seeing how you treated my friend Bill. So you're going to work for me this week. And seven days from now, you'll have some money, and then you can go."

"Doing what?"

Barnes reached down, started pulling off his socks. "What girls are good for."

Charlotte jumped off the bed. She hadn't taken a step before Barnes grabbed her arm. He swung her like she weighed nothing, tossed her on the bed, climbed up toward her.

He smacked her into silence when she screamed. Charlotte had never been hit that hard. She lay back on the bed, in shock and pain.

His shadow loomed over her.

Afterward, Charlotte lay next to Barnes in bed, naked and cold and crying. His body seemed like a mountain next to her.

"You've fucked before," he said. "You need to get better at it, but that won't matter much now." He pulled out his phone, squinted at the screen.

"What do you want?"

Barnes put the phone down. "You're starting tonight. Sofia's got some dates for you."

Charlotte cried.

Barnes watched her.

When she finished, he said, "Men are going to come soon. They get twenty minutes each, so it's going to be fast. There's

Vaseline in the nightstand. Use that on yourself, ass to clit. Make sure they wear rubbers. These men know the deal, they understand what you are. They're not going to help you; don't ask. None of them are as nice as I am. You ask for help, they'll tell me. And if they do, I won't be this nice to you anymore."

Charlotte cried more and begged until Barnes took his gun out, shoved it against her neck, and told her that he'd pull the trigger if she didn't stop. She didn't think she could, she didn't think it would be possible to swallow down this much hysteria.

But she did.

Barnes reached under the bed, took out some lingerie, tossed it to her. Charlotte pulled it over herself. It was stiff black lace and too big, and it only covered her upper body. But she was grateful to wear something, anything.

She hadn't taken in the room yet, but now she could see that the television set and phone had been removed. The windows were covered in dark plastic.

Charlotte pulled the covers over her legs, up to her waist, hoping Barnes wouldn't notice.

He was standing and staring into his phone. Didn't seem to care.

A knock on the door.

Charlotte inhaled sharply.

Barnes opened it a crack, peered out, his gun hidden by his side. He exchanged a few words, then opened the door wider. Flipped the lights out. Someone stepped into the dark room as Barnes stepped outside.

Charlotte saw a large shadow approach the bed and she shrank into the covers, tried to pull them over her but they were yanked off. She whispered, "Please." He laughed and she heard his belt buckle loosen. His weight pressed down.

She didn't dare cry.

There were more that night, a lot more. Charlotte only had a couple of minutes between men, and she did have to use the Vaseline. She was terribly sore and scared and, after what Barnes had told her, didn't think about trying to get the men to help. Charlotte couldn't fight back the tears, but she kept the crying as quiet as she could. The men didn't care, and they didn't stop.

Finally, the door opened, the light came on, and Barnes stood in the doorway. He closed the door behind him and walked over to the bed. Charlotte lay there, staring dully up. He had a paper bag in his hand.

Barnes sat next to her, opened the bag, pulled out a bottle of water and a sandwich.

Charlotte felt like she was near death. Her midsection throbbed in pain. She looked down. The bedsheets had blood on them.

Barnes followed her gaze. "Fucking animals." Something in his tone, the anger when he said those two words, surprised her.

He unscrewed the cap off the water bottle, gave it to her.

"There's no drugs in it."

Charlotte was too thirsty to care. She finished the bottle in a few gulps. Felt the tears start up, looked away.

"Why are you doing this to me?" Her voice sounded strange, as if it belonged to someone else.

"This is how I make my money."

Barnes didn't leave her. He stayed on the other side of the bed while she ate. She lay down when she was done, the covers to her chin, and fell into terrible dreams. He woke her from them, held her, calmed her down. Gave her more water, walked with her as she limped to the bathroom, stood in the doorway as she shit and peed.

When he told her that he was going to leave, he gave her a pill. She swallowed it and, after a minute or two, started to feel dizzy. He walked her to the cage and opened it. Charlotte crawled inside.

CHAPTER THIRTY-SIX

"We have some new leads," Dave says.

Frank and Will had been sitting on the couch, Will eating slices of raisin bread, Frank inhaling from a bong.

Will listens. Frank cranes to see the TV.

"I talked to some detectives," Dave goes on, "who've dealt with sex trafficking. They said some women don't stay at the shelters too long, that they get out of town."

"Where do they go?" Will asks.

"There's some kind of underground network," Dave tells him. "They get sent somewhere else in the country. I got a few names for us to check out today."

He glances at Frank's drug-hazed eyes.

"Will, you take one, I got the other. Yours is some attorney."

CHAPTER THIRTY-SEVEN

Mace feels like a dull spoon is digging out his heart. He looks down at the floor, doesn't think he can look Charlotte in the eyes.

Dory is stoic, writing.

Eve cries.

As for Charlotte, she's in a trance, her voice distant, mind still in that Tucson motel room.

Charlotte woke groggy in the cage. She lay inside, curled on a towel. The memories started to return.

She was crying when the door to the motel room opened and Barnes stepped in. She saw a glimpse of daylight but had no idea what time it was.

Barnes opened the cage, grabbed her by the hair, and pulled her out.

"I don't want to do this anymore."

He smacked her, took her to the shower, threw her inside. Blasted her with cold water and then, when she gasped, warmed it.

"That better?" Barnes growled. He pulled off his clothes, joined her.

Afterwards, he fed her a breakfast of doughnuts and water. Something must have been in the water because Charlotte woke back in the cage. This time she didn't wake scared. She stared dully at the bars until the door to the hotel room opened. Sofia walked in.

"I brought dinner." Sofia opened a bag of fast food, slipped a couple of cheeseburgers through the bars, some fries, a bottle of water.

Charlotte ripped open a cheeseburger and devoured it.

"You lied to me," Charlotte said, when she was finished. "How could you do this?"

"I have to." Sofia's voice was rough.

"What do you mean, you…"

Sofia left.

Barnes came back an hour later. More men came after that. Charlotte's emotions were ragged as she fought back tears. Her body felt like it was going to split in half, no matter how much Vaseline she used.

That was how the week went. Drugged half the time, wishing she was drugged the other half. Charlotte had no idea what day it was, and she lost track of how many men walked into the room.

Sofia stopped by more frequently, even though Charlotte never acknowledged her. She would bring food and ask a couple of random questions that Charlotte ignored. Until the day Sofia said: "He's going to kill you."

"What?"

"He's not going to let you go. He never does. He's going to kill you, and he's going to leave your body in the desert."

Charlotte grabbed the bars of the cage. "Has he done that before?"

Sofia nodded.

"You have to help me."

Sofia started crying. "I can't. He'll kill me."

"We can run off together." Charlotte squeezed the bars. "We'll go someplace he can't find us."

"He'll find us anywhere."

"We'll go to the police. He can't get us there."

"There were policemen here this week."

That made Charlotte pause.

"I don't want you to die," Sofia said. "I don't want anyone else to die."

She walked over to the cage and touched the lock.

Charlotte wanted to say something, but she didn't want to risk changing Sofia's mind. She just stared at Sofia's hand, more intensely than she'd ever stared at anything.

Sofia reached into her pocket, pulled out a key, and opened the cage.

Charlotte was only wearing her lingerie, the lingerie that smelled of sweat and cigarettes and semen, but she didn't care. She rushed to the door.

She didn't make it halfway before it opened.

Barnes walked into the room.

Sofia screamed.

Barnes slammed the door shut, grabbed the girls with one hand each. He threw Charlotte into her cage, then turned his attention to Sofia.

"You helping her?"

"I wasn't," Sofia protested. "She tricked me. She made me open the cage. I didn't want to..."

Barnes tossed Sofia onto the bed. He did worse to her than he'd ever done to Charlotte. She couldn't watch, kept her eyes closed, tried not to listen. Barnes left Sofia curled on the floor when he finished.

Then he sat on the bed, thinking aloud: "I can't keep both of you here. And I can't send you to Mexico, now that my contact at the cartel lost his head. Could give you to the Russians. Send you overseas, never have to deal with you again. It'd be easier to shoot you both and bury you a few miles from here...but you've done good work. Until today. What I should do is kill one of you, send the other away, start over with a new bottom. Get someone loyal, younger. Someone who'll treat me better."

Neither of the girls said anything.

Barnes hopped off the bed and pulled Charlotte out of the

cage. He yanked off her dirty lingerie.

"Get over here," he told Sofia.

Sofia didn't move.

Barnes cursed, walked over to her, and grabbed her by the hair. He threw her toward Charlotte. Charlotte caught Sofia before she fell.

The naked girls stood in front of Barnes.

"Fight for your daddy."

"What?" Charlotte asked.

"Fight for me. Winner lives."

"She's your daughter!"

Barnes squinted. "There's a difference between a daddy and a father, sweetie."

"But—" That's all Charlotte said before Sofia threw herself at her.

Charlotte stumbled back into the wall. Sofia was punching her but they were soft punches, landing on her stomach and hips. Charlotte took them, trying to think, until Sofia bit her on the shoulder.

Charlotte cried out and tried to pull Sofia off, but couldn't. She hit her in the head until Sofia's jaws loosened, then pushed her away.

Charlotte saw Barnes on the bed, pants down.

Sofia launched at her again, but instincts from mixed martial arts kicked in. Charlotte grabbed Sofia by the arm, threw her into the wall. Sofia hit hard, fell to the floor. Charlotte reached down to help her, and Sofia whirled and slammed one of Barnes's boots into her face.

Charlotte was groggy, stunned. Sofia hit her with the boot again. Charlotte fell back, and then the smaller girl was on top of her, hands around her neck.

Blackness sank over Charlotte.

She fought it off.

Her hands found Sofia's throat. She saw the girl's eyes widen like they were about to explode. The hands around her own throat weakened. Charlotte crawled to her feet, pushed Sofia into a corner, kept choking her until someone pulled her off.

Sofia stayed in the corner, staring forward.

Barnes led Charlotte to her cage and guided her inside. Then he walked over to Sofia, knelt, and checked her pulse.

"Is she okay?" Charlotte felt tears on her face.

Barnes looked back at her and grinned. "You just won a trip to Russia."

He left Charlotte in the cage.

And Sofia's body sitting in the corner of the room.

CHAPTER THIRTY-EIGHT

Hours later, Charlotte was led into the back of a van. She was distant, in shock. And she could still feel Sofia's body pressed against hers.

A man sat in the back of the van with her but didn't say a word. He just put on headphones and stared into an iPad.

Charlotte had no idea how long they drove. She stayed awake the entire ride, unable to stop thinking about Sofia.

After a while the van stopped. The back door opened, and a different man climbed in. The man who had been sitting with her headed out.

The new man gave her water, Twinkies, chips, a box of cereal. Charlotte ate it all and fell asleep. She woke with that familiar foggy drugged feeling.

"Where are we going?"

"Baltimore," a new man said.

The men switched places two more times. They gave her a bucket to use the bathroom in, bought her some tampons when they saw the blood. Stared silently at her as she put one in.

A man finally told her, "We're here."

Charlotte was led outside, given to some other men. They took her through a garage, into a house, into a basement. She saw a bed in the dim lighting, chains next to it.

"Is this good?" a nervous voice asked.

She was taken to the bed, handcuffed around her wrists. The handcuffs were loose; not loose enough to pull her hands free, but they didn't constrict her. The dim light extinguished, a distant door closed, sound vanished. She wanted to cry, wanted to scream. Fought both urges until she fell into an uneasy asleep.

She woke later that night when a man came downstairs. He had his way with her and left.

Charlotte didn't cry. Didn't move. But she noticed something, something growing inside her.

Something dangerous.

She slept lightly, woke when the door opened again and someone else came downstairs. The basement was dark, but this man knew his way around. He undid her cuffs and led her to a bathroom. He didn't turn on a light as she felt her way to the toilet and relieved herself. He led her back out, gave her some bread and water. Then he chained her back up.

"I have a couple of things for you."

He wheeled something into the room, a television on a stand. He turned it on and slipped a DVD in. "All Dave has are westerns and kung fu flicks. Sorry about that."

She didn't respond.

"My name's Will. You're Charlotte?"

She kept quiet.

"I got something else," Will said, and he fumbled with one of her handcuffs. Undid it, slipped a different one on. Did the same with her other wrist.

"The chain's longer so you can walk around the room. You can't reach the bathroom, but at least you can get off the bed and switch movies. And just shout if you need the restroom. I'll come down."

Charlotte felt grateful, then hated herself for that feeling.

Charlotte had no idea how many days and nights passed; she was still occasionally drugged, but less often. But she began to learn about the men who were holding her, heard their faint conversations from the floor above. There were four of them: Will, Frank, Dave, and Seth. Will and Frank were brothers. Dave was a cop and in charge. Seth worked at a restaurant called

The Rib Joint.

The chains were bolted into the stone wall. The handcuffs were impossible to remove.

Every night, a different one would come downstairs—but never Will. And after Frank, Dave, or Seth had left, that raw feeling of contempt and hatred would rush over Charlotte, settle inside her like firewood glowing red.

Until one night when Frank was lying on top of her, and Charlotte wrapped the chain around his neck.

She could hear him gasping, and he grabbed the chain and pulled it away; she wasn't as strong as he was. Then he wrapped it around his fist, grabbed her by the hair, and punched her in the cheek.

"Asshole," Frank said when he left.

Charlotte lay on the bed, bleeding, smiling.

Will came downstairs the next morning. He gave her water and a warm pancake. Charlotte dropped it and, when Will went to pick it up, she kicked him in the back.

He howled in pain. She laughed. Charlotte thought he might strike her, but instead he rushed up the stairs.

The pancake was just out of reach.

She stood on the bed to hear them talk about her later that day, but she could only hear snippets of their conversation.

"...not working..."

"...they're not going to want her..."

"...Rib Joint..."

"...just tell them..."

There was silence, and then one of them said something she couldn't make out. The door to the basement opened a few minutes later.

Will walked in.

"You had a chance," he told her. "You could have gone to Russia, worked there, maybe survived. That's not going to happen now. Now they don't want you. They're going to take you somewhere tonight. And that's it."

Charlotte thought he sounded sad.

"I can't do anything for you. We were holding you for them, keeping you a few more days. You just had to play cool and you would have been okay."

Charlotte laughed. She couldn't help it.

"It's not funny!" Will's voice was high. "Those men are going to take you into the woods and cut you into pieces. They've done it to other women. They're going to beat you first, beat you bad. Then cut you apart. And they're coming now."

He left her.

The brutal carelessness Charlotte had been feeling started to recede.

She thought about Sofia. And for the first time since Charlotte had been locked in that basement, she wept.

Wept for her dead friend.

Wept for her lost innocence.

Wept until she heard those two men coming to take her to the woods.

CHAPTER THIRTY-NINE

"That's when Mace found me."

Charlotte blinks back to the present. She looks around the room, at Eve, Dory, and Mace.

"Are you okay?" Mace asks.

"No."

Mace reaches toward her, then stops. "Can I hug you?"

Charlotte nods.

"I believe you," Dory says, as Charlotte buries her head into Mace's shoulder. "And I think you're right. The police can't help you. Not like I can."

Charlotte looks up.

"But," Dory continues, "I have to make some calls to see if what I want to do is even possible."

"Thanks."

"Thank you for talking with us. For trusting us."

Dory walks out of the room. They hear her descend the stairs to the first floor, open and close the front door as she leaves.

"I'm sorry," Eve says.

Charlotte sniffs, gently pulls away. She sits by herself, pulls her knees to her. Wraps her arms around them.

She closes her eyes.

She's teetering at the edge of a cavernous pit, a pit filled with shadows and screams. Hands reach out and grasp her ankles, trying to pull her down. The hands belong to Raúl and that man in the van and those men in the basement and those men in the motel, grasping her clothes and skin, their hands claws.

Charlotte has always felt that pit; until now, she's never seen it. Now she sees the pit clearly, as plainly as Mace and Eve and the empty bedroom, and she realizes how close she is to the edge. She peers into it and there is Barnes, striding out, his giant hand reaching for hers. Charlotte wants to back up, to shrink away as he approaches her, his steps determined but unhurried. The other men blindly, furiously reach for her, but not Barnes. There's a calculated deliberation to him, a practiced slowness in his steps...and that's even worse.

A dog that snaps at you is startling.

A dog hunting you is terrifying.

Mace and Eve are talking. Charlotte looks at them, but she can't hear their voices. She sees their mouths moving, but there are no words, no sound whatsoever. It's as if she's a ghost in this world, a traveler standing in two dimensional realms, her body in the house, her spirit and senses staring down at Barnes and those men. She can't will herself to stand, to join their conversation, to do anything but watch.

Her eyes burn.

Her wrists ache.

CHAPTER FORTY

Will sits in the parking lot outside Dory Anderson's law office, bored out of his mind. He's gone through all of the apps on his phone, texted a girl he'd met at the college who wasn't interested, flipped through radio stations in the car. He wants to walk around the parking lot, escape the cramped confines and the lingering scent of Frank's weed, but knows he can't risk being seen. He stays slouched in his seat.

Privately, he doesn't think there's much of a chance of finding Charlotte. An underground network for battered women seems like too good a place to hide.

The office is in a crappy strip mall, buried in the outlying business districts of Baltimore. This area seems like nothing but strip mall after strip mall, stores always empty of customers with no reason to survive, stores selling carpets and mattresses and off-brand electronics. Will hasn't seen a single customer in hours and had no idea how the stores made enough money to stay in business. Then he thinks about the financial problems Dave told him about—how little they made selling drugs, how much more they could make selling women.

Maybe nobody was making any money. There were the rich people who had it and everyone else, and some invisible border between the two groups neither ever crosses. That idea depresses Will, as do the shops and the whole idea of selling women.

But he can't leave.

Dave wants a photo of Dory Anderson. As if he knows Will

is having doubts and needs proof he's doing his job.

And just then a Grand Cherokee pulls into the lot, parks, and a squarish woman gets out. Will idly watches her, then perks up when she heads to the law office door. She pauses for a minute, searching for her keys.

Will realizes this must be Dory Anderson.

He grabs his phone to take a picture, but he drained the battery playing games all day.

The office door opens. Dory walks in and Will swears to himself. Makes plans to come back in the morning, too frustrated to remember how sad this strip mall made him.

CHAPTER FORTY-ONE

Mace and Charlotte sit on the floor of the living room, watching *The Matrix* on Eve's iPad. Dory and Eve have left for the night, most of the lights in the house are off and, to Mace, the house seems large and lonely.

But only to Mace.

"I love this part!" Charlotte exclaims. "Trinity floating in the air. So badass."

"I can't believe you wanted to see this movie," he says.

"Oh, I love old movies."

"Old?"

"Wasn't this made in the nineties?"

"Okay, shut up."

Charlotte laughs, and Mace looks at her excited face, her eyes intense on the screen. It's hard to imagine, looking at her now, what she's been through. Hard to imagine anyone would do that to a child. Or that the child could recover.

He wonders if that's a difference between men and women. The male soldiers he knew who'd faced traumatic events carried that weight; agony haunted their expressions. But women seem able to compartmentalize their experiences. Like the way Charlotte could hate the men who hurt her, but not all men. Or watch a violent movie hours after recounting her horrific past.

Or maybe that was just Charlotte.

"What kind of name is Keanu?" she asks. "Scottish?"

"I have no idea."

"I don't know why I guessed Scottish. I suck at all that ancestry stuff." Charlotte pushes her hair behind her right shoulder, and Mace is surprised to see an earring high in her ear, a small golden shell clamped over the top curve. He wonders if she's had it this entire time, all these weeks since Barnes first put her in that cage.

"How are you okay?" he asks.

"What?"

"How are you okay, after everything you went through?"

Charlotte doesn't pause the movie, doesn't look up from the screen. He notices her thumb rubbing her index finger.

Mace catches himself.

"I'm sorry. We don't have to talk about this."

But now Charlotte does pause the movie.

"I don't know if I'm okay. I don't know. That man I shot, I have nightmares about him. But I'm glad I did what I did. That at least one of them got what he deserved."

"Really?"

"Yeah. It's like, like I don't have to rationalize it. I just accept it." Her hand touches the bottom of her hair, gently plays and pulls at it. "It was a good thing."

That idea is foreign to Mace, the concept that any death could inherently be good. Even in the Army, when death was understood as necessary for the survival of your brothers and sisters, even then it seemed arguable to Mace. At some point in his life, either by church or school or his parents, he'd been taught that violence was inherently evil. And the lesson had taken root.

Mace doesn't think he believes in fate, but he wonders if some cosmic force brought him and Charlotte together. As if they were meant to balance each other out.

"It's weird that we met," he muses.

"You mean in the woods?" Charlotte asks. "That was kind of random."

"What I meant is, for years, I've worried that there's this

pull to death in me."

Charlotte absent-mindedly scratches her ankle. "What do you mean by pull to death?"

"I come from suicides, my grandfather and my mother. I've just felt like my life is circling it."

A dog barks somewhere outside.

"But you seem like you're the opposite of me," Mace goes on. "You keep fighting for life."

"We're all fighting for it. Most people just don't realize that."

She takes Mace's hand, squeezes it.

That squeeze of the hand, a palm firmly pressing into his own, reminds Mace of Eve, of that trip they took to San Diego. Eve was flying there for a work conference and invited him along. They left a cold and rainy Baltimore behind and, hours later, stood in the warm caress of west coast sunshine.

They'd only been dating for months and were happily drunk on each other; Eve skipped the entire conference and she and Mace spent the week in bed, making love and eating room service and watching rented movies and abruptly stopping meals and movies to make more love. They did emerge once to walk the boardwalk, squinting in the afternoon sunlight, but they were only outside for minutes before hurrying back.

Mace frowns and scratches his knee as Charlotte restarts the movie.

But was that right? Did they only leave the hotel room once that trip? Mace seems to have a memory of San Diego at night, but he and Eve have always joked about spending the week inside.

And was it an entire week? It seems more likely that it was a weekend. He can't imagine taking a sudden week off work.

He and Eve had often returned to that trip, not physically but in conversation, an emotional remembrance of the time they'd been happiest. But now San Diego is swirled in confusion. Had he started taking anti-depressants by then? He can't quite remember, but he assumes it must have been around that time. That would explain the unquestioned happiness. Or was the trip important to him because all of the happiness had been organic, unrelated to any drugs whatsoever?

The memory is confused, hard to grasp, as if it's been complicated by alcohol or exhaustion. Mace wonders if it will further blur the more time distances him, as if the memory is a mix of bright colors that fade until one lone bright emotional hue remains. He hopes it's happiness.

CHAPTER FORTY-TWO

"You want me to move to *Milwaukee*?" Charlotte can't keep the doubt out of her voice.

Dory nods, her smile more unsettling than reassuring. Charlotte had woken to Dory knocking on her door, and she's still a little sleep-confused.

"Just for a few years," Dory says. "I have an associate there who can give you a place to live and a job. After an appropriate amount of time passes, you can move wherever you want. We'll keep in touch, of course. And you may decide to stay in Milwaukee."

"Doesn't it get cold there?"

"You're from California, right?"

Charlotte nods.

"It gets cold."

"I only have one sweatshirt. And it belongs to Mace. And it's ugly."

"Mace and Eve are out buying you new clothes. And Milwaukee won't be that bad. They based *Happy Days* and *Laverne and Shirley* there."

"I don't know what those are."

Dory grimaces. "This isn't ideal, but there aren't a lot of people I trust. I wish I could give you choices in Hawaii or Miami or Paris, but I only have this option. The one thing I can assure you of is you'll be safe. I've worked with this woman in Wisconsin before. She'll help you."

"I guess."

"We leave tomorrow. First thing in the morning."

Charlotte starts. "That soon?"

"You can't stay in this area if you're not going into police protection."

"Yeah." Charlotte thinks about the cop who held her. "I'm not doing that."

"This is the best option. The drive will take two days, and we'll stop at a friend's house on the way. This friend is someone I trust, but she has no idea why we're coming or who you are. For this trip, we need to stay as low-key as possible. You'll be using a different name, and I have a different backstory for you as well."

Charlotte trusts Dory's plan, trusts she'll be safe, but that's not the problem.

"I won't be ready to leave tomorrow," Charlotte tells her. "I need more time."

"For what?" Dory looks around the empty bedroom. "To pack?"

"No, it's not that. Just..." Charlotte can't think of a good excuse.

"It's certainly abrupt. And you've made good friends with Mace and Eve. I'd offer to bring them with us for the trip but, trust me, the less people who know where you're going, the better."

"I guess."

"Be ready tomorrow morning. We're leaving at dawn."

Charlotte nods.

But those men are in her thoughts.

Revenge is in her thoughts.

CHAPTER FORTY-THREE

"Doesn't it feel," Eve asks, as she and Mace push a shopping cart through a sparsely-crowded Target, "like we're buying stuff for a kid going to college?"

"You mean, instead of a sex trafficking victim desperately trying to start a new life?"

Eve glances around. "You might want to keep your voice down."

Mace grimaces. Shopping has always been a chore to him, something he does reluctantly. And he finds stores like Target—places where you can buy lawnmowers in one aisle and groceries in another—overreaching and maybe a little suspicious. He doesn't trust anything that purports to be everything.

Eve has never had that problem. She loves shopping, walks through stores so slowly it's as if she suddenly walking underwater. It always seemed to Mace that Eve views shopping as entirely designed for her pleasure, a weird courting experience between her and the retailer. Which, he supposes, it is.

"Remember," he tells her, "Dory told us not to get anything someone will remember. Just plain clothes."

She's examining a white shirt with a red heart in the middle. She sighs and flips to other shirts on the rack. "I was wrong."

"About what?"

"About not trusting her."

"You don't know that for sure."

"I do though."

155

"You believe everything she told us?"

Eve nods. "For the most part. No memory is perfect, but I do trust her. And it's not like we don't have proof of men trying to kill her."

Mace stays quiet.

"Are you okay?" Eve asks. "You should be happy. She's going to be safe."

"I should be," Mace agrees, and decides to admit the other thing bothering him. "I just didn't think she'd be leaving this soon."

"You're going to miss her."

"I barely know her."

Eve leaves the shirts behind and pushes the shopping cart across the wide aisle. "That doesn't matter," she says, "if you're turning her into your child."

Mace stops walking.

Then, when he realizes Eve isn't going to stop to appreciate his shock, he hurries after her. "What are you talking about?"

Eve picks out a green shirt, shows it to Mace. "You think Charlotte will like this? The color will look good on her."

"I have no idea. And I know she's not my child."

Eve puts the shirt in the cart, along with the other clothes she's picked out. "You care about her."

"Yeah."

She touches his arm.

"You did everything you could for her, you know."

"Doesn't feel like enough."

"Of course not. It's almost never the right time to say goodbye."

Her hand squeezes his arm, leaves.

CHAPTER FORTY-FOUR

Eve had brought the knife over with last night's dinner, left it on the kitchen counter when she and Mace went to the store. It's a steak knife, six inches long, sharp and serrated.

And they're still gone.

Charlotte slides the knife into her sock and pulls her pants leg down low. The cold blade presses against her skin.

She pulls on a hoodie and slips the gun she took from that man in the van, a nine-millimeter the size of her hand, in a front pocket.

She heads out of Eve's rental and tries to get her bearings. She can hear traffic a few blocks away and walks toward the sound, hoping to find a cab.

It takes her ten minutes before she finds a main road, a couple more until she hails a cab.

The driver asks where she wants to go.

Charlotte tells him the one name she's sure of, the name she heard them say upstairs when she was chained in that basement.

"The Rib Joint."

CHAPTER FORTY-FIVE

Dory locks her office door and heads to her car. The energy she had during her conversation with Charlotte is leaving her. She thinks about the drive tomorrow, wonders if she'll be able to stay awake for twelve hours. Maybe she should just head home, get some rest, take a quick afternoon nap.

No chance.

Dory has too much to do. She needs to contact clients, tell them she's going to be unavailable for a couple of days, map out the route she and Charlotte are taking to Milwaukee, make sure the overnight stop is lined up.

But, Jesus, she's tired.

So tired that she doesn't even notice the car following her as she pulls out of the parking lot.

CHAPTER FORTY-SIX

There's not much traffic as Charlotte's cab heads into Baltimore. She stares at the city through her window, the long lines of row houses huddled together, the mix of people walking with purpose and the drifting homeless, the way it seems like you can see every edge of the city. That last one sticks with her, reminds Charlotte of a class trip she once took to New York, and how that city was both gigantic and suffocating. Baltimore seems the opposite.

The cab pulls to a stop.

"We're here?" Charlotte had been lost in thoughts.

The driver points to the passenger side window. They're right outside the restaurant.

The man named Seth worked here.

From the basement, Charlotte would hear the kidnappers say things like, "Seth can't do it. He's at The Rib Joint all day tomorrow." Or, "Seth, Rib Joint called for you." Or, "Seth, the food at The Rib Joint is fucking terrible. Stop bringing it home."

Charlotte slips out, hands the driver one of her twenties. She's too worried about being seen to wait for the change so she waves the driver off, turns her back to the restaurant, hurries across the street. Both sides are lined with businesses and shops. She steps into a drug store, pretends to looks through a display of greeting cards up front, keeps an eye on the restaurant through the window.

It's almost eleven a.m. A few people amble in to The Rib

Joint, but she doesn't see anyone who matches what she remembers of Seth.

The only thing Charlotte knows are the names of the men who held her. She has, at best, a vague idea of their faces. But she does remember their bodies. Seth was medium-height and shockingly thin. And he always smelled like cigarettes.

She stays in the CVS, pretending to look at cards, and waits for him to walk out and smoke. The knife tucked into her sock presses against her skin.

CHAPTER FORTY-SEVEN

Seth opens the restaurant's front door, squints into the sunlight, steps outside.

The street's empty. Not that he's worried about anything, but he always looks around. Lifelong habit.

He pulls out a cigarette and walks into a small alley to the back of the restaurant. He takes a long drag, holds the smoke in his throat, exhales. Doesn't feel as good as it used to, doesn't calm him the way it once did.

He wonders what *would* work. Pot just makes him tired and anything harder leaves him jittery. Seth doesn't like feeling jittery.

He leans against the back wall of The Rib Joint and closes his eyes. Not even getting his dick wet makes him feel that great. Admittedly, the chick they had in the basement was too dry to be fun. Felt like fucking worn carpet.

But Seth missed it, so he tried last night. Went online, went to the personals of some shady site where you can buy anything and everything, and bought someone for the night. Met her in his car just outside of the Block—a neighborhood in Baltimore dedicated to strip clubs and sex shops—drove her to an alley, got pissed when she was going to make him use a condom. Told her he'd pay double, but she still refused. He held her down and fucked her. Kicked her out of the car, pulled up his pants and drove off.

He still wasn't happy.

Seth tries to remember a time when he was truly happy and can't. It wasn't when he was a kid, heading from foster home to foster home after his shit mom got locked up for good—he'd never met his dad, and didn't care to. He finally reached an age where the state couldn't give a damn about him and he was on his own, which is what he wanted. He started dealing drugs with friends he'd made in one of the foster homes, moved into a beat-down apartment with them. Got busted twice for dealing, but one cop just yelled at him, and the other cop bought.

Still, Seth sought stability and knew he couldn't sell drugs forever. He took a job washing dishes and busing tables at the Rib Joint. The job barely paid anything, but Seth didn't care about the money. And he didn't like the work but didn't hate it. It gave him something he'd never had before.

But it wasn't happiness.

Not exactly.

Sometimes he wonders if the way other people live gives them enough. He remembers when he first met Dave, when Dave came to his apartment to buy weed, after he'd busted him and bought from him a week earlier. Dave glanced around the apartment, at the guys passed out in the other room, the stains on the floor, the sound of roaches in the walls, and looked at Seth with pity.

"You live like this?"

Seth shrugged.

"I looked up your record. With all the times you've been busted, you should be making more money."

"What do you mean?"

"I mean you're better than this."

"I'm not."

Dave smiled and left.

Seth didn't think about him again, not until Dave came back a couple of days later.

He didn't come alone. Cops flew in through the door, arresting everyone in sight, leading them out in handcuffs. Seth ended up sitting on the curb, hands behind his back, the plastic cuffs gnawing into his skin.

A shadow fell over him.

He looked up at Dave in his uniform.

Dave stood him up, led him away. None of the other cops seemed to care.

"You stay with these guys," Dave told him. "You'll end up in prison or dead. I can help you. Give you a job."

"I got a job," Seth replied.

Dave sat next to Seth and lowered his voice. "I got a better one."

"Can I keep my other job? At The Rib Joint?"

Dave looked at him curiously. "Really?"

Seth nodded.

"Sure."

"One thing," Seth said. "Why do you want me? You just met me." He pauses. "Is this for some gay shit?"

Dave laughed. A couple of cops turned and looked at them, then turned away.

"No gay shit. I'm putting a crew together, and I could use another person. I got two guys who've been with me about half a year, these two brothers—not black dudes, I mean siblings. They're coming along, but we need muscle. Someone who doesn't give a fuck who he hurts. I busted you on the street, and you didn't get scared. Didn't even react when I asked to buy from you. I went to your apartment, and everyone there was in a drugged haze, but you were sharp. I get the impression you don't like to lose control."

Seth nodded.

"That's what I need. Someone who stays sharp. You come stay with us, get out of the roach motel, and I'll show you how we do things. Trust me, you'll be happier."

Happier.

Seth's cigarette is halfway gone. He holds it up, looks at it.

Happiness, Seth realizes, happens in a moment. Pushing

your dick deep. Getting paid. Sucking a cigarette.

Too bad those moments can't last, he thinks, as he rounds the corner back into the alley. Turn into something longer. Even permanent. Like the warmth from a cigarette before it disappears.

CHAPTER FORTY-EIGHT

The gun is heavy in her pocket and the knife blade bites into Charlotte's ankle as she leaves the store. Her legs are unsteady, have been ever since she saw Seth slink out the front door and disappear behind the restaurant. She breathes slowly, trying to calm her nerves, and crosses the street.

Stands next to the alley entrance, peers in. The alley extends about twenty yards, then curves around the back of the restaurant.

Charlotte takes out the nine-millimeter and slips into the alley.

And almost bumps into Seth when he steps in front of her.

He looks down at her nine, drops the cigarette, and runs back behind the restaurant.

Charlotte follows him.

She rounds a corner and Seth grabs her wrist. The gun flies away, skitters under a dumpster. He shoves her and rushes to where the weapon fell. Charlotte pulls out her knife and shouts.

Seth stops, turns toward her.

The back of the restaurant is closed off by a fence, and the heavy door leading inside is closed.

"You think you're going to do something with that knife?"

Charlotte doesn't say anything.

"You made a big mistake staying. You should be three states away. You and your fucked-up face."

Her fingers tighten around the handle.

"You don't have what it..."

Charlotte lunges forward and stabs his shoulder.

"Shit!" Seth cries out. He staggers back against the restaurant wall and sinks to the ground. His left hand covers the wound in his right shoulder. Charlotte's surprised that the blade didn't go deeper, that she held back.

No one ever held back with her.

Seth's foot lashes out and kicks her knee. Charlotte cries out and drops, still holding the knife. Seth's face is contorted in pain as he uses the restaurant wall to stand, blood from the wound in his shoulder staining his shirt. Charlotte rises, her knee aching, excitement and fear forcing shallow breaths. She can feel her heartbeat in her palms, her feet.

"You think you'll be able to kill me?"

"Always up for a challenge."

But she can't help backing up when he steps toward her.

"I should have killed you while I was fucking you," he tells her.

Charlotte doesn't have an answer for that.

Seth rushes forward and grabs her wrist. She's too surprised to react, feels her knees crumble when he puts pressure on her arm and tries to force the knife away. Her hand starts to open. She hears a cry starting in her, muffled, distant, the same soft sound she'd made when those men would mount her.

Charlotte leans forward and sinks her teeth into Seth's thumb, through the skin. Tastes bone.

Seth lets out a yell and let's go of her wrist. His other hand smashes into Charlotte's cheek but she stubbornly holds on, trying to bite his thumb off. He rears back, punches her in the face again. She sees black for a second and, after that second passes, finds herself sitting on the ground.

She can taste his skin and blood. She wipes her mouth.

Seth is standing in front of her, bent over, clutching his thumb into his gut.

Her knife is on the ground.

He kicks it away.

"I'm going to beat you to death," he rasps. "It's going to be slow, too."

Charlotte lunges for the knife. Seth jumps, and his full weight falls on her back. Air doesn't come easily with him on her. She tries to fight it, her hands scrabbling on the ground until he forces her over.

Charlotte looks into his face, into his small angry eyes. She reaches up and hits him. His fist smashes into her forehead. The back of her head smacks the ground. Again, blackness clouds her vision. She reaches up, pushing him, her hands on his chest, hips, even in his pockets.

"Fuckin' bitch," Seth tells her. He hits her again, this time in the mouth.

Charlotte lays back, hurt and dazed, staring up at the gray sky.

"I'm going to bring you back home." Seth pauses to suck his bloody thumb. "And there's nothing we won't do to you."

He hears something, looks behind himself. Sees his lighter in Charlotte's hand, her thumb running over the igniter.

The lighter she must have pulled from his pocket.

It ignites.

Pain rushes across him as the kitchen grease on his shirt catches fire.

Seth shrieks and rolls away from Charlotte, grabbing his shirt and pulling it off. But it's like pulling off a sheet of fire, and its melting into his skin.

Charlotte stands, her body a giant bruise.

She hears footsteps rushing to the back door.

Charlotte limps out of the alley as Seth screams, burns.

CHAPTER FORTY-NINE

Mace hears Eve running down the stairs.

"She's not there," Eve says, worried.

Mace is checking the front door for damage. "Doesn't look like someone tried to break in. Did you see any broken windows?"

"I didn't check." Eve's voice is strained.

"Maybe she went out. She could have. She did that with me the first night. Didn't tell me where she was going, and just showed up later."

"I though Dory was going to stay with her."

Mace feels weirdly calm, and he's not sure why. Part of it may be because he trusts Charlotte to take care of herself; he doubts she'd do anything dumb. And she did save his life a couple of days ago. That's the kind of thing that earns faith.

And part of it is the dynamic of his relationship with Eve. They've always shifted to opposite ends of the emotional spectrum. When one panics, the other relaxes; when one is dejected, the other comforts. And her worrying now brings him an increasing sense of control.

"Charlotte can take care of herself," he says.

Eve tightly crosses her arms over her chest. "How can you be sure? She's just a kid. And you don't know what these men are like. They kidnapped her before. What if they found her? What if they were waiting for us to leave? What if they have her and Dory?"

168

Mace leaves the door, walks over to Eve, takes her wrists in his hands. Looks into her eyes. "We can't solve anything by worrying."

"Why are you holding my wrists?"

"To relax you?"

Eve shakes his hands off. "It's not working." She walks to the other side of the room, picks her purse up off the floor, pulls out her phone.

"Who are you calling?"

"Dory."

"I'm okay," Charlotte says.

Mace and Eve turn. Charlotte's walking up the stairs from the front door.

"Where were you?" Mace's question is lost in Eve's cry as she rushes past him. That's when he sees Charlotte's face, the new bruises coloring it, the dried blood staining her cheeks and chin.

Eve embraces Charlotte, helps her up the stairs. She staggers over to the wall, leans against it, slides down to the floor. Mace and Eve sit on either side of her.

One of Charlotte's eyes is so swollen that it's almost entirely closed. Her breathing is ragged.

"What happened?" Eve asks.

Charlotte just grimaces and looks down.

"You went to find them, didn't you?" Mace's voice is down to a whisper.

He feels his faith in her slipping away.

Charlotte nods.

Eve looks back and forth between them. "Find who? Those men?"

"Yeah."

"Why?" The word holds desperation.

"She wants to kill them," Mace answers.

The three of them are quiet.

"Did you?"

"Maybe."

"All of them?" Mace is incredulous.

"Just one. I knew where he works, heard them say it when they had me locked up in that basement. I went there."

"Why didn't you tell us?" Mace asks.

Charlotte leans her head against the wall. "Figured you'd say no."

"Well, *yeah*."

"You can't kill those men." Eve's face is distressed. "You're better than that. And where's Dory? Why didn't she stay with you?"

"She said she had to go. She didn't seem worried about leaving me here."

"How'd you get there?" Mace asks. "Did anyone follow you?"

"I took a cab, a few blocks from here. He was by himself. No one followed me."

Eve can't keep still. She keeps starting to pace, rub her hands, pull her braids.

"I'm sorry I didn't tell you," Charlotte says. "I didn't mean to worry you. But I'm tired now. I just want to lie down. Is that okay?"

"We need to..." Eve starts.

"Please?"

Mace and Eve glance at each other.

"I don't know what to do," Eve says.

"I just need a little time," Charlotte replies tiredly, then says, again, "Please."

They help Charlotte up. "I brought over some towels and extra clothes," Eve tells her. "They're in the car."

"Thanks." Charlotte walks over to the steps leading upstairs. "I appreciate it."

Eve turns to Mace after Charlotte is gone. "What the hell? Did you know she was going to do that?"

"I had no idea. And I'm with you. It was a dumb move."

"I need to talk to her."

"Give her time. She's safe. That's all that matters. She's safe."

Eve sinks back to the floor, hands over her face. "Jesus."

CHAPTER FIFTY

Will stares at Charlotte as she limps out of a cab and into the house.

He can't believe his luck. He'd followed Dory to this house earlier, decided to wait down the street.

Just a hunch. Nothing more.

It takes Will a few moments to remember that he needs to call Frank.

He picks up the phone but doesn't dial.

He doesn't want to bring Charlotte back to the basement. Doesn't want to see his friends' faces when he leads her inside. He can imagine the sadistic mix of hate and glee, the easy acceptance of their worst desires.

That's not something he wants.

Will knows the consequences. Charlotte could get to the police before Dave has a chance to stop her. They could be arrested, and it'd be a lot worse than it would have been for the minor shit they were selling in the suburbs.

That's not going to happen, Will thinks.

Charlotte's just happy to be free. She's not going to the cops. She's going to run off.

We'll never hear from her again.

It's like I never saw her.

End of story.

Will turns off the phone, tosses it onto the passenger seat.

Heads home.

CHAPTER FIFTY-ONE

The door to Charlotte's room is closed. Mace knocks.

"Come in."

He walks inside, carrying another shopping bag from Target.

Charlotte's pressed against the wall, peering out the window.

"I'm sorry I worried you," she says.

"What was the plan? Sneak out, kill some guy, be home in time for dinner?"

"Something like that." Charlotte rubs her eyes with her palms.

"What happened? With the man you saw?"

"We tried to kill each other. I won."

At her words Mace feels a sense of unease. Almost like nausea.

"He's dead?"

"Maybe. I didn't stick around to find out. I'm sorry, I don't feel well." Charlotte pushes off the wall and walks to the adjoining bathroom. Mace follows her and stands in the doorway. He's surprised that, empty and a year removed, the bathroom is unfamiliar to him. He wonders if the sink was always close to the door, the shower this small.

"How did you find him?"

"Knew where he works." Charlotte turns on the water, lets it fill her hands, gently rubs the blood from her cheeks, chin, forehead, lips. She gingerly dabs her face with a towel and leaves the towel damp and red.

"Do you need anything?" Mace asks.

She raises an arm and winces. "Maybe some help getting my

shirt off."

"I'll get Eve."

Charlotte shakes her head. "I trust you."

Mace steps in the bathroom. Charlotte leans forward. He pulls her shirt up and over her head and arms. She whimpers a little, but that's all.

There are bruises over her stomach. Bruises startling and detailed and they seem like they'll never fade, as if they're etched into her skin. Bruises like a map of pain and anguish; bruises like a watercolor painted by a sadist; bruises like her skin is a brittle shield barely able to protect her soul. He looks at her skin and sees memories of fists and feet and nails and teeth.

Charlotte notices Mace's stare. But now, unlike when he first saw her face, she doesn't try and hide the marks.

CHAPTER FIFTY-TWO

Will walks up to the house, thinking about what he's going to say when his friends ask him about Charlotte. He plans to lie about everything and hope they don't see through it.

But nobody notices Will when he walks in. Dave strides past him, talking loudly into his phone. "What unit? And don't put me on fucking hold again."

Frank is leaning on the counter, forehead against his palms, staring into his laptop. He looks up at Will. "Where the *fuck* have you been?" His voice is on the verge of breaking. "I've been calling."

Will takes his phone out of his pocket, realizes he never turned it back on.

"I had it off. Sorry."

"Seth got attacked," Frank tells him.

Will blinks. "By who?"

"Charlotte."

Will thinks about Charlotte limping into the house, the bruises on her face.

He must have been too far away to see that her bruises were fresh.

"Where's Seth?" Will asks.

"In the hospital," Dave says. "I'm trying to figure out where."

"Charlotte put him in the hospital?"

Frank ignores his question. "Did you see her at that lawyer's office?"

Dave stops pacing, looks at him.

"No," Will tells them. "She didn't go to the office. What happened? I mean, no way she could take Seth."

Frank chews his thumb knuckle. "She set him on fire."

Will can't speak for a few moments. His concern for Seth, and guilt about hiding Charlotte's location, is thumping inside him like someone pounding on a door.

"Is he...is he going to die?"

"That's what we're trying to find out."

No one says anything for a few moments.

"Seth's been with us too long to lose him," Frank adds, softly.

Will thinks about Seth in the hospital. And he thinks about Frank. About how it could have been his brother.

Something inside him hardens.

"I know where Charlotte is."

CHAPTER FIFTY-THREE

"How is she?" Eve asks, when Mace comes back downstairs from helping Charlotte with her shower.

He sits next to her, back against the wall. "She'll be okay. No broken bones or anything."

"Is it okay for her to go to sleep? What if she has a concussion?"

"I googled concussions. Didn't see any symptoms."

"You googled it?" Eve worriedly scratches her arm. "My brother had some medical training in the military. Should I call him?"

"Hey, I had the same training. And I really think she'll be okay. At least physically."

"I can't believe Dory left her."

Mace shrugs. "She's eighteen. And safe here. And she really did seem okay. Just banged up."

Eve drags her left heel back and forth over the carpet. "What was she thinking?"

"She wants revenge."

"But she's safe! Almost free. All she has to do is stay out of sight."

"I'll ground her. No seeking revenge for a month."

Eve is quiet. She stares at nothing for a few minutes, then rests her head on his shoulder.

"Maybe it's a good thing we didn't have kids," she says. "Is this what it's like? Spending all your time worried about them, and then they actually go and do something stupider than you imagined?"

"From what I've heard, you also don't get tons of sleep," Mace quips, then senses Eve is tiring of his jokes. He changes his tone. "I remember when you and I used to talk about having a kid. Always seemed like it would just happen, but I never pushed it."

"Why not?"

"Honestly, I felt like I'd end up abandoning it."

"Deadbeat dad?"

"Nah. A dead one."

Her heel stops dragging back and forth. "I wish you wouldn't say things like that."

"Sorry."

She closes her eyes, the back of head pressed against the wall. "I thought a child would do the opposite. Give you an anchor. A reason to stick around."

"Didn't work for my family."

"I guess that's true. And no way you're leaving me with a couple of screaming babies." Eve opens her eyes and settles into Mace, her head against the side of his chest, legs stretched out, crossed at the ankles. "You wouldn't get away that easy."

Mace doesn't catch that last part. He's realized something else. Again, he's talked about his depression without it affecting him. Mentioning it used to feel like talking about an injury that still aches, the pain intensifying as it's discussed. But now the idea of depression is distant.

"I mean, babies are sweet," Eve is saying. "And it would be cute to see a little Mace walking around in tiny clothes. All my girlfriends say they're a lot of work, but it's worth it. I guess the idea that you're everything for something, its whole world, and it's yours, is pretty amazing. I just don't see how parents aren't worried about their children every single moment of every single day. Isn't that kind of love scary, as wonderful as it would be…"

Mace listens to Eve talk about children and love.

CHAPTER FIFTY-FOUR

It's late and the house is quiet when Charlotte hears a scrabbling sound outside.

She doesn't move. She stays lying down on the floor, under the blanket and comforter Eve brought her, eyes open, breathing quick and shallow.

She doesn't have a phone or watch, has no idea what time it is. She assumes it's after midnight.

Charlotte wonders if it's Mace, walking around outside for some reason. It could be him, it could be a hundred other things: someone walking a dog, the wind, her imagination. No reason to assume those men found her.

But she isn't about to start taking chances.

Charlotte crawls over to the side of the window, her body sore from the fight that afternoon. She peeks around the edge, tries to see below. No luck.

She tells herself it's just her imagination.

That's when the scratching starts again.

It's faint but close, like someone scratching the pane of her window. But she's two stories up.

Charlotte listens intently.

The sound returns.

A raccoon outside, digging through trash? But she didn't see trash cans out there. A squirrel running through the walls?

The scratching gets louder.

Charlotte can't take anymore. She pulls herself to her feet

and looks outside.

And immediately ducks, worried one of the men trying to undo the lock of the window below saw her.

She's heading out of the room and down the stairs before she's aware of what she's doing. Adrenaline shoves soreness aside. Plans are forming in her mind—how to fight them, how to escape—and another part of Charlotte, a small distant part, is surprised she's not afraid.

Charlotte hurries into the living room. Mace is lying under a pile of comforters. She kneels and shakes his shoulder.

Mace blinks awake.

Another voice: "What?"

Charlotte pulls off the blankets. Eve is lying next to him

"We, um, might be getting back together," Mace explains.

"Those men are outside," Charlotte whispers. "Trying to get in."

"How many are there?" Mace asks.

"Four or five?"

Eve looks scared. "What do we do?"

Glass shatters somewhere.

"Run," Charlotte says.

Eve and Charlotte race up the stairs. Mace pulls on his jeans and stumbles after them. They stop at the top of the landing and listen. A door opens below. Footsteps.

"Where now?" Eve's near panic.

Charlotte and Mace look at each other. There's no place to hide. No way to reach out to anyone. Nothing that can be used as a weapon.

"We can't stay here," he says.

"Go to the bedroom I was in," Charlotte tells them. "Try and get out through the window."

"What are you going to do?"

"Distract them."

"How?"

Eve heads into the bedroom.

The stairs creak.

"Go with her," Charlotte whispers. She hurries down the hall to the bathroom, steps inside, closes the door.

Mace watches her, torn, then slips inside the bedroom after Eve. She's at the window, pushing it open. He hurries to her side and looks out. The drop is too far.

"If Charlotte can distract them," Mace whispers, "they'll walk right past this room. We'll listen to them pass, then open the door. You run out and get help. I'll stay with her."

"I have a better idea," Eve sticks her head out of the window and screams, "Help! Help! Help!"

CHAPTER FIFTY-FIVE

Frank opens the front door for Will.

"Come on," Frank tells him. "They're upstairs. We had to break a window to get in."

"I heard." Will follows his older brother inside.

"You ready?" Frank asks.

Will nods, his throat dry. He touches the gun in the holster on his hip. He's only ever fired it at trees and stop signs.

Dave is waiting at the bottom of the stairs. He points up.

The house is silent.

Dave gestures at Will's head. Will pulls down the ski mask.

The three of them are wearing black sweatshirts and jeans and ski masks, and they're each carrying the same type of Glock 30, given to them by Dave. Frank and Dave climb up the stairs ahead of Will. The nervousness swirling in his stomach grows. His chest is cold with sweat. He wonders if Frank and Dave are just as scared.

Will's not worried about dying, or even about being hurt like Seth was. He's worried about having to kill Charlotte, about that somehow falling to him. That fear echoed through him on the drive here.

She has to die, he tells himself. *For what she did to Seth. What she could do to all of us if she goes to the cops.*

If she dies, we're safe.

"Help! Help! Help!"

The screams stop the three men in their tracks. They look at each other, then rush to the second-floor landing. A hall of closed doors. They hear a window slam down from inside the room directly in front of them.

Another voice calls out: "Hey, guys."

Charlotte. From a room down the hall.

"I'm going after Charlotte." Dave stalks down the hall. "You two go after whoever's in this room."

"And?"

"And kill them."

The knot in Will's throat grows.

CHAPTER FIFTY-SIX

Mace pulls Eve inside. Closes the window.

"What are you doing?" he hisses.

"Screaming for help."

"They'll kill us before—" Mace is interrupted by a rattling sound. Someone's trying to turn the doorknob.

"Get into the bathroom," he tells Eve. "And lock the door."

"What are you going to do?"

"I'll hold them off."

A *thump* from down the hall.

"They're trying to get Charlotte." Eve's voice is breaking.

Now there's a slam against the door to their bedroom.

"Can we tie those bedsheets I gave her together? Make a rope? Lower ourselves out?"

Another slam, another, and the top hinges loosen. Mace shakes his head. "We don't have time."

But that gives him an idea.

He hurries over to the pile of sheets.

A third smash.

The bedroom door leans in and falls.

A man rushes inside.

It's hard to see anything in the confusion. He seems to be wearing all black, and he's holding a gun.

He doesn't see Mace standing by the door.

Mace pulls the pillowcase over the man's head and shoulders, pinning his arms to his side.

The man in the pillowcase swears and jerks awkwardly in surprise, trying to lift his arms, but Mace punches him in the head. The man takes a step back and Mace punches him in the stomach.

"Fuck!" the man swears again. His free hand pulls the top of the pillowcase. Mace grabs the gun and tries to wrench it away. The man abandons the attempt to pull off the pillowcase and, instead, he tackles Mace to the ground.

Mace struggles, but he's not as strong as the other man.

The gun turns toward him.

Then Eve is there, grabbing the weapon, helping to force it away. The man shouts and Mace feels his hand loosening, and then the man rolls to his stomach, lifts himself to his knees, his hands stretched in front. With one yell, he pulls away from Mace and Eve and stands, the pillowcase still blinding him.

Mace is on the ground, behind him. Eve shoves the man and he stumbles, trips over Mace and falls. The back of his head smashes into the wall.

Mace scrambles to his feet. He and Eve turn to the door.

Another masked man is standing there.

He's smaller than the one they were fighting, but he's also holding a gun. He looks at the man on the floor, and then at Mace and Eve.

Something about him, even though he's disguised, seems uncertain. It's the way he's standing, like a brittle leaf about to fall from a tree.

"It's okay." Eve lifts her hand, steps forward.

CHAPTER FIFTY-SEVEN

Maybe, Charlotte thinks, *I should have picked someplace better than the bathroom.*

It's not even a very large bathroom. There's a toilet, sink, and tub.

And a small window.

That's when the idea occurs to her.

She can lure those men to her, escape through the window, and lead them from the house. Away from Mace and Eve.

"Hey, guys," Charlotte calls out and climbs onto the closed toilet seat.

She hears footsteps approach and pushes the window.

It won't budge.

The window is only decorative.

Well, shit.

Someone slams against the bathroom door, angrily, powerfully, and then speaks. The voice is too muffled for Charlotte to identify who it is.

"When I get you out of there. I'm not going to kill you right away. I'm going to make it slow."

Charlotte hops off the toilet seat and looks for a weapon. She pulls open the bathroom drawers. Empty.

Another slam. A splintering sound.

"You're going to want to die. But nope."

Charlotte tries unsuccessfully to pull off the toilet seat. Then she grabs the shower rod and pulls it. Doesn't budge.

Another slam, and the hinges are hanging on. Charlotte looks at the shower rod and realizes it's not bolted into anything, just sitting on two curved bases. She lifts it off.

When the man comes barreling through the door, she smashes the end of the metal rod into his face.

He staggers back into the hall. Charlotte swings the rod up into his nuts. He drops to his knees, gasping. She slashes it against the side of his head.

He drops to the ground. Doesn't move.

Then she hears a shot.

CHAPTER FIFTY-EIGHT

Will had listened to Frank fight, heard the sounds of the struggle. He stood by the door, trying to count down from one hundred and twenty—Frank had told Will to wait two minutes before he came in, to surprise them. He reached zero, inched toward the door, peered inside.

And watched Eve push Frank over Mace. Frank tumbled back into the wall. His head made a sick sound when it hit.

Mace and Eve turned, looked at Will.

Will lifted his arm.

He could barely see them. Not because it was dark, but because of fear. Fear immobilized him, covered his brain like a black cloud rising up his body.

He couldn't feel his finger press the trigger.

Will was somewhere outside of that room, away from this dark house.

"It's okay," a distant voice said.

The sound surprised him—not the voice, but the shot. He feels the Glock 30 in his hand, surprised that he held onto it, surprised it didn't fly out like the first time he shot one. He hears someone fall.

"Hey."

Will remembers this voice but can't quite place it. He turns.

CHAPTER FIFTY-NINE

"Hey."

The small masked man turns toward her, and Charlotte slams the shower rod into his face. He drops. She steps into the room and sees Eve on the floor, Mace holding her.

Charlotte drops the metal rod, slides down next to Eve and Mace.

"Is she okay?"

Mace's voice is uncertain, young. "She got shot."

"Where?" Charlotte looks at Eve's body, but it's impossible to see anything in the dark.

Eve just whimpers, her face pressed into Mace's chest.

"We need to go," Charlotte tells them. She tries to lift Eve to her feet. Eve cries out. Mace picks her up and carries her.

A sound from the corner of the room. A man moaning. Charlotte looks over, puzzled by the pillowcase over the man's head, then sees the Glock next to him. She takes a step toward him.

"What are you doing?" Mace hisses.

"His gun."

But the man's hand comes alive. He grabs the gun. His other hand pulls the pillowcase.

"Go!" Charlotte shouts. Mace rushes out with Eve. Charlotte follows them, just as the gun fires and the doorframe next to her explodes.

Mace's truck is in the driveway. They tumble inside, shoulders hunched in case there's another shot. Charlotte climbs into

189

the passenger seat, pressed next to Eve. Mace starts the truck and roars out of the driveway. He turns so sharply that the truck shifts, nearly topples, and then he races down the road.

"How is she?" Mace asks Charlotte.

Charlotte turns on the interior light, trying to see the wound. It doesn't take long—Eve's shoulder is red and wet.

"We need to go to the hospital."

"Those men will find her there," Charlotte tells Mace.

"She needs help!" he shouts.

"I know!" Charlotte shouts back. "But I don't know what to do! I don't know what to do! I don't know!"

CHAPTER SIXTY

Will stops the car down the street from their house, pulls off his gloves, and drops them in a plastic garbage bag along with the ski masks.

The three men sit in silence for a few moments. Dave breathes wetly. The pipe, or whatever Charlotte hit him with, must have broken his nose. Will was luckier. The pipe hit him in the forehead, but with a glancing blow. Enough to leave a throbbing bruise, but not enough to knock him out.

Will had lain on the ground and pretended to be unconscious. He'd heard Charlotte walk past him, heard Mace say something and, to his immense relief, heard them help Eve out of the room. She might be alive and, for that, Will's grateful.

"How the fuck did that happen?" Frank asks, rubbing the back of his head, feeling the lump from where he slammed into the wall.

Neither Will nor Dave have an answer. The three of them head into the house.

Barnes is sitting on the couch.

Will stops walking. So do Frank and Dave.

"I didn't know you were coming here," Frank manages.

"You don't know much."

Will's unprepared for how large Barnes is, for the way everything on him seems threatening, from his mess of curly black hair to his small angry brown eyes to his giant hands. The couch looks small under him.

"Is Charlotte's head in that garbage bag?"

Will looks down at the bag of masks and gloves he's holding.

"She got away," Frank tells Barnes.

"No!" Barnes exclaims, in mock-surprise. "You got to be shitting me! From the three of you?"

Dave slips past Frank and Will, heads to the kitchen.

"Did she have help?"

Will wonders if Barnes is enjoying this. It sounds like he is.

"Yeah," Frank says. "A man and woman were there. They surprised us."

"You snuck into their house at one in the morning, and *they* surprised *you*?"

Dave walks back from the kitchen, pressing a bag of frozen peas to his nose. "The woman's wounded." His voice is muffled under the peas. "They're going to have to take her to the hospital. Will shot her."

Barnes looks at Will with surprise.

Despite Will's uneasiness, it's hard not to feel a bit of pride.

"Good." Barnes adjusts a black onyx ring on his thumb. "Course, it's hard to do anything in a hospital, what with security. We'll keep an eye on her, see if she gets visitors, who they lead us to. Charlotte's too smart to get caught. Not that it matters. She's going to come to us."

"Why would she?" Will asks.

Barnes stands and heads out of the room.

Will, Frank, and Dave look at each other, then follow him.

Barnes walks into the kitchen, grabs an apple, takes a noisy bite. Keeps walking down into the basement. Heads into the small room where they held Charlotte.

Will can't make anything out until Barnes turns on the lights.

"Who's that?" Frank asks.

Dory Anderson stares at the men, eyes wide and scared, chained to the bed with a ball gag shoved deep in her mouth.

CHAPTER SIXTY-ONE

Mace slams the brakes outside Mt. Sinai Hospital's emergency entrance. He and Charlotte help Eve out of the truck. She's still whimpering, has been the entire way.

"I can't go in there," Charlotte tells Mace.

He's guiding Eve inside, her good arm over his shoulders, his hand around her waist. He scowls back at Charlotte. "Why not?"

"They might try and find us here. And if they see me, it'll just make things worse."

Mace wants to say something, but instead turns and walks Eve through the automatic doors. He glances back as Charlotte climbs into his truck and drives away.

A security guard rushes over. The nurse at registration calls for help. Within seconds, hospital personnel are surrounding Mace and Eve. They guide her into a wheelchair, usher her away.

A police officer leads Mace to an empty office.

"Can you tell me what happened?"

"We were walking to my car. A man came up to us and asked us for money. He had a mask and a gun. I reached for my wallet. He got scared and fired."

"What did he look like?"

Mace shakes his head, hoping there's no way his lies can negatively affect Eve. "I'm not sure. It was dark. He had on a hoodie."

"Was he African-American? Hispanic? Caucasian?"

"I'm not sure."

"Do you need some time?" the officer asks, not unkindly. "Or water?"

"I'm just a little shaken up. I'm sorry."

Eventually the officer does take his statement, and Mace has enough presence of mind to keep his answers vague. The police officer leaves.

Mace spends a half hour fidgeting, pacing, praying, staring out the emergency room's doors, looking for anyone suspicious.

He wonders if he should buy something for Eve from the vending machine. Can't remember if they had dinner. Or if she'll be allowed to eat anything.

Tries to remember what he left at the house. He has his wallet and his phone. Eve's iPad was left behind, and he doesn't know when or if he'll ever be able to retrieve it. All the clothes they bought for Charlotte. The bedding.

Charlotte.

He's done.

Mace's mind is in disorder, unable to calm, but that thought glides easily, like an arrow through clouds. He can't help Charlotte anymore. This world of sex traffickers and murder and hiding and gunshots isn't his, and he never should have dragged Eve down into it. He almost lost everything.

He remembers Eve's cry, a mix of surprise and pain—the twin essences of a lost innocence. The moment that he realized she mattered more than anything else, more than he did, more than Charlotte. He remembers that moment and doesn't feel fear toward those men or the evil they brought; weirdly, he's not afraid. But he won't risk Eve's life again.

A doctor finds him sitting in the waiting area, rubbing his arms, his stomach knotted.

"Is Eve going to be okay?" Mace asks.

The doctor is young and male, late twenties or early thirties. No gray in his hair or creases in his face. All of the emergency room staff, Mace realizes, are fairly young. He wonders why that is, wonders if working here is too physically taxing or emotionally exhausting for anyone over forty.

The doctor is speaking, and Mace strains to concentrate on what he's being told.

"The bullet perforated her shoulder, or passed through, but did chip her upper humerus." The doctor touches Mace on the edge of his shoulder, pressing down with a little pressure. "We didn't see any signs of infection, but there will be some pain from the wound and bone chips. There's no sign of joint damage, so she should regain her full range of motion. We've given her a local sedative. She's resting now."

Mace rubs his forehead with his palms.

"Is there anything you need?" the doctor asks.

"I just wanted to know if she's going to be all right."

"She should be. What about you?"

Mace's default expression has always come off as helpless. He's not sure why that is, but people have often introduced themselves to him by asking if he needs help. It used to irritate him but, without that quality, he might have never met Eve.

He was in his late twenties, working with a team to maintain the web site for a banking company downtown and living in Bolton Hill, a beautiful Baltimore neighborhood filled with historic row houses and dotted throughout with trees. Despite an enthusiastic gentrification, Bolton Hill wasn't unfamiliar with occasional crimes. Mace had been living in the neighborhood for a year, a couple of years removed from the Army, when he found the passenger window of his truck smashed open and the driver's seat slashed.

He complained about the crime to his neighbor, an older man who had lived in Bolton Hill for upwards of twenty years. The old man shrugged. "Happens to all of us. You should park somewhere else."

Anger rarely overtook Mace. He was generally non-confrontational. But the old man's words sparked something.

"I should just accept this?"

"What are you going to do instead?"

"I don't know."

The old man nodded. "There you go."

Mace fumed, repaired his truck, had a security system installed, tried to let his anger go.

But when his window was broken again just two days later, and his security system stolen, Mace flew off the handle.

He was furiously kicking his tire when the old man walked over.

Mace kept kicking the tire.

"Got you again, huh?"

"Those fuckers," Mace said, bitterly.

The old man shrugged. "What are you going to do?"

Mace had an idea. He repaired the window a second time and set a trap.

He took the cards and money out of his wallet and left the wallet tucked into the front seat, as if it had fallen out of his pants. Then he pulled a chair by his bedroom window and peered through the blinds, determined to wait all night.

He was drifting off around one in the morning, his head softly bumping glass, when a voice from outside woke him. Mace separated the blinds further and stared down to the street. He saw three or four silhouettes around his truck. A flashlight clicked on. Mace was about to call the cops when, two to three minutes later, the light vanished, and the men walked off.

Mace headed downstairs. The window was intact, but something was scrawled on the windshield.

He looked closer.

One of them had spray-painted the word "NOPE" across it.

The next morning Mace was using a washrag to scrub away the paint when someone said, "They're persistent, right?"

A woman was standing a few feet behind him. She was black, about five and a half feet tall, and slim with braids pulled back by a rubber band. She looked close to his age, twenty-nine, maybe a year or two younger.

"I'm giving up," Mace told her. "They're better at this than I am."

She smiled.

Despite his irritation, Mace liked looking at her smile.

"A neighbor told me what's been happening with your truck," she said. "I was worried. I thought you might try something stupid, like come out here with a gun."

"I wouldn't do that," Mace said. "I mean, I figure they're kids. And the NOPE thing was kind of funny."

Her expression turned puzzled. "You have a weird attitude about property damage. But nice to hear you say that. I always expect people to shoot first nowadays."

"I don't even own a gun," Mace told her.

"So I could rob you right now?"

"You see my truck. You think I have anything of value?"

She laughed. "My name's Eve."

"Mace."

"But no gun? Why not?"

"Just seems like a cowardly way to solve a problem."

"Huh," Eve commented. "I have one. Does that make me a coward?"

"I wasn't trying to start an argument."

"Good, you'd lose. I'm a lawyer. Arguing's what I do."

"What kind of law do you practice?"

"Family law, in a small practice north of the city. What about you?"

"Web design. Security, stuff like that."

"You do seem good at security."

Now Mace laughed.

They talked for another ten or fifteen minutes, until she pulled out her phone and glanced at the screen.

"Shit," Eve said. "I'm way too late. I'm meeting a client in twenty minutes."

"Need a ride? I can give you one, as long as I don't need to look out the windshield or drive forward."

"Thanks, but I'll take the bus." Eve hunted through her purse, pulled out a bus pass. "See you around."

Mace thought about asking her out, had been thinking about it, but wasn't sure how to do it. And he assumed she had a boyfriend.

He hurried after her anyway.

"Hey, um, Eve?"

"Yeah?" She kept walking.

"I was wondering if you wanted to get dinner sometime, or see a movie, or..."

Eve looked sideways at him. "Or?"

"Just dinner or a movie. Those are the only two date ideas I have."

"We couldn't do dinner and a movie in the same night?"

"Well, then I'd have nothing to offer for a second date."

They reached a bus stop. A city bus lumbered toward them.

"Here's the thing, Mace. You seem nice. And you're cute. But I just got out of a long relationship and I'm sort of messed up by it. I'd be a total wreck if I dated anyone now."

"It's okay," Mace told her. "I understand. Had to ask."

The bus rumbled to a stop. Mace and Eve waited for the noise to die down before they spoke again.

Eve looked at him with kind eyes. "I'm sorry."

He nodded.

Eve headed toward the bus, then turned back. "How'd you get the name Mace? That's a nickname, right?"

He told her the story behind his name.

Eve gave him a weird look. She climbed on the bus and took her seat. She looked out the window at him, that weird expression still on her face.

Then she smiled.

CHAPTER SIXTY-TWO

He blocks the doorway.

Dory can't tell if this is the same man who grabbed her in the parking lot and threw her into the trunk of his car. It's been years since she'd felt that type of strength, that angry male rage. Not since she'd lived in the same house as her father.

But it isn't just the strength.

It's how powerless it makes her feel. How incapable of fighting back.

He steps into the room.

"Dory Anderson?"

It is the same man. She recognizes the heaviness, the faintly southern or western tinge to his words, from when he slammed the trunk closed and told her, "Don't try anything." And she didn't.

Dory doesn't reply. But her arms tense. She feels the chains around her wrist slightly pull from the wall.

He walks into the room, closes the door. Turns on the light and she sees him clearly. Sees how massive he is, how everything on him from his beard to his hanging stomach to his rough hands are threatening, as if moments from touching her.

"Call me Barnes," he tells her. "You heard of me?"

She doesn't trust herself to speak. Her voice is small when she does. "I don't think I have."

"But you know my girl Charlotte."

Dory can't lie. She feels like he knows the truth and lying

will just make things worse.

She nods.

"Know where she is?" Barnes holds up a hand. "Before you answer, know they left that house in Pikesville. They'll take the black chick to the hospital, but no way Charlotte goes inside. I ask you, where did Charlotte go?"

"What happened to Eve? Is she okay?"

"That was not the question."

"Please just tell me if Eve's okay."

"Where is Charlotte?"

"I don't know." Dory is so scared that she honestly doesn't know. Her thoughts seem like they're out of order, a deck of cards shuffled beyond pattern.

Barnes seems to sense her rising panic. Pulls back a little.

"Your work tries to stop my work."

She doesn't want to reply, but he waits until she nods.

"You believe in what you do."

"Yes."

The bed dips as he sits on it.

Near her hips.

He smells like cigarettes.

"I believe in what I do. You understand that, Dory."

His statements aren't questions, but regardless, Dory feels compelled to respond. It's as if he's waiting for her, and if she doesn't do what he says, whatever is keeping him civil will vanish.

She nods.

"You think I'm evil."

Another statement that seems to require a reply. She agrees again.

"All I am is the ship's captain, Dory. I take people where they want to go. I take men to women and women to men. That's it."

"That's not it."

Her words surprise herself. She's still scared, but the short, three-word sentence involuntarily slipped out. The result of a mindset cemented by years of witness and research.

And her words hang in the air, like a body swinging in the silent moments after an execution.

Barnes doesn't seem offended, for which she's terribly relieved. Even grateful.

"What do you mean?" he asks, curiously.

"I...I don't want to make you mad."

"Nothing you say will change how I feel."

Dory suspects there's some truth in his words, even if she isn't entirely sure what he means.

"Men and women would do this without me," he goes on. "They have since the beginning of time."

"Charlotte told me what you did to her."

"Done that since the beginning of time too. And that doesn't happen with most women. Most women don't come through trafficking. They do this because they want to."

Something bending in Dory snaps. "If they told you they wanted to, then they probably had a choice."

Barnes's voice is still mild. Surprisingly.

"Everyone has a choice. And were I allowed to work legally, there would be no Charlottes."

His openness to debate is encouraging. Leads Dory to think that she can change his mind, maybe even get him to let her go.

"You call what you do work?"

A small, almost indiscernible shrug. "Others do."

"It's just a title. It doesn't change anything." Her fear is nearly gone, like a fog dissipating inside her. "And one person shouldn't be able to buy another."

"All owners buy employees. All money is ownership."

"This is different. You don't own them. You can never truly own a person."

Dory is conscious of pushing him too far, but it seems like the argument is having the opposite effect on Barnes. Calming him, keeping him conversational. Keeping him away from using that strength she felt when he kidnapped her.

"Charlotte was never yours."

Barnes moves in one fluid motion, so fast that Dory doesn't have time to react. Her shirt is sliced in half, hanging off either side of her chest. She looks down, looks at the knife that appeared in his hand, watches as he tugs the front of her bra up and slashes it open. Her breasts spill over either side of her chest.

She hears herself breathing hard. "What are you doing?"

"What part of you do I own?" he asks.

Panic rushes through her.

"What?"

He slips his thick index finger under the waist of her jeans, lifts them and her hips rise. His knife flashes. The button on her jeans flies off.

"What part of *you* do I own?"

He pulls her jeans apart, tearing the zipper. Stands, grabs her jeans around the ankles, yanks them off.

"Please," Dory says. "Please don't."

He rips her underwear open.

"What part of you do I own?"

She lies naked.

His hands push down on her hips. Squeeze.

His body towers over her like an avalanche on the verge of collapse.

"What do I own?"

Then he leaves.

Dory cries. It's all she has the power to do.

CHAPTER SIXTY-THREE

The doctor leads Mace to the room where Eve's sleeping. Mace sits by her bed, reaches out to hold her hand, then realizes it's not a good idea to move her wounded arm.

Mace's insides ache from trying to push back his burgeoning resentment—resentment at himself for Eve's condition, resentment at Charlotte for this entire fucking mess. He knows it's unfair, knows Charlotte didn't ask for this either, but he sees Eve's bandaged shoulder and rationality crumbles.

Mace was sprawled out on the couch in his Bolton Hill apartment, watching *Wheel of Fortune*, when he heard a knock.

He pulled himself off the couch, opened the door, saw Eve on the other side.

"What's going on?"

Eve didn't have the carefree air she'd had a few days ago when he'd first met her. Now she looked distraught, eyes troubled, mouth drawn.

"Can I come in?"

Mace opened the door wider.

He gave her some water and sat with her on the couch. Eve took a long drink. It seemed to steady her.

"I'm sorry for barging in," Eve told him. "Did I interrupt you from something?"

Mace looked at *Wheel of Fortune*. She followed his gaze.

"I think I have some free time."

"Someone broke into my apartment."

"You're joking."

Eve shook her head tersely.

"Were you home?"

"No. The door was open when I came home today. I never leave it unlocked so I knew something was wrong. When I went inside, someone had gone through my things, left clothes thrown all over the place, stolen my laptop..." She leaned forward, rested her chin on her fists, closed her eyes.

"You went inside? Did you call the cops first?"

Eve shook her head. "I should have, right?"

"Well, yeah."

Eve opened her eyes. "They took my gun."

"Shit."

"Once I couldn't find it, I called the cops. They just left."

Mace saw how shaken she was. "You want to stay the night? You can take my bed. I'll sleep out here on the couch."

Puzzlement eclipsed Eve's worry. "Why would I want to stay here? I just wanted to talk."

"Figured you didn't want to go back."

"I'm okay." She shook her head, added ruefully, "They didn't take all my jewelry. Left a lot of it. That actually hurts my feelings." She offered a small smile that didn't last long.

"Chances are people have broken into my place," Mace said, "and decided not to take anything. I have no idea."

"I figured you could relate," Eve said. "Did anything else happen to your truck?"

"No. They moved on to nicer vehicles." An idea occurred to him. "Do you want to order dinner? We can have something delivered, watch a shitty TV show?"

He thought she was going to refuse, but Eve surprised him. "I actually could use a little company."

They ordered Chinese from a local restaurant, ate, and talked as *Law and Order* played in the background. Mace was surprised that they'd both spent their lives around Baltimore, but never seen each other.

"We don't have much in common," Eve told him. "Lawyer and computer geek. Black and white…"

"I'm not white."

"You're not?"

Mace shook his head. "I'm mixed. Dad was black, Mom was white."

Eve leaned in close, squinted at Mace. "Really?"

"I'm pretty sure."

Eve sat back, crossed her arms over her chest, frowned. "I thought there was something about you that was different. Couldn't put my finger on it."

"I get that a lot." Mace took another scoop of rice in his chopsticks and managed to steer most of it into his mouth.

"Is that weird? Do you feel, like, distant?"

"Kind of." Mace set the sticks down, wiped his mouth with a napkin. Drank some water to clear the dryness in his throat. "Sometimes it feels like I don't belong anywhere. I've never felt comfortable in any group. Even when I was in the Army. But that was just for four years."

"Why not longer?"

"Ended up not being what I wanted."

Eve faced him, curled on the couch. "Did you go overseas?"

Mace nodded. "Iraq."

"Were you scared?"

CHAPTER SIXTY-FOUR

"Were you scared?"

That was the question everyone asked Mace when he returned from Iraq. It wasn't easy to answer. He'd spent three years in the Reserves training with soldiers who'd already fought, and he felt like he knew what to expect. The unexpected had always scared Mace. Like the night before boot camp, when he spent most of it throwing his guts up, not knowing what was going to happen the next day. Wondering if he'd made an irrevocable mistake.

Boot camp was brutal. The first weeks were a mess of shouting and exhaustion that roughly turned into a routine. After the ten-week training was up, Mace returned to Maryland twenty pounds lighter, but filled with purpose. At first it was jarring to return to work, given how close he'd grown to his fellow reservists; boot camp was the hardest thing any of them had ever done, and they could reminisce about it endlessly. There were times Mace longed for the weekends when he would train. But over the next three years he grew comfortable in civilian life, and training turned into a nagging inconvenience.

"You think we're going to Iraq?" Xander McLean, an accountant who'd befriended Mace during boot camp, asked one day during lunch. The greater war effort had ended by then, but reserves were still being called up.

"Probably," Mace replied. "They say it's not if we go, but when."

Xander took a bite out of his burger, wiped mustard off his mustache with the back of his hand. "They'll send you before me, right? I got a wife and two kids. Figure that has to matter."

"Are you worried?"

Xander shrugged.

They were both deployed a few months later. Mace was assigned to work with Iraqis, helping train their military personnel in everything from security to IT.

"What about you?" he asked Xander, who had moved to Pittsburgh, over the phone.

"Same thing. But bookkeeping instead of IT."

Mace thought he detected a note of disappointment in his friend's voice.

"You bummed?"

"Kind of," Xander admitted. "People are going to ask what I did in Iraq, and I'm going to tell them I showed Iraqis how to upgrade to a calculator from an abacus. Some war story. What about you?"

"I'm glad I'm not being asked to fight," Mace said. "I want a wife and kid someday."

"Maybe you'll find your wife there."

"I'll be too busy ducking."

"Right!"

"I said *ducking*."

He flew one dark cold morning to Kuwait where he, Xander, and a quiet group of reserves received final instruction, situational information about the camp, and grim guidelines about safety. Three days later he boarded a military transit for the VBC, or Victory Base Complex, in Baghdad.

The first mortar attack came the afternoon Mace arrived.

He'd been told the attacks would come, but the raw thunder of the explosions left him shaken. He tried to hide his fear when he saw the narrow-eyed seriousness of the senior soldiers, the way they resumed whatever they'd been doing after the attack ended. He knew the chances of a rocket actually striking him were low—the base was huge, the Iraqis' aim was bad, the Americans brutally quick to respond—but it was hard for Mace to stay calm once he heard those first explosions. Hard to stay calm when there was a chance that the next rocket might be directly overhead.

Hard to stay calm when your life was in real danger.

Some soldiers were unperturbed, refused to show fear, talked and laughed as the world exploded around them. Mace kept his face down, made sure he was indoors. Made sure he had most of his battle rattle—at least his helmet, flak, and soft vest—nearby. He never grew comfortable the way others did.

"So fucking hot here," Xander complained one night during dinner.

Mace had rarely seen his friend since they'd arrived. The VBC was made up of eleven camps and stretched almost twenty-five miles. Xander worked on the opposite perimeter.

"Every time I go outside, first thing I do is shake my fist at the sun."

"It's like a conspiracy," Xander said. "The country trying to get us to take off our gear. I guess we'll get used to it."

Mace nodded but knew he never would. He couldn't shake the sense that he was in the wrong place, that this wasn't who he truly was. Maybe that was why he never found comradery with most of the other soldiers, why he stayed silent during their rough jokes and harsh stories. Physically, he could do everything they could, and they only occasionally called him a shammer or a pussy. But they sensed his distance.

Xander seemed to sense something as well. "You all right, bud?"

"I'm okay," Mace told him. "Just thinking about work."

Xander finished his sandwich, crumpled up the wrapper. He looked over his shoulder at the Cinnabon next to the Subway in the base's food court. "I'm 'bout to do something ungodly to a sweet roll," he announced. "You keep thinking about work. Don't watch me."

When Mace first learned he'd be training Iraqis, he'd imagined bitter bearded men who'd been forced into this role, who'd seen U.S. bombs annihilate their homes. What Mace hadn't expected was that he'd be working with men and women who wanted to learn, who saw the U.S. presence as a chance to share America's talents with their own country.

Mace hadn't expected that he'd actually help.

Some days it was IT training, other days it was drills. Once in a while he had to man a checkpoint just outside the camp. The road leading to the checkpoint was filled with cement blockades designed to prevent cars from rushing the camp with explosives. But it was hard not to feel exposed. And there were days that the line of cars seemed endless, and it shook Mace every time he approached one not manned by Americans. He spent his time at the checkpoint with a tightness in his chest that took days to recede. And he saw how, for the soldiers that patrolled and kicked down doors, that tightness never left. It became part of them.

It was at the checkpoint, late one night, when Mace spotted a shadow in the barricades.

He didn't think much of it. Chalked it up to his nervous imagination.

But then the shadow moved.

Mace squinted, adjusted his night optics, stared as it moved again. He whispered to the Iraqi working with him, a nineteen-year-old named Abrahem, to radio the base.

The young man reached for his radio, quietly spoke into it.

Mace knelt, switched off his optics, lifted his M-4. Next to him, Abrahem did the same. Mace was surprised at how cold he was, how sweat had draped his shirt to his skin. He tried to swallow and couldn't. Tried to remember what he'd been taught.

Slow deep breaths.

The shadow moved closer.

Mace had fired his rifle before, but only as a warning shot in the air when a car refused to reduce their speed. That always brought vehicles to an immediate halt. Mace had never needed to take the next step: shoot the car's engine to disable it.

Or the step after that: shoot the driver.

Slow deep breaths.

Mace blinked sweat out of his eyes. He didn't dare look away from his rifle.

Slow deep breaths.

Spotlights from the camp flooded the barricades in light, illuminating a man crouching in dark clothes. Abrahem shouted something panicked and, somewhere behind him, Mace heard alarms.

The man rose, his arm back in a throwing motion.

His chest turned red.

Mace wasn't even aware his finger had depressed the trigger. The man's shoulder jerked back, his hands flew to his face. He fell.

Later that night, they told Mace that he'd saved his life, and Abrahem's, and likely others in the camp. He'd killed the insurgent before he could get close enough to throw his explosives. Mace sat in the quiet meeting room, listened to the hum of the generator. Soldiers congratulated him.

"How you feeling?" Xander had come over to see Mace, found him lifting weights in a quiet corner of the gym.

"They told me I did the right thing," Mace said.

"You did."

"Doesn't feel like it."

"Why's that?"

Mace didn't look up. He kept his knee pressed down on the padded bench. His triceps strained as he lifted.

"Feels like I'm a different person. I don't like the change. Not sure I wanted it."

"You had to do it. They said he had explosives."

"He did."

"You don't think you should have saved your life? Or the

kid you were with?"

"Just not ready for this," Mace said.

"You did the right thing," Xander replied. "But if you keep feeling this way, you should talk to someone. No shame in that."

Mace didn't talk to anyone. And when he left Iraq two months later, he left the Reserves. His four years were up.

When he saw pictures on the news of the VBC being given to the Iraqi government a couple of years later, it took him a moment to realize what he was looking at; that was how distanced he'd grown. He never talked to Xander again, rarely thought about him. Mace ran from the military, ran from that part of his life.

But he couldn't run far enough.

The memory of that Iraqi returned to him, sometimes relentlessly. He remembered the way that man's hand arced back like he was about to throw a football.

And the anguish in his face as Mace's bullet touched his chest.

And the anguish in Mace after.

CHAPTER SIXTY-FIVE

A hand on his arm shakes Mace free from his thoughts.

He hadn't even heard the door open. He blinks up at Gabe, Eve's brother, then glances at the hospital bed. Eve is still sleeping.

Gabe is six-two, big and burly, bald and black, carrying a backpack. Mace has always privately thought of Gabe as a living moving mountain, both because of his muscular build and silent disposition.

Mace stands. The two men shake hands.

"What happened?" Mace imagines that Gabe's low voice could cause the room's furniture to shake.

"We got held up. I reached for my wallet, I guess too fast..." The sentence trails away.

Mace doesn't want to lie again.

"They said she's going to be okay," Gabe tells him.

Mace nods.

"Thanks for calling me," Gabe continues. "Our parents are coming up from Raleigh, but I wanted to get here first. Give you what you asked for." He slips off his backpack, sets it on a chair. "It's in there."

"Thanks."

"You're not doing anything stupid with it, right? It's just for protection?"

Mace thinks about Eve.

He nods, lying one more time.

CHAPTER SIXTY-SIX

Charlotte watches the hospital entrance through the trees.

She'd parked Mace's truck in a small side street blocks away from the hospital and, after that, had no idea where to go or what to do. She thought about sleeping in the cab, but those men had to suspect that Eve was at a nearby hospital. She didn't think they'd find the truck where she'd left it, but she couldn't risk it.

Charlotte had no phone, no way to contact Mace, nothing to do but wait for him to come out. She slipped into a thicket of trees across the street, found a spot on the ground hidden from the road and curled into it.

She remembers that quick look of disgust Mace gave her outside the hospital. Eve might be dying—Eve, who had risked, and maybe given, her life for her—and Charlotte wouldn't go into the hospital to stay with her, to make sure she was okay.

Charlotte tells herself she didn't have a choice, that she couldn't risk making things worse.

Hopes she can believe it.

She puts her arms inside her sweatshirt to stay warm. Keeps watching the hospital doors.

CHAPTER SIXTY-SEVEN

"This doesn't seem like you," Dory says.

Frank nods too fast, nervously runs a hand through his short hair, feels it spring back into place. He's already high and wishes he was higher. It's been a long time since he did anything other than smoke or eat weed. For a while he was gobbling down mushrooms, but he hasn't been able to bring himself to do it lately.

Frank feels like he needs to be in control.

So, just weed.

He holds the bucket he brought downstairs out to Dory. "Hey, you need to pee or not?"

A disappointed look crosses her face. Her head, lifted at an uncomfortable angle to watch Frank, rests back on the bed. "No."

Frank feels like he let her down, tries to ignore the feeling. Tries to ignore her naked body chained to the bed in front of him, the same way he never looked at Charlotte's body when she was held here. Even when he'd sneak downstairs and...

He shakes his head.

But even then, he never looked at her.

"I'm not like this," he tells Dory, and he remembers being in this room with Will the night Charlotte escaped. How he'd told Will they needed to find Charlotte, said something like "cover that bitch with dirt." Remembered how impressed Will looked, and how impressed Frank felt by the phrase. Or maybe Will wasn't impressed.

Maybe he was surprised.

"That's what I thought," Dory says eagerly. Frank tries to focus on what she's saying without looking at her, which is really difficult when he's high. It took him at least three trips to get downstairs after Barnes told him to look after her. First, he forgot the bucket, then he brought the bucket but forgot why he'd brought it downstairs. Will finally reminded him and tried to do it himself, but Frank wouldn't let him.

He needs to keep Will away from this life.

Everything changed when Charlotte burned Seth.

Not that he was scared of her, but the idea that Charlotte wanted revenge, that she'd taken one of them down, bothered him.

It bothered him because he didn't blame her.

Frank realizes Dory's been talking to him, has no idea what she's said.

"...People are more than bodies. They have souls. That's what I was trying to tell him. That's also why legalization is a flawed concept. It hasn't worked. Like safe spaces for sex work."

Frank nods. Has he been nodding the entire times she's been speaking? What's he agreed to?

"Oh, yeah."

"You know you can't follow him."

"Who?"

Dory looks confused, then pained. "Barnes. Who we've been talking about."

"He scares me," Frank says, honestly.

"Me too."

Frank looks behind himself, turns back toward Dory and speaks in a low whisper, "I think he's going to kill all of us."

"So do I."

"I don't know what to do."

"I can help," Dory says. "If you let me out of here, I'll find help. And you can come with me. I know lots of people. I promise you. We'll be safe."

Frank shakes his head mournfully. "Barnes will find us. We won't even make it out of the house."

"He's going to kill us if we stay. We have to try."

"But...he'll probably kill you first." Frank brightens. "Maybe me and Will can escape when he's killing you!"

"What?"

"Do you think that could work? Honest."

Dory squeezes her eyes shut, keeps them tightly closed for a few seconds.

"Who's Will?"

"My little brother. He's here with me. He's not...he's not like I am."

"Like you are?"

"Will's a good kid," Frank says solemnly. Talking about Will always makes him feel older, gives him a sense of protection. Maturity.

"A nice pimp?"

"He's not a pimp," Frank bristles. "He wouldn't be doing any of this if it wasn't for me."

"And now he's going to die because of you."

Frank wants to respond, wants to argue the point, can't.

He holds his head in his hands.

He should be drinking. Just leave this room and drink until he's unconscious. Wake up days later and see if things have changed for the better. See if Barnes came in here and killed Dory and found and killed Charlotte and left for Arizona and they can go back to selling to suburban kids. Go back to a time when they wanted more money and more danger without taking that first shaky step toward it. That first step into this dark stone room.

He wonders if there's a step out.

"Here's what you do," he hears Dory telling him, her voice a furtive whisper. "You let me out first. Let me escape. When

Barnes comes down here to check on me, you and your brother leave. I'll call and get help. Even if you don't get out in time, we can get someone here. And if you want to disappear once Barnes is in jail, I can help with that too. I'll do anything if you help me."

Frank bites his lip, finally looks up.

"You'd really help me?"

"I promise I would."

He reaches into his pocket, fishes around, pulls out a key.

"And you won't let anything happen to Will? Even if something bad happens to me?"

"He'll be safe."

Frank slides the key into the lock.

"You promise that about Will?"

Dory is watching the key so intensely that she almost doesn't realize he asked another question. "I do."

He turns the lock. The steel circles around Dory's wrists loosen.

They hear Barnes's heavy footsteps upstairs.

On the old creaky hardwood floor, his steps sound like a sledgehammer shattering bones.

Frank hurriedly turns the key again.

Those circles tighten. Dory's arms jerk, snapping the chains tight.

"What are you doing?" she cries. "Help me!"

Frank shakes his head. "Can't do it," he says, and quickly walks to the door. "Can't do it."

"Please! Please!"

Frank closes the door behind himself, praying he doesn't see Barnes on the way to the kitchen.

Barnes is waiting at the foot of the stairs.

"Where did you...I thought you were walking upstairs."

"I came down."

Frank blinks. "You're fast!"

"What were you doing in there?" Barnes asks.

"Nothing. Taking a bucket down to the prisoner."

As frightened as he is of Barnes, Frank couldn't be more relieved that Dory isn't with him.

Barnes cracks a small smile. "The *prisoner*. She trying to make trouble? Get you to get her out? Promise you things?"

"I just, I just left her in there."

Barnes's knife flashes out. Frank isn't even sure where it came from. He's way too high.

"What are you doing?" he asks, his throat dry, eyeing the knife.

Barnes pushes past him, opens the door. Steps inside and closes it.

Frank stays in the hall for a few moments, listens to their low voices inside. And then he hears Dory scream.

Frank needs a drink. He starts to hurry upstairs.

"Frank!" he hears Barnes call. "Come in here."

CHAPTER SIXTY-EIGHT

Eve looks around the room. A TV is perched high on the wall opposite her. A tray with a pink plastic cup is on one side of her bed, Mace sitting awkwardly in a chair on the other. Worry is drawn so deeply in his face it seems permanently etched.

"You awake?" he asks.

"I hope so. If not, heaven is kind of overrated."

A shadow of a smile on his face. "How are you feeling?"

"I'm...okay." Eve tries to remember what led her here—the men breaking into their home, the shot, the rush to the hospital—but something seems missing.

Her wound has stopped hurting.

She gingerly touches the bandage covering her shoulder, winces as pain rushes down her arm.

There it is.

"Where's Charlotte?" she asks.

Mace is quiet for a moment. "I'm not sure, to be honest. And I'm not sure we should find her."

"Excuse me?"

That dangerous tone in Eve's voice; Mace is familiar with it, knows that he's about to lose whatever argument he's making.

But he stubbornly stands his ground.

"This isn't our fight," he says. "And we don't even know her. Or the people looking for her. Maybe we should have just called the cops."

Eve glances at the door, makes sure it's closed.

219

"You'd both be in jail if we had."

"And safe."

Eve gives him a look. "In jail?"

"Maybe."

She pushes herself up to a sitting position with her good arm, grimacing. "Come on, Mace. You know better than that."

"You don't even trust her," he says, accusingly.

Eve doesn't take the bait. "Are you saying this because you're scared?" Her voice isn't unkind.

A beat passes.

"When that gun went off and you fell down," he tells her, "I was scared for a second, and then it changed to something else. I'm not scared anymore."

She nods.

"But you got shot, Eve. And I don't care about anything else but that now."

She reaches out, loosely holds his hand with her good arm. "Right now I'm in a hospital. I'm safe. And Charlotte's out there. I know she seems tough and acts like she can take care of herself, but she's a kid. You need to find her. And after you find her, we need to get her in touch with Dory. Dory can get Charlotte somewhere far away. You really have no idea where she is?"

"No, but she has my truck. I left her the keys."

A moment of pain causes Eve's expression to contort. It passes. "Do you think she's going to go after them?"

"I have no idea what she's going to do. But I'm going to stay here with you."

"No."

"I want to keep you safe."

"I'm safe."

"I just…"

"Mace. She needs us."

Something finally awakens in Mace, the memory of first hearing Charlotte beg for her life, her young fear.

And the resoluteness in Eve's face. And in her voice.

"Okay."

"You promise?"

"Yeah." He looks over his shoulder. "Gabe's here, and your parents will be here soon."

"Gabe's here?"

"I texted him last night. Told him the same thing I told the cops. That it was a robbery." He fidgets with his hands. "It just doesn't seem right to leave you here. Not after what happened."

"I'm in a hospital with my family." Eve touches the end of a braid with her free hand. "Listen, one time this woman visited our office. She wanted a divorce from her husband. I was talking with her when her husband came in shouting. She turned pale and I wanted to say something, but I didn't. He was outside yelling for her and she got up and left. I never heard from her again."

"No one called security?"

"The office I worked for was small. No security."

"You can't put what happened on you. Maybe she wasn't being abused."

"Doesn't matter. What matters is I just sat there. I have to be better than that."

Mace looks away, at the smudged gold of the door handle.

"The man I love has to be better than that."

Silence for a few moments.

"Shit, Eve, ever think about working on your subtlety?"

CHAPTER SIXTY-NINE

Mace hears a low whistle when he walks out of the hospital. A parked ambulance is in front of him, sirens silently flashing. A sleeping overweight man is slouched over the side of a wheelchair, stomach sagging out of a red sweatshirt. Mace looks left, sees Charlotte by the side of the building. She ducks away.

He finds her tucked into a small alcove, pulling leaves out of her hair.

He wants to ask about the leaves, but she speaks first.

"How's Eve?"

"Eve's okay. She won't need surgery. She'll stay in the hospital through the day, then she's going home with her brother."

"Will she be safe with him?"

"He was in the military and collects guns. She'll be fine."

"Good." Charlotte reaches into her pocket, pulls out his car key. Hands it to Mace.

"What are you doing now?" he asks.

"I'm going to find those men."

"And then what do we do?"

Charlotte's surprised. "We?"

A car horn blares angrily in the distance. "They shot Eve," Mace says, simply.

"Yeah?"

"They need to be stopped."

Charlotte's puzzled. "Not to be rude, but how are you going to help stop them? I know you were in the Army, but wasn't that like a hundred years ago?"

"A little less than that."

A mom and a young boy walk past them, the boy holding her hand and skipping. Mace waits until they're close to the hospital entrance.

"Eve's brother gave me a gun."

"What kind?"

"It's a Ruger 380."

"Decent power, but nothing special."

Mace gives her a quizzical look.

"My uncle used to take me shooting." Charlotte crosses her arms, frowns. "So we have one weapon and no plan."

"We have a plan. To find them and stop them."

He's changed.

And Charlotte doesn't like the change. The humor that underlined Mace's voice when she first met him is gone. And whatever that humor was guarding has emerged.

It makes sense. The attack last night, the injury to Eve, all these violent disruptions to his life. And now he's hiding between a hospital and a forest, talking about revenge with a victim of sex trafficking.

Days ago, this hadn't been his life.

It still doesn't have to be.

She can step away from him and Eve. Neither of them needs to be involved. She should have slipped away last night, disappeared into the forest or driven far away, but she wanted to make sure Eve was okay.

And she wanted to say goodbye.

"So listen, Mace..." Charlotte begins.

He's squinting down at his phone and ignoring her, concentrating on dialing in the fierce way that older folks focus on technology.

"Who are you calling?" she asks.

CHAPTER SEVENTY

Will almost drops Dory's phone when it buzzes.

Barnes had told him to search it and find something useful. Will wasn't exactly sure what that meant, but he hadn't found much. Mainly a bunch of apps for volunteer organizations and one defunct dating site. But at least it distracted him from the sounds downstairs.

Will heads to the stairs, yells to the basement, "Someone's calling her phone."

"Bring it here," Barnes yells back.

Will takes a moment to gather his courage, reminds himself that he hasn't heard Dory screaming for a while now. Walks down the stairs to the same small room where they kept Charlotte.

He walks in, and then he can't walk anymore.

He can't move.

Barnes stands next to the bed, a long-bloodied apron covering his bare chest and jeans, hands on his hips, grinning.

Frank is sitting in the corner closest to the door, looking down.

Dory's face is beaten beyond recognition, bloated and bruised. She's naked and curled tightly, her breasts ballooned flat against her thighs.

Her back bleeds from knife lines. Barnes grabs a white towel forever stained red, runs it over her back, drops it on the floor.

Will looks away as Dory stares at him, her mouth covered in

tape, her eyes wild and desperate.

Barnes wipes his hands on his apron and takes the phone.

"This is Luther Ford." His voice smooth and light, the gruffness gone.

He listens, then says, "Who's this?"

Barnes waits, listens. Then he grins, picks up a knife from the floor and holds the phone in front of Dory's face with his other hand. "Want to say hi?"

She stares hard at the knife. Doesn't move.

Barnes sits next to Dory and sets the phone to speaker.

"Dory can't talk right now."

"Where is she?" a man asks, his voice encumbered by static, like thorns holding back someone emerging from a forest.

Frank hasn't acknowledged his brother, lifted his head, moved a muscle.

Will desperately wants to leave the room. Wants to forever forget Dory's desperate, fearful eyes, the blood rising from her back.

"Dory's here," Barnes is saying. "But like I told you, she isn't much for talking right now. You said my friend Charlotte wanted her. She with you?"

No response for a few moments.

"Barnes, you stupid sick fuck." Right away, even with the static, Will can tell the voice belongs to Charlotte. "What'd you do to her? What are you doing here?"

"Came to see you. And Dory's fine." He swings his giant fist down to Dory's face. Everyone in the room flinches. His hand stops inches from her nose.

Barnes extends his thumb up.

"Prove it," Charlotte says. "Let me talk to her."

"You were a good worker, Charlotte," Barnes replies. "That was what, a hundred men in a week?"

"You're going to burn," Charlotte threatens, thickly. "Let me talk to her."

"You want her?" Barnes's mood abruptly changes. His face

darkens, fist opens. He grabs the edge of the masking tape and rips it off of Dory's mouth. She cries out. He slams the phone down on the bed and climbs on top of her, like a car running over an injured deer. Will wants to say something, do something to stop him, but can't. He just stands there as Barnes pushes her chin up and presses the knife against her neck.

"Dory?" Charlotte is calling out. "Dory? Are you there?"

Dory whimpers. Doesn't say a word.

"Beg," Barnes tells her. The blade pushes into her neck.

"Please!" Dory cries out. "Please! Someone help me. Please, do anything, do whatever he wants."

Barnes takes the knife away from her neck, climbs off her, grabs the phone.

"I'll help you," Charlotte is saying. "I'll help you. I'll—"

Barnes interrupts her.

"You want to save your fat friend, you come down to the old police station at Fells Point at midnight tonight. Go there and we'll trade. And if I find out you told someone, she dies quick."

"Trade what?" Charlotte asks.

"You for her."

He hangs up the phone, tosses it to Will.

"Take out the card, smash it, lose the phone."

"She's not going to be there," Frank says.

It's the first time Will's heard his brother speak since he came downstairs. His voice is hushed.

"She'll be there," Barnes replies. He looks down at Dory's terrified face, runs his fingers down her back. "Otherwise, this woman dies."

CHAPTER SEVENTY-ONE

"We have to call the cops," Mace says.

"No."

Mace looks at Charlotte, dumbfounded. "No?"

He takes the phone from her and dials 9-1-1.

Charlotte touches his arm. It's enough to stop him before he can press SEND.

"They can't help," she says. "We don't know where Barnes and his men are, where they're holding Dory, nothing. And you heard him. If he finds out we went to the police, she dies."

Mace hesitates, then turns off the phone.

"What do we do?"

Charlotte breathes in the scent of the forest on her clothes from the night before. Pulls another leaf from her hair.

"We do what he wants."

CHAPTER SEVENTY-TWO

Officer Dave Baker hangs up, thoughtfully taps his phone against his chin.

Checks his bank account.

Under a thousand.

Dave wonders if he should have asked Barnes when he was getting paid. Or even if Barnes was still planning on paying him, since his only job had been to hold Charlotte for a few weeks and that hadn't worked out.

Looks like they'll be getting her back. Dave has to admit Barnes has a good plan for tonight, assuming Charlotte shows up.

He has a feeling she will.

Something about her.

His mind goes back to his bank account. The entire reason he went down this path was the money. Half his paycheck goes to Cate, his ex-wife in Annapolis, and it's not like cops make that much to begin with.

Dave's pretty sure he's doing something wrong with the money. He'd spent five or six years busting dealers and bangers and finding more cash on them than he'd make in months. And these were kids. Sneering at him like they knew how much he made, how poor he was.

He can't stop thinking about money, especially since his divorce a couple of years ago. Cate had moved back with her family, left him after some woman he'd been texting had emailed the texts to his wife. He was surprised how much he missed Cate, surprised at how powerful loneliness was when she left.

He gets to see the kids every once in a while, and that's fine. He's never been that comfortable around them—a boy and a girl, eleven and nine. Even so, sometimes Dave wakes at night from a dream of them, confused to realize he'd cried himself awake. Confused because, as soon as he wakes, whatever sadness was plaguing his dreams has vanished.

But he does find it hard not to wonder how they're growing up.

Cate's looking out for them. That's a good thing. She's tough, a workaholic nurse who doesn't take shit. And she's a good mother, much better than he is a father.

Some of his buddies on the force pad their pockets with cash they take off dealers. Dave isn't too proud to do different, but he needs more than a couple of hundred dollars here or there. He needs regular money coming in.

He was tired of barely getting by. So he busted some small-time dealer, rattled him, found out he got his junk through a man named Stephon. Dave showed up at a club on the Block, Baltimore's row of strip clubs and sex stores, inexplicably just a few turns away from the tourist-filled Inner Harbor, down the street from a police station. The proximity to the police had always surprised Dave; supposedly, it meant the Block was on close watch, but Dave saw it as the Block defiantly sticking a middle finger at authority. The same way kids he busted sometimes refused to hide the joints stuck in their mouths. The same way prostitution didn't feel like a real crime. They always let the johns go. Threw the women in jail, but the johns scurried back to their families. No sense ruining more lives than they had to. Dave knew all about that.

Word was Stephon liked to hang at a club called Bare that had a pink neon sign blinking LIVE GIRLS. Dave found the sign, remembered a conversation with a guy on the force about signs like that. "We can assume they're live, right?"

His friend shrugged. "Rather they be girls instead of women."

The dancers at this club were definitely women; they all had at least a decade on Dave's thirty-odd years. He spotted Stephon, sidled up next to him. Told him what he was thinking underneath a dancer's low-swinging tits.

He'd run his own crew, work the places he knew cops didn't check.

Stephon thought about it and told him, "Yeah, fuck you."

Dave insisted he was legit, told Stephon he wasn't part of an undercover op. "What'll it take to convince you?"

It took a trip to the restroom with Stephon and his body-guard. They stripped Dave down to his boxers looking for a wire, then Stephon and Dave snorted a little coke together.

"You passed the first test," Stephon told him, rubbing his nose. "Lemme look into you, see if you pass the second. Come back in a week."

Dave showed up after a week of being followed, a week of men staring at his apartment from across the street, strangers standing too close to his car. Stephon was more connected than he thought, had more resources than he realized.

It made Dave nervous.

His fellow cops acted like gods to everyone else, aloof, re-moved, only occasionally kind. Dave pretended to be the same, but that wasn't him. He was scared but drawn. Like with that woman he'd been texting. He'd known his wife would find out, felt the inevitability. And still couldn't stop.

Dave had thought it was excitement. But now he knew it was fear.

He went back to the club after a week, back tense until Stephon told him he'd passed.

"Here's how it works," Stephon said. "Every Thursday night, you leave an envelope with three hundred in your mail-box. An hour later, that cash will have magically changed."

"You care what I sell it for?"

"Shit do I care?"

And that's why Dave assumed he must be doing something wrong. Stephon had hooked him up with Frank and Will, and Dave brought Seth on board a few months later. Frank and Will didn't understand how poor they were, and Seth didn't care. But Dave was different. He knew he was poor, cared, and couldn't figure out what he was doing wrong.

His first thought was that one of his three men was stealing from him, but Frank and Will didn't have it in them, and Seth was too stupid.

When someone told him that a man named Barnes was looking to move women, and he'd pay thousands for someone to house them, Dave figured it was worth a shot.

The hookers he'd arrested weren't standing on streets anymore, flashing ass. Now it was raids, apartments where scared women were carted away from angry men. Dave had never thought about expanding into that market, mainly because he'd heard horror stories about eastern European pimps and didn't want to fuck with them. He remembered a story about a cop who tried to get a woman brought over from Moldova to testify. She'd been brought to the states by Albanians, forced to work in a brothel, only thirteen. Amazingly, a john took pity on her, got her out of the brothel, and dropped her off at the cops. They made a deal for her to testify.

She ended up dead, found with Polaroids of her family being tortured and killed scattered around her.

The john's lower body was found in the desert bordering one side of Vegas, his upper body in the other.

After that, no one said shit against the Albanians.

Dave wasn't sure how his crew would react about holding women, but they were predictable when he explained his plans during a "family meeting" at the dining room table. He'd been staying with them in the house recently; he had a tiny efficiency and the crew all paid for this house together. Dave knew it was dumb for a cop to be anywhere with a drug crew. Especially living with them.

But Cate had met someone else and he was just so goddamn lonely.

Seth was happy to start selling women, the way Seth liked anything illegal. Frank shrugged, didn't even look up from the joint he was rolling. Only Will seemed doubtful. He glanced at Frank for approval, looked back at Dave and nodded.

Three nights later a van pulled up in front of the house. A couple of men brought Charlotte in, hood over her face, and led her downstairs to the small room Dave and his men had prepared. Gave Dave the girl, but no money.

He'd hoped for a deposit. Should have asked. Didn't.

That first night Dave heard Seth leave his bedroom and creep downstairs. He thought about stopping him but, honestly, didn't care. Barnes had said they could have at her. Not like they were doing anything she wasn't used to.

Seth didn't mention it the next day and Dave didn't bring it up.

Frank went down that night and Dave realized that, without communicating verbally, they'd established a system. They'd each get one night with her. Every night, at midnight, they'd lie in their rooms, wait to hear the neighboring door open. That third night Dave gave Will his chance, but no doors opened. No one went downstairs.

Dave was up that fourth night and oddly, excited about it. He wasn't excited about getting laid; that was nice but, ever since his divorce, pussy was just pussy. Women were nice warm places and that's it.

Dave thought, as he headed down for his turn in the basement, that his excitement could have something to do with the illicitness of the act. It wasn't rape, not exactly. He wasn't even sure if, technically, you could rape a prostitute.

Besides, he knew what rape was. There'd been a girl in high school. They went on a date, went back to her place, and he got carried away and couldn't stop. It was half her fault, he told her afterward; she'd got him way too worked up and, after a certain point, a man *can't* stop. She'd agreed.

Or hadn't disagreed.

But she'd never mentioned it again and they never went back out.

Sometimes he imagined how he'd feel if this happened to his own daughter. He'd heard men say how their views on sex and violence changed after they'd had kids, but he'd seen enough busted married-with-children pedophiles to understand that, if children did change men, the change wasn't permanent.

Dave walked into Charlotte's room and closed the door behind him. He kept the lights off and felt his way to the bed. He touched Charlotte's legs, let his hands travel up to her waist. Pulled down her pants. Entered that nice warm place, moaning in her ear while she stayed quiet.

Afterward he was disappointed that the sex was bland. He hadn't been rough with her, hadn't fucked her ass or stuffed his dick down her throat, nothing that would hurt her. He figured, after he'd fucked her every fourth night for two weeks, that she'd start to slip to her old prostitute ways. But she never changed.

He'd expected more. Expected fucking a pro would have benefits.

Then again, he'd expected Barnes would pay him.

The thing he hadn't expected was that Charlotte would fight back. She was getting resistant, not caring about beatings, becoming a problem. He told Barnes, and Barnes said the deal was off.

He'd wanted her broken.

And he was sending a couple of men to get her, finish her.

No mention of payment. And Barnes sounded so angry that Dave didn't ask.

He couldn't figure out what he was doing wrong.

CHAPTER SEVENTY-THREE

Charlotte sits on the hood of Mace's truck, one foot resting on the front bumper. "I don't need you there. I got this."

"There's no way you're going alone." Mace is staring at a map of Baltimore spread next to her. "You shouldn't be going at all."

They're parked at a remote end of a parking lot in Dundalk, outside of a grocery store. Charlotte's not sure if they're in Baltimore or not, but this whole area is incomprehensible to her. The cities and towns bleed into each other, without break. Different from the west coast, where everything is separated by mountains and desert.

Nature never had a chance here.

"I'm tired of arguing." Charlotte leans over to peer at the map. "Where's this place again?"

Mace points at a section of the city next to the water. "Fells Point. It's crowded. College kids, tourists, locals, even at night. Eve and I used to go there with friends." He pauses. "Wonder why Barnes picked a place that's so public? It's risky if anything happens."

Charlotte draws her knee to her chest, rests her chin on it. "He doesn't need to make a scene. Remember, he has a cop working for him. He could have me arrested in front of everyone, then driven somewhere and shot."

"The cop...right." Mace thinks about it. "Makes sense why he picked the police station then. Although it's not an actual police station anymore."

"It's not?"

He shakes his head. "It closed down a few years ago. Then they used it for a TV show. Now it just sits there." He straightens, stretches his neck until it pops. "You think they're really going to bring Dory?"

Charlotte folds her arms hard over her thin frame. "Too risky. They'll just put her on the phone."

"We have no idea how many of his men are going to be there, what's going to happen, or if they're even going to honor the trade. Just a place and a time."

"Stop saying *we*. You're not coming with me."

"Yeah I am."

"I'll make sure Dory's free, make sure he honors the deal. Once she is and she's safe, then you find Barnes. I'll stay alive until you find us. I'll do whatever it takes. I've done it before."

"That's insane."

"I can't let anything else happen because of me. Everyone around me gets hurt. All of you. Eve. Dory." She swallows painfully. "Sofia."

"None of that is your fault."

Charlotte says something too low for Mace to hear.

"What?"

"I'm not worth it."

Mace reaches out to comfort her, but she recoils.

The way she does now whenever someone touches her.

"You believe that?"

Charlotte doesn't respond.

"When my mother died," Mace says, "I blamed myself. I felt like I should have done more. But the truth is I couldn't have done enough. Something bothered her that was beyond me. It was stronger than me. I couldn't have fought it." His throat is growing hoarse. "But I wished I had the chance. I wish I had just one chance to spend a day with her, telling her that she had me, that she had someone. That she didn't have to face this monster alone."

Charlotte seems small, hunched on the hood.

"You're not alone," Mace tells her. "You don't have to fight this monster by yourself."

Silence between them.

Charlotte uncrosses her legs, slides off the hood, and hugs Mace.

Mace wants to hold her tight, squeeze her so she realizes how much she's come to mean to him, but knows that might make her uncomfortable. Instead, he keeps his arms loose and lets her hold him.

And realizes, in a sharp moment, what drew him to Charlotte when he first heard her voice that night in the woods.

He hasn't understood it until now, hasn't known it's something parallel in him, something that's been an unrecognized constant in his life.

Their desperate twin hopes to live.

CHAPTER SEVENTY-FOUR

It's hard for Dory to see through her swollen eyes, but she doesn't dare close them. She can't risk not being aware of everything around her, even in this small, square, stone-walled room.

Her thoughts are coherent and have been ever since that phone call with Charlotte, when she realized there was a chance she could live. It's not much of a chance, but they haven't killed her yet.

A door opens somewhere above. She hears footsteps.

The cuffs around her wrists are tight, and her arms ache from being in the same stretched position.

The footsteps are coming down the stairs.

Dory's body turns stiff.

She whimpers.

The door opens. A man walks in, the youngest of them, the one who brought down the phone. He stands uneasily before the bed, before her naked body.

"Do you need to go to the bathroom?"

"What?" The single word hurts Dory's lips. Blood has dried them together.

"The bathroom." He looks back to the door. "I can take you, if you need to go. My name's Will."

"Oh. Yes. Please."

Will walks around the bed and lifts her hand. His touch is gentle, unlike Barnes, where every gesture seems intended to cause pain.

Will undoes the first cuff, guides her wrist out of it, lowers her arm to the bed. Then he walks around her and does the same with the second cuff.

Dory tries to sit up and cries out.

"He cut up your back pretty bad. I think the blood stuck to the sheets."

Will puts his hands under Dory's shoulders and gently lifts her. She tries not to cry out again as the blanket pulls away. It takes a few minutes.

"The bathroom is across the other room," Will tells her.

He puts her arm over his shoulders and helps Dory out of the small room. They walk into a larger one, too dark for Dory to see anything. He guides her to a door at the far wall. Her hips hurt, and she has to walk in a plodding motion.

Will opens the door. "Light's out," he tells her. "But there's a sink and a toilet."

"Okay."

"I can…"

Dory whirls, grabs his head, and slams it into the door.

He makes a surprised sound and goes down to a knee. She sees the shadow of his body before her, kicks his head with her bare foot. The movement is agony to her sore limbs, but he collapses to the floor.

Dory turns and hobbles past him, toward the stairs. She touches the railing and starts climbing, pulling herself up. She hears Will moaning behind her, calling out, and she thinks a thousand thoughts as she climbs: did he have a weapon she could have taken, can she find help, will she be caught? She hears something moving behind her and climbs faster, her sore legs feeling like they're on the verge of breaking.

It's suddenly bright, so bright she's nearly blinded.

All she can see is light from above, and an immense figure in the middle of it.

And then there's pain, coming from his fist to her nose to her eyes to her brain. Dory's hand releases the railing and her feet slide out, and fear overwhelms her as the cement floor rushes up.

CHAPTER SEVENTY-FIVE

"Meet back here in four hours?" Mace asks Charlotte. They're sitting in his truck in Baltimore's Federal Hill neighborhood, staring out into the night. He tries to keep his voice light. "You're sure you're sure about this?"

"I'm sure I'm sure."

"You're not going to run off, try and find them without me? Like you did with that guy at the restaurant?"

A half-smile. "Nah. I need the backup this time."

The cab of the truck is dark where they're parked, in the shadows of a side street.

"I just don't think this is a good idea," Mace tells her. "You know?"

Charlotte scratches the side of her head. "Like I said, I want to spend some time alone. If that's okay."

"Yeah." Mace wants to say more but doesn't know how. The past week has been a whirlwind, but that wild wind seems to be settling.

Eve will heal, and she's safe.

Dory's not safe, but they're going to get her back.

All of the uncertainty and fear will resolve tonight. And the only people at risk are him and Charlotte.

Mace truly isn't concerned about himself. Maybe his depression has taken deeper root than he realized, but he treats whatever's going to happen to him as matter of fact. Then again, the plan he and Charlotte came up with is fairly safe and the area where they're meeting will be crowded. The risk seems low.

But he doesn't want to leave her.

He has to keep reminding himself of what he told Eve, that Charlotte's nearly an adult.

"Just be safe until I see you again." His voice has a breaking edge.

"I'll be okay. Just got something I want to do, especially if tonight's the last chance I have to do it."

"I don't like how you keep thinking tonight could be the end."

"It could be."

He tries to lighten the atmosphere. "I figure some mysterious disease will probably take me out. I'll be the happy patient who cheers everyone else up." Mace pauses. "I'm looking forward to being inspirational."

Charlotte leans over, gives him a quick hard hug. "You're stupid."

"I know."

She breaks away, pushes open her door and steps out.

"Hey!" Mace calls. "You got my watch, right?" He pulls out his phone and glances at the screen. "We're back here at eleven?"

Charlotte pulls up her sleeve to show Mace his watch. It's far too large for her wrist. Something about that makes Mace ache. "Back here at eleven, yup."

She closes the door.

Charlotte walks through Federal Hill, heading to the bright lights of the inner harbor. The harbor isn't crowded this late in the year, but she still has to walk through loud groups of people or sidestep the occasional running child. Charlotte has to admit that the harbor is pretty—a tiled path that passes bobbing boats and wandering tourists, a pair of musicians, loud teens, the constant homeless. Lights from the high buildings sparkle on the water like a handful of diamonds tossed across a black blanket.

But Mace told her about the city this afternoon, about how the harbor isn't truly representative, how Baltimore's beautiful grit isn't found in these manicured walkways. It leads Charlotte to wonder if anything is as simple as it seems, or if everything has a hidden side.

Like her mother, and the aneurysm waiting inside her.

Like her life in Tucson, and the future that awaited her.

Like her friendship with Sofia.

Charlotte reaches the Landmark Movie Theater, buys a ticket for a show, and slips into a theater where a movie is already playing. She takes a seat in the back, starts to watch one of the films in the *Transformers* franchise.

Charlotte loved going to the movies when she lived in San Diego. It was easy for her to escape, to stare at the actors and their problems, to slip inside the story. Sometimes she would go with her uncle, sometimes she would skip school and go alone.

But it's hard for her to concentrate on this movie. The actors are too perfect, the violence without real consequence. There are no bruises.

Nothing is messy.

And something about that is unsatisfying. Despite how much Charlotte longs to disappear into some other world, even for a few hours, she can't escape reality. It's waiting for her.

She feels it.

Charlotte stays until the end. Then she heads back out into the night.

The other thing Charlotte wants to do, before she meets with Mace, is eat ice cream.

She finds a stand in one of the shopping arcades in the Harbor, orders caramel vanilla in a waffle cone, sits in a spot secluded from the crowd. Takes a bite. She hears the happy sounds of people talking, smells seafood from a nearby restaurant. Charlotte slows her breathing as she chews. Closes her eyes. Narrows the world until it's only a sweet salty taste.

Nothing more.

CHAPTER SEVENTY-SIX

It's hard for Eve to focus on Gabe's face, and not just because it's dark in his bedroom. She's disoriented after the phone conversation she just had with Mace, too distracted to concentrate.

Gabe is standing across from her, his back to the door, thick arms crossed over his tank top.

"Why are you crying?"

She shakes her head. Everything seems unnaturally loud after her whispered, frantic talk with Mace: a neighbor shouting at his child; a truck roaring down the street; a high-pitched, excited conversation between Gabe's wife and ten-year-old daughter from the living room down the hall in his Silver Spring rambler.

"Eve, what's going on?"

"I'm telling you the truth," Mace told her, *"because I don't want to lie to you. Not tonight. I don't know what's going to happen, but I know that I don't want to lie to you."*

That throbbing pain returns to her shoulder, the way it's receded and returned all day, like an alarm clock faintly echoing in your dreams and becoming shriller until you wake.

"Eve."

She tells him, finds that talking helps. Allows the tears. Tells Gabe everything that's happened.

Gabe sits on the bed next to her, listens quietly. Chin on his fists.

"We have to call the cops," he says, when she's done.

"Maybe."

"There's no maybe about it."

242

"Mace said they'll kill her if the cops find out."

"Look at me."

Eve does.

"Those men shot you." Gabe's voice is low and measured. "They kidnapped your friend. And they're hunting that Charlotte girl. You have to tell the police."

Eve squeezes her eyes shut. "Mace is with Charlotte. He'll help her."

"It doesn't seem that you and Mace have been the help she needs."

Eve opens her eyes, looks away.

"I'm sorry," Gabe adds, not unkindly. "I get you're trying. But doesn't seem like you're helping."

"All I know is what not to do." Eve's fingers glide over the wound in her shoulder, desperate to soothe the ache, careful not to let her fingers touch it. "And I'm not going to get Dory killed. And that's what will happen."

Gabe is about to argue, but something in Eve's face stops him.

He's known her his entire life.

And he knows she's not going to change her mind.

"You really think Mace can handle this?"

"I don't know," Eve admits. "And, God, Gabe, I fucking hate just sitting here. Not doing anything. But there's nothing I can do! Mace turned off his phone and I don't have a way to reach Charlotte. If those men find out I went to the cops, Dory might die. And Mace wouldn't tell me where they're meeting. I don't know where any of them are."

His arm gently draws her to him.

She leans in.

"You got shot," Gabe says, brokenly. "I just want to help."

"I know. Me too."

"I hope your friend will be okay."

Eve nods, thinks about Dory held by those men. And helplessness and fear courses through her body, searching for a release. Finding none.

CHAPTER SEVENTY-SEVEN

Will walks down the stairs to the basement, finds Frank struggling to screw in a new lock on the door leading to the stone room.

"Dory is dead," Will says.

Frank takes a moment, then goes back to struggling with the lock.

"She was bleeding everywhere after cracking her head like that," Will goes on. "And he wouldn't take her to a doctor. She was begging him, and he just stood there. Her voice was all thick and slow."

"You really thought he would?"

Will shakes his head, winces.

"You okay?"

Will touches the knot from Dory's kick on the side of his head. "It's okay. Hurts a little."

"Two hits in the head for you this week."

"Yeah, it's not a good week." A beat passes. "Why'd Barnes get a new lock?"

Frank grunts.

"He wants to keep us out of this room."

"Barnes told you that?"

"He said he has special plans for her. And wants privacy."

Guilt starts rustling in Will.

Frank gestures to a screwdriver on the bed. "Grab that, help me with this."

"Okay." The brothers work in silence, test the lock when they're done.

"All right." Frank motions for Will to follow him into the bedroom.

He closes the door quietly.

"Something about this shit doesn't feel right anymore," Frank says. "I thought I'd be okay with it, but I can't. Not after what he did to that woman. We were never that bad. Barnes is...something about him scares me. Like he could kill any of us. You feel that way too?"

Frank is looking at Will earnestly, hopefully.

"Yeah," Will admits.

"We can't do anything tonight. Barnes has some other men coming in, hitters from New York. If we disappear too soon, he'll think something's up. We wait for the dust to settle and then, little brother, we're gone. You with me?"

Will feels a familial longing he hasn't felt in years.

He feels the blood between them.

"Yeah."

CHAPTER SEVENTY-EIGHT

The police station in Fells Point is the most beautiful one Charlotte has ever seen—although, come to think about it, she realizes she's only seen a couple. But this red-bricked building is gigantic, perched over the harbor and sprawling over water, with a cavernous half-oval entrance underneath a row of pillars and, near the top, two statues posed on either side of a stone shield. The cobblestone street in front of it is crowded with people, smiling and laughing and wandering around restaurants and bars even now, well past midnight.

Charlotte and Mace stare into the crowd across the street from the station, sitting at a table in the Fells Gate Tavern.

Someone shouts outside, an inebriated man yelling at someone. His friends restrain him, pull him away.

Mace takes a long drink. "Scared?"

"Yeah."

"We don't have to do this. There are other ways. You can leave town. I can call the cops and see if they can get Dory back. Take the chance they find her before Barnes finds out we went to them."

For a quick moment, the idea appeals to Charlotte. The longer she and Mace have waited in this bar, the more reluctant she's grown.

He sees fear creeping over her, but knows she'll never back out.

"What are we doing?" Mace asks. "Tell me the plan."

"You create the diversion, I lead them to the alley on Fells Street," Charlotte recites. "You come up behind them with the gun and force them to give us Dory. Hold them until she's free. If they try anything, we bring in the cops."

"And we all pay the consequences," Mace finishes.

Charlotte rubs her thumb over her index finger. "Speaking of, you see those cops?"

Mace looks to where she's pointing. Four police officers are huddled together on the corner.

"What about them?"

"One of them has a white bandage over his nose."

"You think it's the same man? The guy you hit at the house?"

"Maybe."

Mace glances at his watch. "Ten till one."

She wonders if Mace is as scared as she is.

She can't pinpoint what's affecting her, whether it's seeing Barnes, or her guilt about Dory, or the specter of going to jail.

Or if it's something else, something she doesn't quite understand—a reckoning.

Her entire life has been created and lived in the reflection of what others wanted: her mother; Raúl; Sofia; even, in a way, Barnes. Nothing is hers. She's separated from her heritage by language, from her true name because it reminds her of Raúl, from her home in sun-drenched San Diego.

Everything's been taken from her. And she doesn't know what's left.

And she's not sure she wants to know.

Charlotte pushes all of her thoughts, everything, aside.

"This is the only way," she says.

Mace looks at his watch. "It's time." He stands, tries to give her an encouraging smile, but it comes off weird. He pulls his baseball cap low.

"Hey, Mace?"

"Yeah."

"Be really careful."

He lifts a thumb before walking out into the street.
Charlotte watches him, relieved he didn't say goodbye.
It would have felt permanent.

CHAPTER SEVENTY-NINE

"Let's just grab him," Rob Welsh whispers, watching Mace walk to his truck.

"Nah, bro," Jake Childs whispers back. "He's right there in the open."

Rob grunts. "Just want to get this over with. Get back home."

Jake can hear the nervousness in his friend's voice, even though Rob's not lying—they're both tired. He got a call from Barnes at eight tonight, telling them he had a job in Baltimore. Good money, a thousand each, but they had to do it tonight. That meant driving down from New York to fucking Maryland, making a four-hour drive in three, and that was *after* they'd spent the day at the gym.

"He's not that big," Jake tells Rob, his voice low. "I mean, he looks big but, like, *used* to be athletic. Like it was a long time ago."

"Yeah, he's soft."

"Don't you got that in common?"

"Fuck you."

Jake doesn't press it. He and Rob are practically brothers. They grew up best friends in the same neighborhood in the Bronx, went to the same middle school, dropped out of the same high school. Went to juvie together when Rob beat some kid into a coma and Jake lied and said he'd helped him out. Jake wasn't going to let Rob spend time behind bars alone.

They got out, got shit jobs, got a basement apartment together, got drunk a lot. Tried every crime they could until they started running girls. That's the one that stuck.

The girls were usually sixteen or seventeen, black or brown. They got attitude the minute they got comfortable, so the trick was not to let them get comfortable. Keep them on edge with sudden mood swings, keep them drugged, match them with a rough john. Then turn on the sympathy and let the girls come back to you. Earn their hard trust.

Business got good. Prices rose, ages lowered. The client list grew. One time a girl went missing and they couldn't find the client either. The police found the girl's fourteen-year-old body strewn all over an alley somewhere. Rob and Jake didn't care, but it was bad for business. Their girls got scared, and all the heroin in the world wouldn't relax them. They slowed things down, kept a lower profile.

After all, they weren't in this for the money.

In fact, Jake and Rob couldn't tell you what they were in it for. Hard to figure out. But when they walked into those Manhattan bars and saw that something in the women's eyes, that fear...that's what they liked.

But they needed money and contacts. When their old friend Barnes called and said he needed a favor, they took him up on it. All they had to do was kidnap some man and a whore, bring them both back to his house. No real threats, but the whore was a scrapper. Names were Mace and Charlotte.

Rob and Jake had found Mace's truck easy enough, parked on the side of a dark quiet street, shuttered warehouses on either side. Then they waited until Mace came walking back to it.

"We should just grab him," Rob says again.

This time, Jake's inclined to agree.

Mace stops, pulls out a gun, points it into the air and fires three times. Then he shoves the gun into his jacket pocket and starts walking back in the direction he just came.

Lights are turning on in the neighborhood down the street.

People are shouting.

Rob and Jake are staring at each other.

"The fuck just happened?" Jake asks.

CHAPTER EIGHTY

Charlotte knows the shots are coming, but still flinches when she hears them. Three in quick succession.

Surprised shouts and screams come from the crowd. People start running.

But Charlotte's watching the cops, not the crowd. Three of the four run off in the direction of the gun fire. One stays behind. You wouldn't notice it if you weren't looking at him; the crowd is everywhere, scattering on the rough cobblestone, pushing into whatever bars and restaurants and shops are still open.

Soon it's just Officer David Baker standing in front of the old police station.

And there's that white bandage over his nose.

Charlotte doesn't have long. Other police officers could come by. The ones he was with could return. She walks out in clear view of Baker.

He stares at her, sharks darting through his eyes.

Charlotte hurries down the little cobblestone-lined street, water on one side and a row of closed shops on the other. She looks back and sees Baker about forty or fifty feet behind her. She walks faster and reaches the end of the narrow walkway. It turns into a tiled road with residential-looking buildings to her left. She finds the small alley Mace marked on the map and ducks into it.

High brick walls are on either side of her. The other narrow end opens into a dark street. Charlotte turns. Dave Baker's standing at the entrance.

"You're fast," she tells him.

Charlotte looks for Mace. She doesn't see him.

She tries to think of a way to stall as Baker approaches.

CHAPTER EIGHTY-ONE

"Why was he shooting?" Jake asks.

"Fuck should I know?" Rob replies. "Maybe he saw some freaky bird. Should we follow him?"

Jake nods. They each reach into their coat pockets.

"Wait." Rob and Jake watch three cops run toward Mace. They ask him something, and he shakes his head and points in another direction. The cops hurry past.

Rob and Jake wait for the cops to run by, then they step around the corner. Mace is about a hundred feet ahead of them, trying too hard to walk casually. They pick up the pace. When Mace turns around, they're right behind him.

He looks down at their coat pockets, sees the bulges.

"Who are you?"

"Where's Charlotte?" Rob asks back.

"Who?"

Jake looks around. A few people are peering out of their windows.

"Let's not play this game here," he says. "You know what we got in our pockets?"

Mace nods.

"Then keep your hands where we can see them. And walk where we tell you to walk."

CHAPTER EIGHTY-TWO

"Where's Dory?" Charlotte asks.

"Waiting for you."

"Is she here? Let me see her."

Dave shakes his head. "You don't call the shots."

Charlotte takes a step back. She looks at him, remembers him now. Remembers his body weighing down on hers. His voice in her ear.

She forces those thoughts away. "The deal was me for Dory. I want to see her."

"And I'm here to take you to her. But I figure you have some kind of plan." Dave walks toward her. "Figured you and your friend were the ones behind those shots. Make me come to you, right?"

"You're good."

He's about ten feet away.

"You fucked up my nose. Still hurts like hell. But I kind of respect that. I like it when women fight."

He keeps walking toward her.

"We did have a plan," Charlotte tells Dave. "But it fell apart."

He stops. "Yeah?"

"My friend was supposed to be here by now, and he was going to shoot you in the back."

To Charlotte's surprise, Dave doesn't look over his shoulder.

"I figured that the minute I entered this little alley. It's not a bad idea."

Charlotte shrugs.

"Problem is," he tells her, "you're not the only one with friends."

Charlotte tries to keep her voice from wavering, can't.

"Listen," she tells him. "We don't have to do this. You can leave."

She pauses.

"One of us doesn't have to die."

Dave stares at her, then his face breaks out into a smile. He throws his head back and laughs. Loudly.

Charlotte's surprised—it was a real offer. But she knows this is the only chance she might have. She turns and runs.

She hears Dave following her. She emerges into a small side street and ends up facing a fence. A clump of bushes to her right. The metal fence in front of her is so tall it's impassable. Charlotte fingers the knife tucked under her sweater, tries to think of what to do.

CHAPTER EIGHTY-THREE

Dave Baker sees Charlotte turn into the alley, then the night goes quiet.

The silence is sudden. Charlotte is a loud runner, her shoes fiercely slapping the pavement. Even if he hadn't been able to see her, he could follow her by the sound alone. The silence brings him to a stop.

He pulls out his revolver.

There's every chance Charlotte's hiding around the corner, waiting with a weapon. He's familiar with this neighborhood, knows a tall fence is on the other side. A fence too high for her to climb.

Dave keeps his gun low, walks around the corner.

Just as he thought. Fence in front of him, bushes to his right.

But something is lying on the ground in front of the metal fence, crumpled in a small pile. He leans closer to get a better look. It's the sweater Charlotte was wearing.

The bushes to his right explode. Dave sees the shine of the blade as it rushes to his neck.

He grabs Charlotte's wrist and bends it.

The blade clatters to the ground. Charlotte sinks to her knees.

"Got you," Dave says.

Charlotte bites his hand.

Dave yelps, releases her. She rises, rushes out of the alley.

Dave picks up the knife.

CHAPTER EIGHTY-FOUR

Charlotte turns a corner, sees nothing but water.

Dave is just a few feet behind her.

They stop running.

There's nowhere for her to go.

"Lots of buildings around." Charlotte's breathing hard. "You can't shoot me here."

"Sure, I can." Dave touches his badge. "I can do anything I want."

He grabs her, pulls her close.

And then Charlotte slips under his arm and behind him. His feet are swept out from underneath. Dave almost laughs as he falls; he can't believe that a girl who weighs one hundred pounds took him down. He lands perplexed, not hurt.

She learned some MMA, he thinks.

Should have just shot her.

And, panicked, remembers his revolver.

Dave reaches for it, but Charlotte's not going for the gun. Her hands are on the back of his head.

His face is driven down.

It happens too quickly and violently for him to fight back, so fast he's surprised to realize his head is underwater.

The idea is still crazy. No way this little girl can hope to drown him. No way he's going to let that happen. He rises to his knees, lifting her with him.

That's when the knife sinks under his ribs.

Head back in the water.

Dave cries out, swallows water, chokes. It's either the pain in his side or the blood, but everything is red. He tries to rise. It hurts too much. He lifts his head, eyes just breaking the surface, hears the knife stab him.

Hears it, doesn't feel it anymore.

Dave's head is driven back into the water. He stares down dully, and remembers those nights when he wakes from those dreams he has of his children, his face helplessly wet.

His children.

He sees them down there, deep in the water. Feels himself drift toward them.

CHAPTER EIGHTY-FIVE

Charlotte takes off her shirt and turns it inside out to hide Dave's blood. She slips it back on, tucks the bloody knife into her sock, lowers her pant leg over it. She hates feeling Dave's blood against her skin but doesn't have a lot of options. Charlotte wants to keep his revolver, but the police are going to be everywhere.

She tosses his weapon in the water, walks away from his body.

Two people, Charlotte thinks. *That man in the van, and now Dave.*

Maybe three, if Seth's dead.

And Sofia.

Don't think.

Don't stop and think.

Charlotte walks back out into the heart of Fells Point. She passes cops shouting, using anger and the threat of violence to return order. She heads toward Mace's truck.

She finds it, doesn't find Mace.

Charlotte looks up and down the street. Lights are on in nearby houses, but she doesn't see anyone outside.

Except for…

Charlotte squints and hurries. She saw a flicker of something. It could have just been her imagination, but she needs to make sure.

She heads to the end of the street and sees three men. She pulls the knife out of her sock and slips it into her jacket pocket.

"Hey!" Charlotte shouts. They all turn toward her. Mace is

between two men she doesn't recognize. She heads toward them, makes the knife bulge like a gun.

She gets closer, sees the two strangers also have their hands in their pockets.

"That was easy," one of them says. They're both big, bodies like they spend all day lifting weights. Short hair, New York accent. One's a brunet, the other a blond.

"Come with us," the blond orders Charlotte. "Or I shoot Mace."

"You shoot him," she replies, "and I shoot your friend."

The blond gestures at her with his free hand. "Then I'll shoot you next."

"Not if I shoot you first," Charlotte retorts.

"I'll shoot you, too!"

"You know," Mace offers, "I have to think there's an easier way."

"Shut up," the brunet tells him. "Jake, take Mace here with you. I'll deal with her."

"You sure?"

Not-Jake grins. "I'm sure."

Mace looks at Charlotte, nothing but pain and disappointment in his face.

"It wasn't a great plan," Mace says. "My bad."

Jake guides him away.

Charlotte watches them go, stares at Mace, worried hard as he and Jake disappear into the darkness down the street.

"How do you want to do this?" not-Jake asks. "You come with me, it'll be easier for everyone. I'll take you to your friend."

"You work with Barnes?"

"Doing a favor for him."

"What's your name?"

He thinks about it for a moment. "Rob."

"You from New York, Rob? Your accent sounds like you're from New York."

Rob smiles. "Maybe you don't need to learn anything else about me."

"Okay."

"Why don't we take our guns out of our pockets? See what we're working with."

Charlotte clutches the knife harder. Unfortunately, that doesn't turn it into a gun.

Rob removes his.

The gun is big; Charlotte imagines that, if ever she shot it, the propulsion would send her sailing back into a wall. The night is too dark for Charlotte to tell what type, but she's impressed.

She shows him the knife.

He looks at it and laughs. "Come on, give me the knife. Let's go get your friend."

Charlotte tosses the knife to him and it clatters on the street.

Rob picks it up. "Jesus, that's a lot of blood."

Charlotte turns and runs.

She heads back around the corner, back tight, tensed for a shot. The shot doesn't come. She just hears a surprised "Hey!" and footsteps. She reaches the corner, runs around it, has no idea what to do next.

She screams.

It's piercing. Full of panic and fear and more pent-up than she'd realized. She screams so hard that she stumbles, so hard her throat aches.

"Fuck!" Rob curses, somewhere close behind her.

Charlotte screams again, just as she feels his hand on the back of her jacket. He yanks her down to the ground.

She lands painfully on her knees and rolls to her back. They're in the middle of the street, but nobody comes out of their houses.

"Fuck are you doing?" Rob asks.

"Hey!" a sharp voice shouts.

Charlotte and Rob both turn. A pair of cops are approaching.

"He's trying to kill me!" Charlotte exclaims. She pushes away from Rob. "He has a gun!"

The cops have their guns out before either she or Rob can react.

"He told me he stabbed a cop," Charlotte tells them.

"What?" Rob explodes. "That's bullshit!" But the cops are on him, pushing him toward a wall. They turn him around, pull out the bloody knife.

"He forced me out of my house. Told me he needs a place to hide."

"Are you kidding?" Rob yells.

One of the cops asks her, "Where do you live?"

"Right there," she points at the furthest house. "The one on the corner."

"Go inside," he orders her. "Get some water, something to calm down. I'll be there soon."

Charlotte hurries away. She hears Rob shout, "I didn't kill a cop!"

She reaches the house on the corner, ducks around it as a sedan passes. She presses herself to the shadows and sees Mace in the passenger seat. Jake's driving. The car passes the cops and Rob.

Charlotte hurries across the street to find Mace's truck and climbs inside.

She waits for the sedan to get some distance from her, follows it.

CHAPTER EIGHTY-SIX

Mace watches the cops arresting Rob with interest. Jake glances over, curses, and speeds up the sedan.

"Did you see her?"

"No."

"Shit." Jake takes his hand off the wheel and chews the skin next to his thumbnail. His left hand holds a gun in his lap, pointed at Mace.

"Can you point that somewhere else? If you hit a speed-bump or stop suddenly, you might shoot me."

"Maybe I should have you hold the gun."

"You'd do that?"

Jake glances at Mace.

"Oh." Mace is quiet for a few moments. "Where are you taking me?"

"To Barnes. So we can figure out how to find Charlotte."

"Is Dory there?"

"She's there."

That sounds ominous, bur Mace decides not to follow up.

"I can't tell Barnes where to find Charlotte," he says. "I have no idea."

"Doesn't matter to me. I figure he'll want to ask you himself."

That idea makes Mace uncomfortable. More than uncomfortable. He wonders if he can fling open the door and lunge outside before Jake fires.

Doubts it.

They're passing through downtown Baltimore, and the tall buildings thin as they get close to the highway. It's late, but a few people are still out. Mace wonders about Charlotte. How she escaped. Where she is.

"Fucking Rob!" Jake suddenly exclaims. "Can't believe that asshole got nabbed. The shit they're going to find on him."

"What kind of shit?"

"I knew we shouldn't have come to Baltimore. None of this...none of this is what I wanted."

He lapses into silence. Mace follows his lead. They pass the edge of Baltimore and enter a dark highway, leaving the lights of the city and the half-moon of the harbor's high bright buildings behind.

CHAPTER EIGHTY-SEVEN

Charlotte follows the taillights as they head up I-83, staying one to two cars back, careful not to get close. Her heart's beating like an angry boxer punching a bag, her forehead clammy, stomach roiling. The sound of the knife sinking into that man's body, the way the skin seemed to suck back every time she pulled it out, won't leave her.

I had to do it. I had to.

That urge she felt at the bar, that desire to run, pounds in her.

It's tempting to turn around and drive off, to take the truck and drive to some small town and start over. Put the killing and those men and Mace and Eve and everything else behind her.

But Mace and Dory could die.

And that scares her more than anything.

Charlotte realizes she's almost pulled up alongside the sedan and slows.

This is the first time in a long time she's been afraid and had a choice in the matter. She's been under someone else's control for so long, and so ruthlessly, that the chance to do something else—to run from her fear—is stronger than she expected.

It's the helplessness, she realizes. She doesn't have a weapon, an ally, nothing.

She's going to try to save Mace and Dory by herself.

And she has no idea how.

CHAPTER EIGHTY-EIGHT

Will wonders how stoned Frank is.

He figures he can walk across the room, take the remote from Frank, and change the channel from college volleyball to something else, anything else. Frank's staring hard at the television, but Will's almost positive he has no idea what's happening.

Will doesn't want to watch any more volleyball, but he also doesn't want to leave the living room and risk running into Barnes. And no matter what room he picks, Barnes will be there, with his unkempt eyebrows, bushy beard. Dark glaring eyes.

The front door bursts open. Mace steps in.

Will yelps. Frank blinks, reaches into the couch and whips out the remote control. He points it at Mace and presses a button. The channel changes.

A hand pushes Mace forward. He takes a couple of steps and the new guy, Jake, walks in after him.

Barnes is somehow already in the room. Will has no idea where he came from.

"Where's Charlotte?" the big man growls.

Jake closes the door behind himself. Shakes his head. "No idea. Rob got nabbed."

Barnes squints. "What do you mean, *nabbed*?"

"Charlotte and Rob got in a stand-off. I loaded this guy in the car. When I drove back she was gone and Rob was getting arrested. That was the last I saw of her."

Barnes looks at the ceiling for a long moment. Will watches

Mace. Notices his hand is shaking.

"Where's Dave?"

Jake shrugs. "Saw him standing by that old police station, then we went looking for him—" Jake slaps Mace in the back of the head, Mace flinches, "—and never saw Dave again."

Barnes pulls out his phone, makes a call. No answer.

He looks at Mace.

"What was the plan tonight?"

"Where's Dory?" Mace asks, instead. The two words sound uncertain, as if his voice is teetering on a ledge.

Barnes steps forward and smacks Mace. The sound echoes in Will's ears. He looks over at Frank again. Frank is leaning forward, trying to pick a potato chip up off the floor.

"Buried."

Will sees the shock pass over Mace's face, like a shadow.

"You killed her?"

"What was your plan?"

"I don't—"

Barnes smacks him again, so hard that Mace crashes into the door. Barnes grabs him, lifts him up, slams him to the floor.

Mace isn't a small guy.

Will had never realized how strong Barnes is.

Barnes puts his knee on Mace's chest, pulls Mace's right hand up. He grabs Mace's pinkie.

"What was the plan?"

"I don't—"

Barnes twists the pinkie, breaks it.

Mace's scream is so loud, and Barnes's motion so violent, that everybody has a reaction. Jake exclaims, "Shit!" Frank falls off the couch. Will hurries to a corner of the room.

Only Barnes stays still, perched over Mace.

He grabs his ring finger.

Will watches Mace's feet kick.

"She was going to kill you." Mace's voice is hoarse, as if the scream ripped his throat raw.

"Dave was there. The cop. Did she kill him?"

"I don't know."

Barnes breaks his ring finger.

Another scream. Mace's next two words are said in a sob: "I don't."

Will's worried that Barnes is going to do more, but he stands and stares down at Mace.

"Chain him to the bed downstairs."

"Why?" Jake asks.

"I got at least eight more questions."

CHAPTER EIGHTY-NINE

Charlotte parks a block away from the sedan and searches Mace's truck for a weapon. She settles on a tire jack.

She doesn't remember anything about this neighborhood, has no idea if this is even where she was held. The houses here are spread far apart, but they're not wealthy. Most are ramblers, except for the one the sedan is parked in front of. That house is two stories with a forgotten yard and dark windows.

Charlotte walks around the side, cautiously, worried about making a sound. She looks through a window, sees an unlit kitchen.

The backyard is fenced but the fence isn't high. Charlotte climbs it, the tire jack tucked under one arm. She slips a leg over the top and lowers herself down to the other side. The backyard is all concrete, with a couple of aged lawn chairs and a rusty grill. The glass sliding doors leading inside the house are dark, and there's a low narrow window on the far end of the house. Charlotte crouches down and peers inside.

She sees the basement.

And remembers it.

Charlotte can't feel her hands on the coarse ground, the bend in her knees.

She couldn't hear the men upstairs during those long weeks, except for when they'd get drunk and their voices would rise to shouts. She'd grow terrified the louder and rougher their voices grew. The chains bit into her wrists, especially when that door opened, and she'd hear one of the men clumsily stomping downstairs.

At first, she tried not to listen to whatever they were saying, tried to block everything about the experience out of her mind, put herself into a black box none of them could open.

But those men gave her nowhere to hide.

She remembers feeling their skin, the stench from their armpits. The way their fingers pressed into her, the soreness all over her body when they were done and left her on the bed, her wrists chained.

Her body is so tense it could snap in half.

Charlotte breathes deeply, then peers through the window again. She tries it. It's locked. She looks up, sees a couple of windows too high to reach.

The patio door slides open.

A man stumbles out. He walks over to one of the lawn chairs and collapses in it without looking in her direction.

Charlotte can't see him very well, can't tell who he is. He's not tall, which means he's not Barnes. And he's not Seth. If Seth's still alive, then there's no way he's walking this easily. Not with a body covered in burns. It could be Jake, but Jake had a muscular, bulky build. This man is thinner, slight.

Charlotte figures him for one of the brothers, then smells pot. She realizes which brother it is.

Frank.

After Frank was done, he'd lie next to her and smoke a joint.

She imagines herself standing behind him as he sits in the chair, holding the tire jack high, bringing it crashing down on his skull.

But she can't. Not yet. She has to find Mace first, make sure he's safe. She can't risk getting into a fight out here and alerting the house.

All she can do is get Mace, free him and escape with him. Then regroup and figure out what to do next.

Frank is slouched in the chair, staring into the sky. It

wouldn't take much for him to glance back and see her crouched in the shadows.

Charlotte inches to the door and peers inside. The kitchen is still dark. She takes a step in, hears him getting up behind her.

She slips into the dark kitchen and makes out a long island, fridge at one end, table with chairs at the other. She hurries around the island, ducks down as Frank comes in from the patio and walks over to the fridge.

He opens the door. A square of light lands next to her.

She forgot the tire jack on the patio.

He takes something from the fridge, lets the door smack shut. Walks back outside. She listens to the patio door close and breathes deep. Touches her chest. Her heart's shivering.

Charlotte rises, but not completely. She heads to the counter, where something flashed in her eyes when she rushed past.

A long, rusty screwdriver.

CHAPTER NINETY

At least, Mace figures, the pain from the ball-gag pressing into his mouth distracts him from the burning ache in his hand. It's hard for him to breathe, hard for him to swallow. Saliva trickles down his throat.

But at least it distracts him from the pain.

He turns his head to look up at his handcuffs, one end of the cuffs tight around his wrist, the other end attached to a hook on the wall. Each of his wrists is cuffed in the same fashion, his arms spread to either side.

As scared and hurt as he is, it crushes Mace to think about Dory.

And to think that this is how Charlotte was held.

He doesn't hold out any hope for rescue. Charlotte may have freed herself of Rob, but she'd never be able to find him here. And even if she does, he'll be dead before she arrives.

After all, they didn't keep Dory alive for long.

It makes him happy—somewhere distantly inside him, like a star flickering far away—that he didn't give up everything he knew. He wanted to, especially when Barnes broke his index finger, and the world had turned into a red and white swirl of pain.

He'd passed out. But he hadn't told Barnes the most important thing: his best guess about Charlotte.

Mace assumes she'll somehow end up with Eve.

That's his hope, although it doesn't seem possible. Mace

doesn't know if Charlotte ever learned Eve's last name, where she lives, or how to find her. But he hopes Charlotte ends up back with Eve, and Eve will help Charlotte find her freedom.

As for him, these men will kill him. No reason to keep him alive.

He just hopes it's quick.

He doesn't want to be in more pain.

CHAPTER NINETY-ONE

Charlotte can hear the men from where she's hiding in the hall.

They're in a room to her right. A staircase on her left leads up to the second floor, and a door next to it leads down to the basement.

Charlotte slips halfway up the dark stairs and hides in the shadows with the screwdriver.

Frank wanders toward the living room, a beer bottle dangling from his fingers.

He stops, leans against the doorway.

"We figure out what we're doing?" he asks.

Charlotte hears a "Nope."

Frank heads into the living room.

"She's still in Baltimore," Jake says. "We should be back there, trying to find her. And getting Rob out of jail."

"We're not going to find her driving around the city." Charlotte recognizes this voice. It belongs to Frank's brother, the nervous guy who brought her food, took her to the bathroom, walked her around the basement. He never did anything to her, but he never helped her either.

Will.

"We're just supposed to sit here? That's my partner!"

"Yeah," Frank puts in, "and Dave was our friend. And he's...we're just..." His voice drifts away.

"Look," Will says, "Barnes is downstairs with that Mace guy. He'll have answers for us soon."

Charlotte stops breathing.

She'd been listening for Barnes, wondering if he was just sitting silently among them. She hadn't thought he was with Mace.

As if he heard his name, the door to the basement opens and Barnes walks through. Charlotte watches him as he heads into the living room.

She's holding the screwdriver tightly; her hand nearly cramps. She forces herself to relax her grip.

"Good news is, he told me everything he knows."

"What's the bad news?" Jake asks.

"He doesn't know much. Has no idea where Charlotte went."

The room is silent for a few moments.

"What'd you do to him?"

"Broke another finger."

Charlotte squeezes her eyes shut.

A chair moves.

"He talked, then went lights out."

Frank stumbles out of the room with his beer and sits ten steps beneath her, on the bottom of the stairs. Shakes his head. Drinks.

Above him, Charlotte tries to calm herself.

She needs to get Mace out of here.

Frank finishes his beer, stands, and walks down the hall.

Charlotte guesses where Frank's going and, when she hears the bathroom door open, she hurries down the stairs and softly opens the door to the basement. She slips inside and closes it behind her.

CHAPTER NINETY-TWO

"Mace?"

He feels her hands in the dark as she removes the ball gag.

"Are you okay?" Charlotte whispers.

Mace wants to answer but his throat is raw. He turns and buries his face into the side of her neck.

He weeps.

He and Charlotte need to leave, but Mace thinks about Charlotte in this basement and everything inside him seems to collapse. He hates this world, this world that celebrates madness and violence; a world of stupid men who proudly defend their savagery; a world only populated by abusers and their abused; a world where every foot sinks into blood-soaked land.

"Dory's dead," he whispers.

Charlotte exhales. "She is?"

"They killed her."

There's a flicker inside Charlotte, not grief or sadness. Anger. She tries to push it aside. "We have to go. Did they leave the key in here?"

The door leading upstairs opens. The stairwell light turns on.

"Shit." Charlotte hurries to the bedroom door.

The light to the outer room flickers on.

Footsteps come closer.

Will walks into the room, doesn't see Charlotte hiding by the door.

Charlotte kicks his leg out from underneath him and wraps

her arm around his neck.

Will stumbles and cries out, but Charlotte's arm is wrapped so tight that his cry is gurgled. His fingers reach up, trying to create space between her arm and his neck.

He can't.

Mace watches his feet kick, listens to him try and speak, but Will can only make a wet nasal sound.

Charlotte loosens her arm. "Do you have the key?"

"No," Will whispers hoarsely. "But I can get it. I'll help you escape."

"Like you helped me before? Or Dory?"

"That was different. Now I..."

"Hey!"

Charlotte looks over her shoulder at Barnes.

He's holding a gun.

Charlotte pushes Will to the side and rushes Barnes. Mace flinches, expecting him to shoot, but Barnes raises the weapon and smashes the handle butt into Charlotte's head. She goes down.

"You okay?" Barnes asks Will.

Will stands, still coughing. Nods.

Barnes grabs Will, puts one giant hand over his mouth, breaks his neck.

Mace struggles, pulling the chains tight.

"The lesson, kids?" Barnes lets Will's body drop to the floor. "Be quiet when you're talking about helping someone escape."

He looks down at Charlotte.

CHAPTER NINETY-THREE

"Sorry about your brother," Barnes tells Frank.

Frank wants to be upstairs with Will's body. Instead he's in this small room, watching Jake and Barnes finish tying Mace to a chair next to the bed. Charlotte's handcuffed to the chains in the wall. Both are gagged.

After Mace is secured to the chair, Jake and Barnes rise and stand next to Frank, each on either side of him.

"I'm sorry too," Jake tells him.

Frank nods.

"He's the last one of us she'll kill." Barnes touches Frank's shoulder. "What do you want to do with them?"

"I want them dead. But you should do it."

"Why?"

"They're your prisoners." He looks at Jake. "Let's go."

Jake follows Frank out.

They start heading up the stairs, but Frank stops at the bottom step. "I don't want to be up there with his body," Frank lies. "I'm going to wait down here."

Jake heads up and closes the door behind him. Frank walks back toward the small bedroom and sits against the door leading into it.

Frank's face is still wet with tears, his nose helplessly running, his breaths coming hard. He keeps hoping that if he goes upstairs, there's a chance Will might be alive.

But he won't.

And soon enough, Frank will be gone too.

Frank's felt this way ever since Dave first told them about Barnes and the plan to hold this woman. Felt that way when Will looked at him for reassurance, because he knew it was beyond what they wanted to do.

When he dies, people are going to think of him the same way a part of him feels.

That he got what he deserved.

Frank closes his eyes in the darkness, leans the back of his head against the door. Hears a murmur. The gags must have been taken off Mace and Charlotte.

Barnes is speaking.

"...and then, after you killed Sofia, I figured I was doing you a favor. You were a wildcat, knew you couldn't be tamed. Gave you a choice—go somewhere in Russia or stay here and die."

He pauses. Neither Mace or Charlotte says anything. Or anything Frank can hear.

"You two think I'm the devil. But all I do is fill men's appetites. I'm not the devil. I'm Charon."

Silence again.

"You know who that is? Old Charon took souls across the river Styx, brought them to Hades. Those men who want you, those men who fuck you, they're the passengers. All I do is take them where they're going, a salesman. Those men can always refuse, decide not to step in the boat. Let me tell you, I've served thousands of customers. Maybe tens of thousands. Probably that many. All across America. Ran operations from New York to Los Angeles, San Francisco to Miami. Let me tell you, none of those men ever once said no."

Another pause.

"If they had, I'd have given them their money back. Better believe I would have. Because that's what being a businessman is about. And, yeah, maybe I take a little of my own product, break the girls in, but better they're broken in with me instead of someone else. Everything I do, I do with honor."

"Do me a favor." To Frank, Mace sounds weary. "Kill me. But let her go. She won't do anything. She won't tell anyone a thing. You'll never see her again."

"What do you think, Charlotte?"

"You let me go and I'll come back here and gut you, you fat fucking piece of shit."

"Looks like we don't have a deal." Barnes's tone is calm. "Not that I'd have made one. Here's what going to happen. I'm going to give this girl what she deserves and you're going to watch me do it. Then I'm going to do the same thing to you.

"Just kidding. I ain't a faggot.

"But I am going to shoot you in the forehead after."

Silence.

"Shit," Barnes says. "No rubbers."

Frank hears footsteps approach the door. He moves away, presses himself against the wall. The door opens, and Barnes walks out. He passes Frank without seeing him, heads up the basement stairs.

Frank walks into the room. Charlotte is whispering something to Mace. She stops talking the moment she sees his shadow.

"Who's that?" Mace asks.

The flashlight from Frank's phone turns on.

"You killed Will," Frank tells Charlotte.

"She didn't!" Mace's voice is urgent. "Barnes did. It wasn't her."

Frank and Charlotte stare at each other.

"Did he?" Frank asks.

"You won't believe me. What's the point?"

"I do believe it. Barnes is an animal." Frank pauses. "If I let you go, will you run off, never come back?"

"Yes," Mace answers, quickly. "Please, untie us."

Charlotte is quiet.

"How about it?"

"Yes."

"No, you won't. You'll try to kill everyone here."

Charlotte doesn't reply.

Footsteps upstairs.

Frank walks over to the bed. He reaches for the handcuff on Charlotte's wrist and puts the key in the lock.

The cuffs pop open. Charlotte turns toward Mace, starts tugging at the knots binding his arms to the chair.

Frank turns off the flashlight and walks out of the room.

CHAPTER NINETY-FOUR

Charlotte frees Mace's left arm, but she can't loosen the knots over his right wrist. They're both breathing hard, anxious, waiting for the door to the basement to open and Barnes to descend back down those stairs. Mace reaches over with his free hand, tugs at the knot, pulls his hand out. He stands.

"There's no way out down here, right?"

"No." It's dark, but he can see the outline of Charlotte's body in front of him. "We have to go up."

"Listen." Mace winces as he accidentally touches his broken fingers. The pain is there but distanced by adrenaline. "The door's right in front of the stairs. We push open the basement door, run through the front, get the hell out of here. There are other houses nearby. If they chase us, we make a commotion. Nothing they can do to us when we're..."

"Yeah, I don't like that plan." Charlotte turns and walks out of the room.

"What, what do you mean? What are you doing?"

Charlotte doesn't answer, just keeps walking.

"Why do this?" Mace hurries after her, whispering harshly. He grabs her arm with his good hand. "Why risk your life? You can be free!"

"No, I can't. And you don't have to stay with me. Besides, I'm not sure how much you'll help."

That stings. "I'm not leaving you here."

"I know," Charlotte answers. They climb the stairs, walking

as softly as possible. They stop at the top.

A line of light shines under the door.

Charlotte leans close to Mace's ear.

"I don't want you to risk your life," she whispers. "It's important to me that you…"

The door swings open.

Barnes stands in the doorway, wearing a T-shirt and boxers. He's holding a flashlight in one hand, a dangling condom in the other.

"What are—"

That's all Barnes gets out before Mace rushes up the two stairs, inadvertently knocking Charlotte into the wall.

Barnes is a big man. Stands over six feet, weighs well over two hundred pounds. But there's something about being in your underwear that leaves you ill-equipped to defend yourself.

Barnes isn't ready for Mace's shoulder to slam into his gut. He stumbles backward into the living room, falls to the ground.

But he has enough presence of mind to grab Mace and take him with him.

Even though Charlotte's face smacked into the wall when Mace rushes past her, she's only a little stunned. She enters the hallway, looks for Mace and Barnes. Doesn't see them.

But Charlotte does see, sitting shiny on the stairs leading to the second floor, the screwdriver.

She's about to take it when someone calls her name.

Jake is standing at the other end of the hallway, near the kitchen.

"How'd you get out of the basement?"

Charlotte grabs the tool.

"We don't have to do this," she says. "You can leave. One of us doesn't have to die."

Jake's expression changes.

"Really?" he asks, hopefully. "Cool. This isn't what I signed up for. I'm not into killing people. So, okay, I'm going home."

"Oh." Charlotte's taken aback. "I didn't expect that."

"Yeah, this sucks. And I need to go get my boy."

Jake reaches behind himself, pulls out a gun.

Charlotte turns numb.

He holds it out to her, handle-first.

"You'll need this to save your friend."

Charlotte exhales, takes the gun.

She watches Jake leave, disappearing into the kitchen, heading out the back-sliding door.

And then hears Mace scream.

CHAPTER NINETY-FIVE

Down the hall, Mace's fight with Barnes isn't going well.

Barnes rolled him over, sat on his chest, and is raining punches on Mace's face. The punches are solid; Mace feels like he's being pelted with stones. He tries to fight back and can't. All he can do is lift his arms, cover his head.

The blows stop.

Mace is surprised. He looks up just in time to see Barnes's forearm driving down toward his throat.

Mace squirms out of the way and Barnes's forearm slams into the floor. He slips out from under the big man, quickly straddles his back, wraps an arm around his neck.

And squeezes, his hands clasped together as tightly as a sinner hanging onto heaven's gates.

Barnes slaps the floor, his feet kicking wildly. Mace keeps up the pressure, feels Barnes slowly give, weaken.

"It's over," Mace tells him. "You lost. It's over."

Like the snap of a scorpion's tail, Barnes reaches back with one hand, scrabbling. His fingers find Mace's face.

His thumb buries itself in Mace's right eye.

Everything leaves Mace.

He no longer feels Barnes underneath him, doesn't feel pain from his mangled fingers, doesn't feel the short breath panic from his fight. Doesn't wonder about Charlotte in the other room.

Mace is nothing but a flash of pain as Barnes's thumb wrestles its way deeper inside his eye socket.

Somehow he's standing. Time is distant now. Hours could have passed.

His back touches the wall, palms pressed to his face.

Now his knees are on the floor.

His damaged eye is sealed closed, as if it will never open.

With his other eye, he blearily sees Barnes's boot rushing toward his face.

CHAPTER NINETY-SIX

Barnes staggers out of the living room. He looks at Charlotte.

She lifts the gun and fires.

The bullet sails past him. Barnes throws open the basement door and runs down the stairs.

Charlotte tries to fire again, but the gun clicks. Empty.

Well, Jake, she thinks, *thanks anyway.*

She rushes down the hall and stops at the doorway to the basement. There's no sound from below. Charlotte touches the wall as she walks down, the empty weapon in her other hand. She stops near the bottom of the stairway.

Turns on the light switch.

The room is flooded with light and, for the first time, Charlotte sees the outer area. A couch is pressed against the corner, a television set mounted to the wall, a small rectangular table in another corner—the furniture's been pushed out of the center, but the room has all the makings of a den. She's stunned that she was held next to this family-styled room, held and tortured and raped.

She also sees Barnes crouched against the wall, holding a lamp, waiting to surprise her.

Charlotte points the empty gun at him. He lowers the lamp.

"Forgot about the lights," Barnes says.

She descends the last three steps. "Back away."

Barnes doesn't move. He stays standing against the wall, only a few feet from her.

"Pretty sure you're out of bullets."

Charlotte doesn't change expression. "One way to find out."

They stare at each other.

"Guess so." Barnes take a step toward her.

It's a quick step and takes her by surprise. Charlotte retreats, bumps the stairs, but still doesn't pull the trigger.

Barnes smiles. "You'd have shot me."

"Change of heart?"

Barnes lunges at her.

Charlotte turns to run up the stairs. He grabs her shirt and yanks her back down.

She spins and slams the gun against the side of his head. Barnes backhands her.

It reminds her of when he first hit her in Tucson, the shock echoing through her body. Charlotte doesn't even realize she's airborne until she lands hard on the carpet. She struggles to her knees, shakes her head, and sees Barnes's boots in front of her.

He pulls her up.

"Going to bury you next to your friend upstairs. After I have some fun."

Barnes throws her back into the room where she'd been held captive. She stumbles against the bed and turns. Barnes is reaching toward her.

And then she hears Mace.

Mace is shouting and running through the large room in the basement. His face is a mask of blood, the shout full of pain and rage. He sounds like a wild animal.

He runs right into the door frame.

Mace falls back and sits on the floor, stunned.

Barnes laughs and turns back toward Charlotte.

She snaps the handcuff chained to the wall over his outstretched wrist.

"The fuck?" Barnes looks down incredulously.

Charlotte slides off the bed, but Barnes grabs her with his free hand, clawing for her throat. Charlotte smashes the empty gun into his head.

She does it over and over until the hand over her throat drops.

CHAPTER NINETY-SEVEN

Barnes wakes up.

His head is killing him. It takes him a moment to remember what happened.

Then he does.

He tries to stand, almost pulls his arms out of their sockets.

Barnes cries out in pain. Looks at the wall. Sees each of his wrists handcuffed.

Barnes tugs at the chains. He can almost see the hook shaking a little. Or he imagines it's shaking. Hard to tell in the dark, feels like his mind's playing tricks on him.

He works the chain rhythmically, tugging it hard for twenty to thirty seconds, resting, then yanking as hard as he can, trying to dislodge the hook from stone. Every time it feels a little looser, but it's been...Barnes has no idea how long it's been since Charlotte left. An hour? A couple of hours?

He shouts. No response.

He's not worried. Someone will come for him. All he has to do is stay alive until then.

Barnes wishes he'd eaten a heavier meal. His stomach is growling, so loud the sound escapes him, and fills the room along with his breaths and the smells of semen and sweat.

When he gets out of here, Barnes tells himself, he's going to twist that skinny no-titted dead-eyed cumbucket fuckfaced bitch's head off.

He pulls the chain, waits, lets the strength return to his arm, and pulls. Cries out as he does it, as the chains chew into his wrist.

He remembers some story about a guy who got caught in a rock and cut his arm off. Barnes would eat his own shoulder if he had to, but he can't turn his head that far.

He tries to bend his body, bring his knees to his chin, and reach over to the wall hook with his foot. His gut gets in the way. It flops down on his face, all sweaty hairy skin. Practically suffocates him.

It's going to be embarrassing when someone finds him here, but Barnes has a story in mind. How that Mace guy led him here at gunpoint, chained him to the bed. No way he's going to let Charlotte get the better of him, even in a memory.

Tug, rest, pull.

Tug, rest, pull.

Tug, rest, pull!

This time Barnes feels it move, he's sure of it. He tugs the chain and it wobbles. He smiles.

CHAPTER NINETY-EIGHT

"Are you safe?" Eve asks.

Eve and Charlotte are in Eve's apartment. It's nicer than Charlotte expected—perfectly clean and stylish, like a page out of some furniture magazine. Eve is sitting on a white leather couch and Charlotte in an ornately-carved wooden chair with thin cushions, her elbows pressed into her knees, fists pressed against her lips. The room smells like roses.

She can't believe Eve is asking her this question, can't believe she's even concerned for her welfare. "It's been a few days. I don't think anyone's coming for us."

"Good."

"Is Mace is going to get his sight back?"

Eve shakes her head. "Not in his left eye. That's gone."

Charlotte looks away. "How's he doing?"

"Not good."

Charlotte thinks she detects something accusatory in the other woman's tone. But she understands it, even welcomes it. "I'm sorry for what happened. I'm sorry for…"

"I don't blame you."

"This would never have happened if he hadn't met me."

"Mace made choices from the moment he met you. And he thought they were the right choices."

Charlotte wraps her arms around herself. "I can't visit him?"

Eve shifts. "Look, it's not your fault. And Mace will understand that soon. But in the state, he's in, he doesn't understand it now. So, no, you shouldn't visit him."

"I wish I could."

Eve looks closely at her.

"You feel guilty."

Charlotte feels tears starting. "You all gave up so much for me. And you shouldn't have."

Eve stands, holds the crying girl.

"I said Mace made choices. We all did. And we made the right ones. He'll understand that, I promise you. He'll come around."

"I like that about him," Charlotte sniffs. "How...simple things are. I get how that sounds, but I mean it in a nice way."

"All men are simple. Not many in a nice way."

Charlotte pulls away. "I've seen a lot of terrible things. And I've done some. I can move past a lot of that stuff, for some reason. But not Mace."

"Of course. You care about him."

Charlotte's surprised she didn't realize it before. Or, at least, how much.

"And he cared about you," Eve adds. "He'll recover. You both will."

"When I left my uncle, I didn't have a plan. I just wanted to get away from him. Then I got to Tucson, and I was happy for a while. But I still felt like there was something else I should do. I couldn't work at Applebee's forever. I definitely couldn't eat there much longer."

Eve smiles.

"What do I do next?"

CHAPTER NINETY-NINE

After the taxi pulls away, Charlotte tests the front door.

It's still unlocked.

She looks around, wraps a scarf around her nose and mouth, walks back into the house.

She knew the smell of death would be strong, but it's worse than she expected. It's been a week, and the house smells like she's pushing past piles of rotted fruit.

Charlotte doesn't bother going upstairs. She presses her hand over her scarf and heads down to the basement.

The lights are still on. Charlotte walks down the stairs, hurries across the empty room, pushes open the bedroom door.

The smell burns her eyes.

Barnes is lying there, the handcuffs still around his wrists, the chains still attached to the hooks in the wall. His body is bigger, bloated. His stomach blocks her view of his head.

It should be enough.

It's not.

Charlotte stands next to his head, touches his neck.

Cold. No pulse.

Charlotte heads back up and out and closes the front door behind her.

She sits on the front porch and breathes greedily. Sucks in air like she's drowning.

Her eyes are still burning, to the point of tears. She blinks fast, rubs them with her palms.

Charlotte stands, heads off the porch. She has no idea where to find a cab, but the walk will do her good.

It's hard for her not to shake. Her legs feel unstable, like she's stepping onto cracking glass.

She looks back at the house.

Charlotte opens the front door one last time, just enough to reach inside and lock it. She pulls it closed.

CHAPTER ONE HUNDRED

Three Weeks Later

Rose tries to look confident as she walks in heels higher than any she's ever worn, in a street where everyone is staring her down. It's cold this time of year, and her fifteen-year-old bare legs are freezing in the late night.

She doesn't walk far from the apartment building. Anthony will beat her if she gives up, but that's safer than what might be waiting in one of these cars. A few are idling at the corner, a couple cruising by. She stays back against the building, in the shadows, trying to get the courage to walk out onto the sidewalk.

Rose sees some other women out here, three talking at the end of the block. Anthony's told her how territorial these blocks can get. About new girls getting put in the hospital.

Don't trust anyone.

She scratches her arm and steps out of the shadows.

Right away, a car slows down. It creeps past her like a hungry wolf, stops, backs up. The window lowers.

Rose takes a step closer and bends down, conscious of how her cleavage is showing in front, of how her skirt's rising in the back.

"How much?"

"Forty," Rose tells him. That's what Anthony told her to charge. Not too much. ATM-friendly.

"Forty for what? Suck or fuck?"

"Just one. Not both. Both is another twenty."

"How old are you?"

"Old enough." She pauses, trying to remember what Anthony told her. "Or young enough."

"Good answer."

Something's not right. Rose isn't sure what it is, but uneasiness overtakes her. She steps back.

"I got a room a couple of blocks away," he goes on. "Give you a hundred for an hour. Drive you back here when I'm done."

Rose shakes her head. "I'm not supposed to leave the street."

"You'll be fine. Get in."

"No thanks."

He calls Rose something that makes her take another step back. The window rolls up and the car drives off.

Rose is back in the shadows, breathing hard, squeezing her hands. If Anthony knew she passed up a hundred dollars, he'd kick her until she threw up. And that was worth at least two to three jobs. She should have taken the money, no matter her nerves. She expects that the first time she does this will feel terrible.

Rose wraps her arms around herself and can't stop thinking about that hundred. About how much it would have helped Anthony. Given him enough to inject himself with some peace, bring back his smile, his warmth.

Sharp laughter from the women at the corner. Rose hadn't realized they were watching her.

She's staring at the women so intensely that she doesn't notice the next vehicle pulling to a stop in front of her. She doesn't even look away from the laughing women until she hears, "Hey."

Rose steps back into the light, determined not to back out this time.

"What are you looking for?" She bends lower this time.

"I just want to talk."

Rose checks out the car. A large black sedan. Nothing fancy.

"Talk about what?"

"Options." He leans closer to the passenger window. Rose can see him clearly now. A black man with a shaved head and serious face. He looks at her without lust or threat, but something about his terse replies worries Rose.

"I don't..." she starts.

The back window rolls down and a woman says, "Options? Jesus, that sounds creepy."

Rose looks around. "What's happening right now?"

The woman pokes her head out of the window, a black woman with braids and a wide smile. "Listen, my driver here's not that great with ladies."

"Driver?" he asks.

"But he's right," she goes on. "We just want to talk. And we'll pay you for your time. Fifty dollars. We don't even have to leave the street."

"Are you reporters or something? Christians?"

Laughter from inside the car, but it doesn't intimidate Rose in the way that the laughs from the women on the corner did. "We're not reporters, and not that religious. We just want to offer you some help. You don't have to accept it. We'll still give you the fifty dollars."

"What are your names?"

"I'm Eve. My driver is Gabe."

"I'm not her driver."

Eve opens the door and scoots back to give Rose room as she cautiously climbs inside.

Rose keeps her hand on the door. "You promise you'll give me the fifty?"

Gabe hands her a fifty-dollar bill. Rose takes it, and holds the money tight in her other hand.

"We promise," Eve tells her. "We just want to help."

CHAPTER ONE HUNDRED ONE

Mace's hands are heavy. He lowers his arms and steps back, but steps too slow. A left hook from Marcus darkens the world.

Moments later, Mace doesn't remember how he got back in the corner, or when Marcus removed his headgear and knelt next to him.

"That was on me," Marcus is saying. "Should have held back."

Mace nods, confused. He pushes his mouth guard out with his tongue, lets the guard fall to the mat. He hopes no teeth came out with it.

Nausea swirls.

"I need a second."

"Cool." Marcus pats Mace on the knee, stands, and shadow boxes his way to the middle of the ring.

Mace watches him dully, listening to Marcus's hands slice the air, his sharp breaths following a second later. Marcus won a state championship in boxing and, even though he stopped fighting years ago, he still has that solid boxer build, his body padded with muscle. Mace watches him, mesmerized by his hands, how fast they move in a combination.

Marcus glances at Mace. "Don't get down. It's only been a couple of weeks."

"Yeah."

Marcus dances to his left, out of Mace's vision. Mace's left eye is still heavily taped but, once that tape comes off, his eye will be useless.

His sight isn't going to return.

Mace reaches for the ropes and tries to stand. Marcus reappears, his hand on Mace's arm. It's still hard for Mace to adjust to wearing boxing gloves, still hard to remember that he doesn't yet have the complete use of his fingers. He accepts Marcus' help, lets the other man pull him to his feet.

"We got five more minutes," Marcus tells him. "But we can go to the bag."

Their training sessions are an hour, three nights a week, after the small gym in Towson has closed to regular students and competitors. Most of that hour is spent on form, stance, combination, and endurance, but Marcus likes to leave the last ten minutes open to light sparring.

"Best way to learn," he'd told Mace at the end of their first session.

Mace can feel the difference in his body. His legs have more resilience than they did, and that nausea has settled. His cheek hurts from Marcus's blow, but the pain lacks permanence. He ambles out to the middle of the ring, slaps his gloves together.

Marcus advances on him.

Mace makes a point of keeping his hands high as he peers at Marcus over the tops of his gloves. His damaged eye is still dangerously sensitive, and Marcus is too good to accidentally hit him there, but it's hard for Mace to relax. He keeps his left hand with his healing fingers a little higher, shielding the wound.

He remembers Eve's surprise when she'd found out he'd started boxing.

"You have?" she'd asked, standing in front of his recliner. "Why?"

"Just something I wanted to do."

"You've *never* said that before."

"I didn't say it was something I *always* wanted to do."

Eve smiled. "Then we have to get you back home. You'll

need lots of TLC. And concussion tests."

Mace didn't respond.

"That Seth guy, the one Charlotte burned? He's out of the hospital."

"Yeah?"

"He left town, went down south. We've been watching him. Hopefully he realized there's nothing left for him here."

"Good."

Eve's voice dropped a tone. "Come on, Mace. You're not still staying here, are you?"

"I don't know where I'm going."

Eve slid down to the floor. Mace watched her hands, one thumb nervously rubbing the other.

"I thought we were, I thought things were going back to what we had," she said. "What we liked."

"I can't do that right now."

"But why not?" Sorrow clouds Eve's face. "Why are you punishing me?"

"I'm not." Mace got off the recliner and sat on the floor, facing his ex-wife. "But I look at you, or I think about Charlotte, and I see them."

"Who?"

"The men we killed."

"You told me she killed them."

"I helped her."

"You don't think they deserved it?"

Mace stared at the flat brown carpet. "Just not sure that matters."

Marcus's feints in and Mace pulls back. He keeps his elbows tight so, when Marcus goes for his midsection, Mace absorbs the punches on his arms. It still hurts, even if Marcus is holding back. If Marcus used all his strength, Mace figures the bones in his arms would shatter.

He steps away, still giving Marcus the center of the ring. Mace has realized, over his weeks of training, that being on the outside takes so much more energy. He has to keep moving so he doesn't get trapped against the ropes or corner, but he's running out of steam. He still feels a bit lightheaded from Marcus's punch, and it's hard to breathe. He's gulping in air.

He stops moving, lifts a hand. Marcus lowers his arms.

"Need a break?"

Mace nods, hands on his knees. He uselessly wipes his forehead with the back of his sweaty wrist.

He wonders how Charlotte is. Eve's been taking care of her, letting Charlotte live with her. Mace likes that. It gives them both something they need. And he hopes Charlotte doesn't think he's angry with her or blames her for what happened to his eye.

Even if he can't tell her himself.

Mace straightens and walks around the ring, gloves on his hips, still trying to catch his breath. He doesn't blame Charlotte but, like he told Eve, something about her distances him. That's not something he wants to admit. Seeing her feels like it would be an acknowledgement of something he doesn't understand, something dark and dangerous.

Something else that drew him to her.

The same reason he pulled that trigger in Iraq.

The reason he wanted to.

"I'm okay," he tells Marcus. "Let's finish off the night."

Marcus shrugs. Mace dances toward him, aims high with a jab then tries a shot to the gut. Marcus twists, absorbs it and grins. It's an easy grin, but a truly happy one, and Mace realizes Marcus is proud of his effort.

He grins back and Marcus strikes.

One punch to his shoulder and a solid one right on his chest.

Mace steps back, dazed, and then he's on the ground again, one knee pressed into the mat.

"You okay?" Marcus's voice is worried, distant, an echo.

Mace nods, his heart beating like the wings of a frightened bird.

His forehead touches the mat.

CHAPTER ONE HUNDRED TWO

Charlotte steps out of the airport and into Nevada's heat.

The fake driver's license Eve gave her hasn't failed yet. Eve told her not to worry, said her new network—Dory's old network—was looking out for her. But Charlotte couldn't help it. Has to be scary to be the new Dory after what happened. But there was a determination in Eve that didn't allow for questions.

Charlotte had asked if she could help her out. There was still an urge to hide, to run to some other state and lose herself in seclusion. But that fear would always be with her.

She understands that.

And she understands the memories that have started reappearing, as sudden as explosions. The expressions on the faces of the men she'd killed, their pain and their fear. Those memories keep her staring hard into the dark at night.

What Charlotte doesn't entirely understand is why those memories stopped when she'd decided to stay with Eve. She'd told Eve she'd do what she could to help other women, stay with her and Mace (if he ever returned). After that decision, the memories hadn't come back.

Maybe there is a path.

Charlotte finds her rental car in the parking lot, gives her paperwork to the attendant, drives out of the lot.

Heads to the address Eve found for her.

* * *

When she'd learned the address was in Nevada, Charlotte had expected she'd end up in Las Vegas. She's never been but has seen so many depictions of it in movies that she feels like she had an accurate image of the city.

She did not, however, have a mental picture of Reno, which is fortunate, because Reno sucks. Neon-tinged, but not in a good-natured way. The city has a dirty, desperate quality to it, as if it had been intended for better times than it was experiencing. The streets aren't as crowded as they should be for ones with this many store, and the entrances to its biggest businesses—hotels, casinos—are dark and foreboding, like the openings to wet caves.

Charlotte drives through the city and into the desert. She passes brown land pockmarked with green cacti, desert flora, and small hills until she reaches a tiny town. She drives through it, finds the unmarked building she's looking for on the outskirts. Charlotte parks next to it and steps out into dusty heat. She walks up to the front door and presses a buzzer.

Nothing.

Charlotte presses the buzzer again. A woman's tired voice answers.

"Yeah?"

"Is Brandi here?"

Silence, then a buzz. Charlotte pulls open the door and walks inside.

A narrow stairway leading up is in front of her, a small hall next to it. One room is on the right side of the hall, another all the way at the end.

A woman calls out, "Upstairs."

Charlotte climbs the stairs, sees the same configuration as the first floor: one room down the hall in front of her, one to the right.

She pushes open the door to the first room. A stained mattress is on the floor. A woman is lying on her back, squinting up into a cell phone.

"Brandi?"

"Yeah."

"My name's Charlotte. I knew your daughter. Sofia."

Brandi brings the phone down, sets it on her chest, cranes her head to look at Charlotte.

Eve had told her that her sources were confident they'd found the right woman. And Charlotte can see some resemblance. Dark skin curled black hair, Sofia's wide eyes and small mouth.

"I don't have a daughter. Sorry."

Brandi picks up her phone and stares into it.

"Okay." Charlotte walks into the room and stands near the wall.

"What do you want?" Brandi asks, irritated.

"She was my friend. Sort of."

"Charlotte? That's your name?"

"Yeah."

"Why'd you think she was my daughter, Charlotte? And how do you know who I am?"

"I heard you might be her mother."

"Yeah?" Brandi rolls over on the mattress to her elbows. "Where you from?"

"San Diego."

"Never been there."

"I met Sofia in Tucson."

Brandi shrugs. "How'd you find this place? Doesn't exactly advertise."

"Sofia was my same age. She was funny. Smart. Pretty. But she was in a bad situation and made some bad decisions."

"Okay."

"I was there when she died." Charlotte feels her voice breaking. And not just her voice. Something else inside her. "I was there when she died. She didn't deserve to end up that way."

Charlotte wipes her eyes.

"Sofia deserved more of a life than what she got."

"We all do," Brandi tells her, resolutely. "Nothing any of us can do about it. But I don't know her."

"She was with a terrible man."

"That's usually why."

"You're not going to admit it, are you? You're not going to admit you were her mother?"

Charlotte's anger seems to surprise Brandi, breaks through her barrier. "I...I don't have any idea who you're talking about."

"I couldn't help Sofia. I should have."

Brandi doesn't answer.

"But none of us can be perfect. None of us can be perfect."

Brandi bites her lip.

"None of us can be perfect. None of us do what's right. You lost her. I don't think she hated you. That was just the only life she knew."

Brandi shrugs it off. "Jesus, girl, I told you, I don't have any kids."

Charlotte feels a hand on her shoulder and turns. A man is standing in the doorway.

"You brought a friend?"

"She's not my friend."

The man looks up and down at Charlotte's body. "You sure?"

Charlotte twists away from him and walks out the room. The door closes behind her.

She's about to walk down the hall and leave this brothel. Head back to Maryland. Instead, she stops.

"Why are you going there?" Eve had asked her. *"What do you expect to find?"*

Charlotte didn't have an answer then and doesn't have one now. Something inside her has felt shaky ever since she left Barnes's house, like the smell from those bodies is still lingering.

I did what I needed to do, Charlotte thinks. *I saved my life. Saved others.*

But it doesn't add up. Whatever cosmic scale balances these

things is missing.

Or never existed.

Charlotte feels her nails digging into her palms. She wipes her eyes again.

No, she doesn't know why she came here.

Charlotte still has an urge to knock on the door, to force Brandi to admit who she is. To beat the hell out of that man.

She walks down the hall.

Charlotte heads down the stairs, toward the exit and the rental car and the hot Nevada night.

Behind her, in that room, the man grunts.

The woman cries.

ACKNOWLEDGMENTS

I owe a lot to a lot of people; frankly, this acknowledgements section could last pages. To avoid your very understandable tendency to skim, I'll be brief.

Thank you, as always, to my wonderful agent Michelle Richter, and all of the shrewd agents and talented writers at Fuse Literary.

Thanks to all my early readers for their feedback and guidance: Jennifer Hillier, Alan Orloff, Wendy Tyson, Michele Greene, Jenny Drummey, and Amy Roach.

Thank you to David Swinson and M.K. Haddad for their information on policing and soldiering, respectively.

Thanks to Down & Out Books for their belief and support, and for taking chances in crime fiction. With a special nod to Chantelle Aimee Osman for her thoroughness with this book.

Thank you to ITW for all the wonderful things they do for writers, and to my Murderers' Row and editing staff at *The Thrill Begins*.

Thanks to the *Washington Independent Review of Books* for giving me a monthly column years ago, and for warily allowing me to write whatever I want.

Thank you to the wonderful writing conferences and festivals and all they do to bring writers to readers, especially the Gaithersburg Book Festival; the National Book Festival; Creatures, Crimes, and Creativity; Bouchercon; ThrillerFest; Malice Domestic; Fall for the Book; Books Alive; and many more.

A seemingly countless number of books are published each year. That's a good thing, even if it presents a challenge to writers. If you read this book, chances are a reviewer or blogger brought it to your attention. There are many great ones out there, but I'm particularly indebted to BOLO Books, Dru's

Books Musings, Detectives Beyond Borders, Unlawful Acts, and Dan and Kate Malmon.

I'm also indebted to a number of bookstores, particularly the lovely people at One More Page Books, East City Bookshop, The Ivy Bookshop, Kramerbooks, and many more.

Thanks to everyone who's come to D.C. to read at one of our Noir at the Bars. And thanks to other organizers (Eryk Pruitt, Jen Conley, Nik Korpon, Marietta Miles, David Nemeth, and others) for continuing to put on such outstanding events.

Speaking of D.C., our D.C./MD/VA triangle has one of the sharpest crime fiction communities out there. I'd invariably, unforgivably forget someone, but I would like to call attention to our region's wonderful crime fiction writers as a whole. And the fantastic writing teams at Marymount and George Mason universities.

I've been fortunate to find a place in crime fiction's family. You people, especially the ones not mentioned in some capacity above (Sarah M. Chen, Jamie Mason, Alex Segura, Chris Holm, Radha Vatsal, and more), genuinely make me happy. Thanks for being there.

And speaking of family, to my parents, my wife, and my son, thank you for giving me every opportunity to write. I love you.

E.A. AYMAR'S thrillers include the novel-in-stories *The Night of the Flood* (in which he served as co-editor and contributor) and "The Dead" trilogy. His column, "Decisions and Revisions," appears monthly in the *Washington Independent Review of Books*, and he is the Managing Editor of The Thrill Begins, ITW's online resource for aspiring and debut thriller writers. He also runs the Noir at the Bar series for Washington, D.C., and has hosted and spoken at a variety of crime fiction, writing, and publishing events nationwide. Aymar lives just outside of D.C.

BOOKS

On the following pages are a few
more great titles from the
Down & Out Books publishing family.

For a complete list of books and to
sign up for our newsletter,
go to DownAndOutBooks.com.

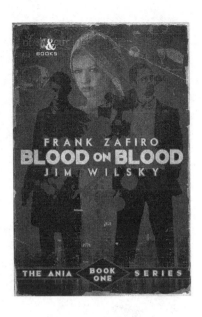

Blood on Blood
The Ania Trilogy Book One
Frank Zafiro and Jim Wilsky

Down & Out Books
December 2018
978-1-946502-71-1

Estranged half-brothers Mick and Jerzy Sawyer are summoned to their father's prison deathbed. The spiteful old man tells them about missing diamonds, setting them on a path of cooperation and competition to recover them.

Along the way, Jerzy, the quintessential career criminal and Mick, the failed cop and tainted hero, encounter the mysterious, blonde Ania, resulting in a hardboiled Hardy Boys meets Cain and Abel.

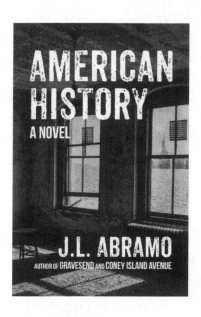

American History
J.L. Abramo

Down & Out Books
September 2018
978-1-946502-70-4

A panoramic tale, as uniquely American as Franklin Roosevelt and Al Capone...

Crossing the Atlantic Ocean and the American continent, from Sicily to New York City and San Francisco, the fierce hostility and mistrust between the Agnello and Leone families parallel the turbulent events of the twentieth century in a nation struggling to find its identity in the wake of two world wars.

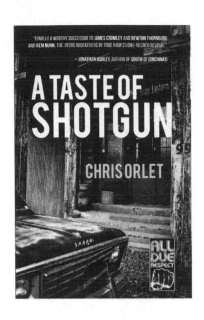

A Taste of Shotgun
Chris Orlet

All Due Respect, an imprint of
Down & Out Books
July 2018
978-1-946502-92-6

A local drug dealer has the goods on Denis Carroll. That shooting at his tavern five years ago? Turns out the cops got it all wrong. Now, after five years of blackmail, the Carrolls have had enough. When the drug dealer turns up dead, Denis is the prime suspect. As more bodies pile up, they too appear to have Denis' name all over them. Is Denis really a cold-blooded killer or could this be the work of someone with a grudge of her own?

In this darkly humorous small-town noir everyone has something to hide and nothing is at seems.

Texas, Hold Your Queens
A Mason Page & Farrah Tyler Novella
Marie S. Crosswell

Shotgun Honey, an imprint of
Down & Out Books
September 2017
978-1-943402-74-8

When the body of an undocumented Mexican immigrant is found abandoned on a roadside, Detectives Mason Page and Farrah Tyler have no clue how a throwaway case that neither wants to let go will affect their lives.

On the job, Page and Tyler are the only two female detectives in El Paso CID's Crimes Against Persons unit. Off the clock, the two have developed an intimate friendship, one that will be jeopardized when the murder case puts them on the suspect's trail.